The more he discovered about this woman...

The more he thought there was something special about her.

As he watched Madison examine Sniff, he felt an odd churning in his gut. Yeah, he'd had breakfast at six, grabbed a quick sandwich for lunch and it was almost five now, but he didn't think his reaction had anything to do with being hungry.

Rick shoved both hands back into his pants pockets. He didn't want to dwell on the fact that all of a sudden he was tempted to reach out and discover the texture of the veterinarian's springy red hair or how smooth her flawless complexion really was. He liked women, sure. Too much sometimes. This felt *different* somehow, and he'd just met her. He considered how gentle and sweet—not a word he used often, but it seemed right—she was with his dog.

That's it! It was Sniff, he rationalized. Anyone who loved his dog was okay by him.

That was it. That was all.

D1550966

Dear Reader,

Thank you for choosing to read the second book in my K-9 trilogy. This book tells the story of San Diego Police Department K-9 unit sergeant Rick Vasquez, veterinarian Madison Long and Rick's narcotics detection dogs Sniff and Nitro. While both Rick and Madison do important and meaningful work in their day jobs, they share a passion for making a difference to those in need. Rick is determined to do what he can to keep susceptible youth from getting involved with drugs, and Madison is leading groundbreaking research to help injured animals heal. When two such deeply moral people come into conflict, finding common ground can be surprisingly elusive.

If you enjoyed the first book in the trilogy, *When the Right One Comes Along*, this book also provides an opportunity to revisit old friends San Diego Police Department search and rescue officer Cal Palmer and Dr. Jessica Hansen (now Palmer).

I hope you enjoy getting to know Rick, Madison and their dogs. If you do, watch for the third and final book of the trilogy, planned for release in early 2016. It's the story of K-9 unit captain Logan O'Connor and San Diego International Airport chief of security Arianna Atkins. When these two come together, their interaction promises to be explosive!

I would love to hear from you. You can connect with me by email (readers@kate-james.com), through my website (kate-james.com), Facebook page (facebook.com/katejamesbooks), Twitter (@katejamesbooks), or mail me at PO Box 446, Schomberg, ON, L0G 1T0, Canada.

I've also provided some discussion questions on my website, in case you'd like to use this story in your book group.

Happy reading!

Kate

HEARTWARMING

When Love Matters Most

—

Kate James

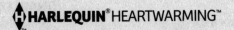

Recycling programs
for this product may
not exist in your area.

ISBN-13: 978-0-373-36771-9

When Love Matters Most

Copyright © 2016 by Kate James

HARLEQUIN®
www.Harlequin.com

Printed in U.S.A.

Kate James spent much of her childhood abroad before attending university in Canada. She built a successful business career, but her passion has always been literature. As a result, Kate turned her energy to her love of the written word. Kate's goal is to entertain her readers with engaging stories featuring strong, likable characters. Kate has been honored with numerous awards for her writing. She and her husband, Ken, enjoy traveling and the outdoors with their beloved Labrador retrievers.

Books by Kate James

A Child's Christmas
The Truth About Hope

The K-9 Trilogy

When the Right One Comes Along

To Wil Cohn. With love.
And
To the men and women who dedicate their lives
to law enforcement.

Acknowledgments

Thank you to my editor Paula Eykelhof for always making my books stronger and continuously challenging me to tell the very best stories in the very best way that I can. Also, thank you to Harlequin Heartwarming senior editor Victoria Curran for her unwavering vision, good humor and warmth.

Once again, much thanks to the York Regional Police (Ontario, Canada) and Constable Jim Hilton, in particular. Constable Hilton, a YRP canine unit officer and trainer, was generous with his time, resource materials and limitless knowledge as I conducted my research for this trilogy. I would also like to thank him for introducing me to his explosives detection dog, Max, and proudly showing off some of Max's considerable skills for me!

CHAPTER ONE

ENRIQUE FLINCHED AT the burst of gunfire. That slight motion nearly made him lose his balance. He'd been hiding in the corner of his closet for a while, as high up as possible, bracing himself with his back against one wall and his feet against the facing wall. It wasn't the first time he'd hidden there, trying to avoid discovery, but at twelve he was almost too big to fit. His muscles spasmed from the exertion. He rubbed his thigh, trying to get the blood circulating.

The next round of gunfire sounded as if it came from the hall. Despite the stifling heat in the dark, cramped space, he felt icy perspiration on his brow. The door to his room banged open, accompanied by a rapid exchange in Spanish and the clatter of booted feet rushing in. He bit down on his lower lip to keep from crying out. He heard a swooshing sound, which he guessed was the cover being torn off his bed; under it, he'd stuffed a couple of pillows to resemble a body. He'd prayed they'd take their shot and not bother to check if he was there.

He wasn't that lucky.

A loud crash—likely a piece of furniture toppling—startled him. Movement halted as the cartel enforcer yelled again to someone outside the room.

Then he heard heavy footsteps approaching. His closet door was yanked open and light flooded in. Looking sideways, he saw the barrel of a machine gun slide in and ruffle the hanging clothes that were concealing him.

The barrel paused a mere six inches from his hip. He knew he was as good as dead if they found him. Petrified, the boy held his breath…

And waking from his nightmare, the man bolted up in bed, drenched in sweat and gasping for air.

Rick Vasquez raked back the damp hair from his forehead with both hands and glanced at the glowing red numerals of his bedside clock. Still shy of five in the morning. He'd barely had three hours' sleep, but getting any more was out of the question. This was *not* how he'd hoped to start his day.

He swung his legs over the side of the bed. With his elbows on his knees and his head in his hands, he gave himself a moment to let the vestiges of the nightmare fade and his heart rate level out.

Sniff, his narcotics-detection canine partner, scurried to his side and nuzzled him.

Rick straightened and stroked the yellow Labrador retriever's head. He felt Sniff's tension subside. He and Sniff had been working together since the day he'd joined the San Diego Police Department's K-9 Unit six years ago. They were as connected as it was possible for any man and dog to be. The contact steadied him as much as the dog.

Sniff slid down and stretched out across Rick's bare feet, head nestled between his paws.

Rick exhaled heavily. It had been a while since he'd had the nightmare. He recalled the fourteen-year-old kid he'd caught the night before, crossing the San Ysidro border from Tijuana into San Diego with a kilo of marijuana, and he should've expected that the nightmare would revisit him.

He gently nudged Sniff off his feet and stood. Placing his hands on the small of his back, he stretched and yawned. He wasn't due at work until the evening shift, but he'd go in and have a strenuous workout to clear his mind. He had plenty of time before he and Sniff were scheduled to be at La Valencia High School for their drug-abuse awareness session. His yawn turned into a smile. He and Sniff loved the work they did counseling inner-city youth about the dangers of drug use. If, through their efforts, they managed to keep just one kid from using or selling drugs, that made it worthwhile. But he hoped their influence was much wider-reaching than one kid.

Rick tugged on a pair of gym shorts and a San Diego Police Department T-shirt that had seen better days before letting Sniff out in the backyard. He winced at the dog's awkward little hop as he navigated the final step of the deck. He'd make a point of taking him to the veterinarian again, although there wasn't much that could be done for the dog's morning stiffness.

It was all part of the aging process, he acknowledged philosophically but with regret. He had to face it: Sniff was no longer a young dog. Police dogs tended to be retired early because they had a dangerous and demanding job. Sniff was exceptional at what he did and enjoyed doing it. That was the main reason Rick hadn't already initiated the process to retire him, but well aware of Sniff's physical limitations, Rick was careful not to overexert him.

Maybe it was time. Sniff had more than earned the right to retire, Rick thought as he stuffed street clothes into his duffel.

After Sniff had his breakfast, Rick helped him into the back of his police-issue Ford Explorer. On the way to the division, he pulled into a Starbucks to grab a breakfast sandwich and a coffee. Before he had a chance to indulge in his meal, his radio signaled.

"We have a situation," the dispatcher announced.

Rick took a sip of his coffee and cursed as the hot liquid burned his tongue. In sharp contrast, apprehension chilled his skin.

"What kind of situation?"

"We have an officer down."

The chill slithered up his spine. Rick knew it would be one of his team if they were contacting him. "Who?" he inquired.

The voice on the other end was barely audible. "It's Jeff."

"What happened?" Jeff Bradford was one of his best officers and specialized in narcotics, just as he did. Rick prayed the injury wasn't serious.

"We received a tip at oh-four-hundred this morning about a drug shipment coming in. We got the route, the vehicle description and the estimated time of travel. Jeff and a couple of guys from the Narcotics Task Force took the call. Jeff was shot."

A million questions crowded Rick's mind, but he asked the one that mattered most. "What's Jeff's condition?"

"It doesn't sound good, Rick," the dispatcher responded. "Jeff took a bullet in the neck above his body armor. He was unconscious and was transported by ambulance to Ocean Crest Hospital."

"How did it happen?"

"The captain is certain it was a setup."

"Is Jagger in?" Rick asked about K-9 Unit captain Logan O'Connor by his alias. He needed the details.

"No. He's at the hospital. Jeff's family has been notified, and they're being taken there by a couple of uniforms."

Rick thought of Jeff's young wife and their two-year-old son, and grief and anger warred within him. He placed the coffee cup in the center console holder, tossed the unopened sandwich on the passenger seat and switched on his lights. "I'm on my way to the hospital."

"No. Wait! The captain and half the unit are already at the hospital or headed there. Jeff'll be in surgery for a couple of hours at least. Logan asked me to contact you," she said. "He wants you at the scene. He wants you to find Zeke." Zeke was Jeff's narcotics-detection dog.

"What do you mean, *find* him? He's trained in handler protection. Even if he wasn't, he would've stayed with Jeff until the ambulance took him away. Why didn't someone from the division get Zeke? There must've been others on the scene by then."

He heard a drawn-out sigh. "From what I understand, Zeke was injured trying to protect Jeff. Also a gunshot wound, we suspect. No one's seen him since Jeff was loaded into the ambulance for transport. Logan figures that Zeke stayed with Jeff as long as he could, but his injury must be serious. In all the confusion, he must've gone off…"

She couldn't finish the thought. None of them wanted to think about losing an officer or one of their dogs. Rick assumed Logan was correct. Injured animals tended to find a

quiet place to be on their own. If Zeke hadn't
been hurt, there was no way he would've left
like that.

There wasn't anything Rick could do for
Jeff right now, except pray, but maybe he
could help the dog. "I'm on it," he said in a
flat voice as he drove out of the parking lot.

If Rick hadn't taken all that extra time to
do what he had for that Mexican kid coming
across the border the night before, detain-
ing him well beyond the end of his shift, he
was sure he would've been the one called in
to respond to the tip instead of Jeff. Would
that have made a difference? Would he have
done anything different? Would he have seen
something because of his intimate knowledge of the cartels that Jeff or the others had
missed?

As Rick sped along I-5, he spoke to the
detectives conducting the investigation so he
could gather as much information about the
incident as possible. From what he was told,
Jeff had done everything right. They'd found
the cube van parked at the side of the road,
apparently abandoned. Jeff and Zeke had
been doing the perimeter check for narcotics to establish probable cause to search the
inside of the van. When they'd approached

the back, the doors had swung open and the shooting started. One of the Narcotics cops had been at the side of the van, out of the line of fire. He'd taken down the shooter, but it had been too late for Jeff.

There'd been no drugs in the van. Just the shooter. It had to have been a setup, as Logan thought. Their unit had been making a huge dent in the activities of a number of the cartels. This must have been payback from one of them. The guilt burned through Rick and settled in his gut, a hard, uncompromising knot. It *should've* been him, if anyone. Not one of his men. Not a cop with a young family.

His assumption about his own absence was confirmed when he spoke to Logan. They'd decided not to call him for the reason he'd surmised. If he hadn't helped that kid the night before, it would've been him at the back of that cube van when the scum with the rifle had taken his shot. If he'd been there instead, Jeff wouldn't have taken the bullet and wouldn't be in the hospital with critical injuries.

It was hard enough when one of their own got hit, but to make matters worse for Rick, the burden of guilt weighed heavily on him.

As for Jeff, they were hopeful he was going to make it through the operation. After that… the doctors couldn't say. The guilt surged up again and Rick tasted bile in his throat.

Rick had to take comfort in the fact that Jeff was receiving the best possible care. Right now his concern was Zeke. He knew Zeke well. He'd helped train him when he'd come to the K-9 Unit from the Czech Republic as a cute, floppy-eared shepherd puppy. Rick wanted to stay positive, but if Zeke had gone off on his own, it wasn't a good sign. Rick rubbed his eyes when the road blurred in front of him. He stopped by a cordoned-off area, a cube van at its center. Leaving the air-conditioning on in the back of his SUV for Sniff, he jumped out.

By the time he got to the crime scene, there were cops everywhere. He greeted the ones he knew and headed to where the detectives were gathered. It was obvious where Jeff had been shot from the pool of blood on the pavement, but Rick could see a second, smaller pool, too…and the trail of drops that led away from it.

He followed the trail at a fast jog to a residential yard, where it ended by a wooden step at the base of a deck.

Rick crouched down and peered into the dark, confined space. Relief flooded through him when he heard the panting. Even before he dropped to his belly and shone his light in, he started to murmur to Zeke in a calm, reassuring tone. He wanted to reduce the chances of the injured animal—out of pain or self-defense—lashing out at him.

He needn't have worried. Large chocolate-brown eyes stared up at him and a warm, dry tongue brushed the back of his hand when he reached in. Zeke was lying on his left side. From what Rick could see, he must have taken a bullet on his right side. Judging by the dark crimson stain on the packed dirt, he'd lost a considerable amount of blood.

But Zeke was alive and conscious. Rick needed to get him to a vet. And fast.

Resting his flashlight on the grass, Rick elbowed into the tight space and maneuvered the big dog gently out from under the deck. He could tell from the whimpers that he was hurting Zeke, but there wasn't anything he could do about it. The dog remained stoic, seeming to trust him implicitly.

"I've got you, pal," he murmured. "You're going to be okay."

Rick carried Zeke to his truck as fast as

he dared. He didn't want to jostle him too much, didn't want to cause him more pain, or aggravate his injuries and blood loss. At his vehicle, he looked around quickly. Not wanting to set Zeke down only to have to lift him again, he needed help. He saw another cop from his division and called out, "Give me a hand, would you, Steve?"

The cop glanced at Zeke. His brows drew together and his mouth formed a hard, straight line. "It's terrible what happened to Jeff. Is his dog going to be okay?"

"If I have anything to do with it, yeah. There's a blanket on the floor just behind the passenger seat. Get it for me, and help me wrap it around Zeke. I want to stem the flow of blood, and keep him warm and still, if possible."

"Sure." The cop did as he was asked.

"Now recline that seat all the way."

"Why don't you put him in the back? Wouldn't it be more comfortable for him?"

"My dog's in there, and there isn't room for both of them." Almost as if on cue, a short bark and a whine came from the back compartment of the SUV. Sniff must have sensed Zeke's presence and his distress.

"Besides, I want Zeke up front with me so I can keep an eye on him," Rick added.

"All right," Steve said, and complied with Rick's directions.

They slid Zeke carefully onto the near-horizontal seat.

"Thanks, man. I owe you one," Rick said, slapping the other cop on the back. Then he skirted his truck at a run.

He buckled himself in, put a reassuring hand briefly on Zeke's head and turned on his lights. He needed to get Zeke to the Mission Bay Veterinary Clinic as swiftly and smoothly as possible. He called ahead to make sure they could see Zeke right away.

Despite the short interval, by the time Rick drove into the clinic's parking lot, Zeke's breathing had become shallow and labored. His eyes had drifted closed.

Rick carried the dog as fast as he could into the clinic.

"Oh, my gosh! What happened?" The receptionist—not Heather, the clinic's regular one, but the college kid who filled in sometimes—sprang up from her desk and rushed around the counter.

"He's been shot. As I told you on the phone,

he needs attention right away." Rick's voice was hoarse with emotion. They couldn't lose Zeke.

"Here! We're ready for you." She indicated an examination room and quickly opened the door for him. "You're Sergeant Rick Vasquez, with the SDPD, correct?"

Rick laid Zeke down on the examination table. "Yeah. Good memory, but can you hurry, please? Zeke needs help urgently."

"Okay, I'll get Madison right now."

Rick's head whipped up. "What? Why not Jane? I need the best for Zeke."

The girl took a stumbling step back. "I... I'm sorry, but Jane's off this week."

Rick fought to keep his temper in check, more for Zeke's sake than the receptionist's. He didn't want the dog to be any more agitated than he already was. "What about Don, then?" He inquired about the other partner in the practice.

She shook her head. "He's at a conference."

"Fine," Rick said tersely. "Get whoever you mentioned in here, then." Recognizing the girl's distress through his haze of anger and fear, he added in a more controlled voice, "As fast as possible, please."

The girl nodded briskly and rushed out of the room.

Rick could see that Zeke's condition had deteriorated considerably during transport. It made the wait seem interminable, although it couldn't have been more than a couple of minutes before the door finally swung open again.

Seeing the vet enter, he felt a jolt. His immediate reaction was elemental and hormone-driven. The woman standing in the doorway was of average height, with impressive curves obvious even in the boxy white lab coat, and she had long, curly red hair. When she introduced herself as Madison Long, he heard Texas in her sultry voice. He was unaccustomed to his shock at the sight of an attractive woman. He ignored the feeling, astonished that he'd even noticed her appearance when all he cared about was Zeke and his survival.

She narrowed her eyes and he realized he must have been scowling. "Are you qualified to deal with trauma?" he blurted out, to re-establish focus on Zeke and his care. *Stupid question*, he chastised himself as soon as the words were out of his mouth, but there was no taking them back.

The V that had formed between her brows

deepened. Her curt "Of course" sounded haughty, and made him angry for some reason...probably at himself, if he was honest. During the drive to the clinic, his feelings of guilt had extended from Jeff to Zeke, and that hadn't helped his disposition. He was desperate for them both to pull through.

Then the veterinarian was all business. She asked him to explain what had happened and began her examination.

When she manipulated Zeke's leg and the dog yelped, Rick's angst spewed forth. "You're hurting him," he accused.

She looked aggravated. "I'm trying to *diagnose* him."

"Well, can't you give him an anesthetic or something to ease the pain?" He couldn't stand to see the dog suffer. "You..."

The door opening interrupted Rick, and one of the techs rushed in.

Ignoring Rick, the veterinarian spoke to the tech. "Oh, good, Sean. Can you please hold Zeke still and try to keep him calm while I finish my examination?"

"Sure," Sean replied, and moved into position beside the examination table.

When Zeke whimpered again, Rick threw

his hands up. "You can't let him suffer like this! Can't you just…"

"I have to determine the extent of his injuries before I can sedate him," she cut in. "I need you to stay quiet and let me do my job."

"But…"

"Sean," Madison interrupted and addressed the tech with a voice that brooked no argument. Her gaze, steady and angry, rose to meet Rick's. "Since the officer is being a distraction, please escort him out so he can wait in the reception area and we can do our best for his dog." As she lowered her eyes to Zeke, her expression softened and her whole demeanor changed. "We don't have time to waste quarreling."

Rick was about to object, insist that he had to stay. He *needed* to know what was happening with Zeke. When he felt Sean's hand on his arm, he wanted to argue or resist, but realized it wouldn't help anyone, least of all Zeke. It would only take valuable time and energy away from his care. Whether Rick liked it or not, this doctor was Zeke's only chance, and antagonizing her would do no good. He didn't bother to correct her that he was a sergeant or that Zeke wasn't his dog. Both facts were irrelevant.

He shrugged off Sean's grasp. "I can manage on my own," he grumbled, and left the room, with Sean closing the door none too gently behind him.

Rick moved restlessly about the waiting area, occasionally stopping to stare out the window. He worried about Jeff. He worried about Zeke. He fumed at the way the bust had fallen apart, and berated himself for not having been there to begin with. The guilt, anger and worry were an ugly maelstrom in his gut.

He called his parents to tell them he was okay. He knew they'd be worried because they would've heard the news by now. He called his sister, Sophie, as well, since she'd left him a couple of frantic messages. He assured her, too, and asked that she call their brother, Daniel. Rick phoned Logan next to get another update on Jeff's condition and the state of the investigation.

Jeff was out of surgery, but the doctors still couldn't give any guarantees that he'd make it. They'd done all they could for him, Logan reported, but Jeff had lost too much blood, and the internal damage had been extensive. There were no developments with respect to the investigation. All they knew of the shooter at this point was that he was probably Mexican.

Rick couldn't believe how what should've been a straightforward bust had gone so wrong. They'd received a tip, as they often did. It wasn't from one of their usual confidential informants, although they'd dealt with this CI in the past. Nothing major, but enough to establish a degree of credibility. With the time frame so short, they'd never properly validated the tip.

Would he have taken any additional precautionary measures if he'd been called in? In retrospect, he felt that an abandoned vehicle would have been a yellow if not a red flag for him, but would he have thought so in the moment? Or would he have been so anxious to get the bust that he would've done exactly the same thing they had? He let out a string of expletives as he spun away from the window.

And nearly bumped into Andrea or Angela or whatever the part-time receptionist's name was. He hadn't realized she'd approached him.

"Um, would you like some coffee or water…while you wait?" she asked.

Her eyes were round, and she linked and

relinked her fingers in front of her. Rick exhaled heavily. It wasn't like him to take his feelings out on other people. It was also rare that his temper got the best of him. He sighed and smoothed the harsh edge to his voice. "I'm sorry. Yeah, a coffee would be good. Thanks."

When she left to get it for him, he stared at the closed door to the exam room. Why was it taking so long?

His cell phone rang, and he answered it.

Jeff had gone into cardiac arrest.

CHAPTER TWO

MADISON HELPED SEAN wheel the gurney on which the sedated dog was lying to the clinic's recovery area. Once Zeke was settled and she'd given Sean strict instructions for his care, she washed up the best she could. She was a mess; it had taken nearly two hours, but she was optimistic that Zeke would be fine. That was worth anything to her. Fortunately, the injury wasn't as bad as she'd first suspected. The bullet must have just grazed him, and the damage was limited to the muscle and nerves in his right rear leg. An artery had been nicked, accounting for the significant blood loss, but his handler had been smart and acted quickly to stanch the flow. He'd likely saved the dog's life.

With some rehab therapy, Zeke would recover, as long as he didn't develop an infection. That was always a risk in cases like this, and she'd watch for it. She'd have to talk to the dog's handler, though—Rick, Angela had told her—and strongly urge him to consider retiring Zeke. The dog might only be six years old, but he shouldn't work again. With any luck, he'd enjoy eight or nine more years of just being a dog. However unpleasant the handler had been, it was clear he cared about his dog, so she figured it would be an easy sell.

Madison stripped off her soiled lab coat and stuffed it in a hamper. She thought about the groundbreaking platelet-rich plasma research she was part of at the San Diego Animal Rehabilitation Center. Zeke could be a candidate for a trial because of his muscle and possible nerve injury. But she was getting ahead of herself in her enthusiasm for the early success of her research. Whether platelet-rich plasma therapy was right for Zeke or not, she'd see to his rehab. If not through PRP, then definitely through aqua therapy.

She washed and dried her hands, then took a deep breath. She didn't relish facing the truculent cop, but at least she had encouraging news for him. She didn't want to consider what his reaction might have been otherwise. Was it just her personal experience, or did great-looking guys always have attitudes or tempers that were off the charts? This cop certainly proved her theory.

The cop in question was standing by the window when she entered the reception area. He had one hand jammed in the pocket of his pants and was holding a Styrofoam cup in the other. There were no other clients waiting. Fortunate, she mused, because if the strained look on Angela's face was any indication, the cop's disposition hadn't improved.

Madison had a definite aversion to ill-tempered people, but she accepted that in this case he had a legitimate reason. She would've been surly, too, if it was her Alaskan malamute, Owen, who'd been injured. Yes, police dogs had a job to do, but it didn't mean there wasn't a very real attachment between a handler and his dog. Perhaps it was even greater, since their very lives could depend on each other.

He was looking outside, and yet with the tension almost visibly rippling off him, she doubted his mind was on the tranquil green space the practice maintained for its patients next to the building. The slope of his shoulders and the fatigue evident on his face told their own story. He was hurting and vulnerable.

He must have been deep in thought, too,

since he seemed oblivious to her presence when she approached him. Of course, the comfortable, soft-soled clogs she wore might have had something to do with it.

She took another minute to study him. Tall, with wide shoulders that narrowed to a lean waist, he was obviously fit. She knew K-9 cops had to be. He had thick, jet-black hair, not closely cropped as many cops favored, but more stylish with loose waves. She guessed that, working narcotics, he'd go undercover at times, and a brush cut on a physique like his all but screamed cop.

She took a couple more steps forward. "Excuse me, Officer…"

His head snapped toward her. She must have observed him in a weak moment. Now his shoulders were squared and there was no sign of vulnerability.

"How's Zeke?" he demanded.

Madison raised an eyebrow at his brusque tone. She tried to rationalize again that it was out of concern for his dog and rushed to give him the good news. "Zeke's prognosis is positive. I was able to repair most of the internal damage. There might be some sustained muscle and nerve injury, but we'll have to assess that once he's recovered from the immediate trauma and the surgery. I'll watch for infection. Barring that, Zeke should recover well." She could see the relief on his face, softening the harsh lines, and his whole body appeared to sag. She glimpsed the vulnerability again and warmed to him a little. He *must* care deeply about his dog, she concluded.

"My expectation is that he'll require rehab," she said. "At the appropriate time, once we've assessed his needs, I'd like to discuss some experimental work that I'm involved in that might be beneficial for Zeke."

"Experimental? What are the risks? I don't want Zeke to be a guinea pig if there are any risks."

So much for warming to him. Did he really think she'd do anything that wasn't in the absolute best interest of an animal? "As I said," she continued in clipped tones, "we can discuss the options at the appropriate time. In the meanwhile, I want to talk to you about his future."

He frowned. "What about his future?"

She might not intimidate easily, but this cop set her nerves on edge. She thought she heard her own gulp and hoped it wasn't audible to him. Thinking of Zeke and what he'd been through firmed her resolve. Whether he'd like what she had to say or not, she had a responsibility to her patient. "You should retire Zeke," she said emphatically.

He paused, and seemed to reflect on it. "Is that a medical opinion?" he asked curtly.

"No. It's a humane one," she retorted.

"Well, it's not up to me. How long will you need to keep Zeke here?"

"Probably a week but, as I said, he'll likely need rehab. And he *should* be retired from active duty."

"Yeah. I heard you the first time." He dragged a hand through his hair. "Unless you need anything else from me, I should get going."

Need anything from him? How about a personality? Or a little courtesy? A simple thank-you would've been nice. He couldn't fathom how much it took out of her when she feared she might not be able to save a life. With Zeke, it had been touch and go because of the amount of blood he'd lost. "No. We've got everything we need."

He crushed the coffee cup, tossed it in a waste receptacle and started to walk away. Unexpectedly, he paused. "Look, thank you for what you did for Zeke. For saving his life."

It was almost as if he'd been reading her mind. Without the harsh undertones, she liked the deep timbre of his voice. How strange that goose bumps formed on her arms.

"Just doing my job," she said, wanting him gone because of the sudden discomfort she felt in his presence. When the front door chime sounded, she glanced toward it, and the tightness in her chest eased. She smiled broadly when she saw her next clients, twelve-year-old Tammy Montpelier, her mother and their miniature Doberman, Gustav. "I'll be right with you," she said before shifting her attention back to the cop. In that brief moment, his frown had returned. What was it that made him so moody? It had to be more than concern for his dog, since she'd told him the dog would be fine.

"I'll be in touch tomorrow to check on Zeke," he said.

"No problem." *What an odd man*, she thought as she watched him walk out the door. Leading Gustav, Tammy and Mrs. Montpelier to an examination room, she tried to block Rick—and the disconcerting sensation he stirred in her—out of her mind.

RICK'S EMOTIONS WERE a muddle. He felt light-headed with relief over Zeke. At least the dog was going to be fine. He wished the same could be said for Jeff. The last he'd heard, the doctors had restored Jeff's heart function with a defibrillator, but he was back in the OR. The doctors were concerned, although they said he had a fighting chance. And Jeff *was* a fighter.

Rick tried to ignore the worry, but that just left the anger and guilt to consume him.

He couldn't shake the feeling that what had happened to Jeff and Zeke was his fault. Intellectually he rationalized that it was nonsense, but it didn't negate the *feeling*. Jeff was a good cop but relatively young. With his own experience and more personal insights into how the cartels operated, Rick wondered again if he would've been able to detect that it was a trap. The simple fact that they'd had a tip—from a questionable informant—and that the van was found apparently abandoned should've been reason enough to exercise extreme caution. Who'd abandon a vehicle voluntarily if it contained drugs? Why hadn't the Narcotics Task Force guys see that, if Jeff hadn't?

Rick had no answers. Second-guessing

was futile, but Jeff was part of his team, so Jeff was his responsibility. Rick had decided to go to the San Ysidro border area the night before because the Sinaloa Cartel was rumored to be active there. Then he'd caught that boy trying to smuggle the kilo of marijuana across the border. Although Rick had never run drugs as a kid, it had struck too close to home, and he'd taken pity on the boy. He'd made arrangements to get him to Child Services instead of booking him. And that skirting of the law, even with the best of intentions, had taken considerably more time than arresting him would have. The result was Jeff and the Narcotics cops handling the incident without him.

Was his fixation on the Sinaloa Cartel all these years later—although they were no longer the SDPD's biggest concern since the Los Zetas Cartel had risen to prominence—a contributing factor? Rick had to admit that, right or wrong, he couldn't forgive or forget. Had his personal grudge caused him to make the wrong decision, and consequently a good cop, a young father, was fighting for his life?

And if it was an ambush, why? To send a message to the SDPD K-9 Unit because of the significant headway they'd made in shutting down the cartel's usual smuggling routes? It was plausible.

When he reached his SUV, he let Sniff out to relieve himself and stretch his legs before they headed back to the police division. He watched Sniff favor his left rear leg as he ambled about. Lying down for long stretches wasn't good for his partner. Watching Sniff, he considered next steps.

The unit needed to debrief, and he planned to have a one-on-one with Logan. He was almost certain that the Los Zetas Cartel was behind the trap. That made sense, since they were the ones who'd been impacted the most. Yet they were still the dominant force. The SDPD needed to take down their operations in San Diego.

Rick checked his watch. Logan should be back from the hospital by the time he got to the division.

Helping Sniff into the vehicle because he couldn't make the jump on his own reminded him that he wanted to take him to the clinic for a checkup. And that got him thinking of the new veterinarian, Madison Long.

He'd treated her terribly. She hadn't done anything to deserve it. It was just that he was angry, worried and—if he was rationalizing—

he might as well add sleep deprived. He felt rotten about having questioned her competence. She had to be good at what she did. Jane and Don wouldn't have brought her into the practice and entrusted her with the care of the SDPD canines if she wasn't.

Rick wasn't rude or ungrateful. His parents had raised him better than that. All the more reason for him to feel ashamed of the way he'd behaved. He knew he'd made a horrible impression, and couldn't really blame her for being abrupt with him. He could come up with all the excuses he wanted, but the bottom line was that he'd been a jerk. The vet had saved Zeke, and he should've shown her all the gratitude in the world for that alone.

Then she'd voiced his own thoughts about Zeke's having earned an early retirement. She was clearly a caring person. He wished he could have said yes, but Zeke wasn't his dog. With Jeff in the hospital, he'd make the recommendation. The decision, however, was Logan's. Something else he'd have to discuss with the captain. Had it been just that morning that he'd contemplated approaching him about retiring Sniff?

He and Logan had been talking about a renewal of the canines, planning for the future by bringing in some younger dogs. If they were going to be training, they might as well train a few young dogs at the same time. Those dogs would have to be checked over by the vet to ensure that they were physically sound…and that brought his thoughts full circle to the beautiful redhead.

It had been an emotional day, and he needed some sleep. That was all. Nothing more. He had to cancel his drug-awareness counseling session at the school, which he hated to do, but he just couldn't take the time. That didn't help his mood. It had turned out to be one of his worst days in recent memory.

He'd stop by the division, talk with Logan, find someone to cover his shift that night, set the wheels in motion for a debrief at oh-seven-hundred hours the next day, then go home, have a beer, get some sleep.

If he could shut his brain down long enough…

CHAPTER THREE

As it turned out, Logan wasn't back at the division when Rick got there. He'd apparently gone from the hospital straight to the scene of the shooting. Couldn't blame him. Rick would've done that, too, if he hadn't been with Zeke. In fact, he might just go there now, catch up with Logan at the scene.

"Where're you going, Pitbull?" Shannon Clemens, the sole female officer in their unit and one of the most recent additions to their team, called out to him as he started to pack up his gear. "You just got here." She made a sweeping motion around the mostly empty squad room. The few cops who were present had their eyes on him. "Everyone's asking what we're going to do about Jeff. About what happened to him."

Rick ran his fingers through his hair for what must have been the thousandth time that day, something he did when he was frustrated or overtired. "If I knew anything, I'd tell you. But I don't. Not any more than you already know." There'd been no updates since Jeff had gone back into the OR. He looked around, scanned the furious faces. They were all aware of what had gone down and praying for Jeff to pull through.

"The good news is Zeke's going to be okay." He could at least give them that much. "I'm going to try to catch Logan in the field."

"You won't get him there," Shannon said. "I was just speaking with Dispatch. Jagger's coming in," she said. "But he plans to make a couple of stops first."

She took a long look at Rick, so intense and appraising it made his skin itch. He was just about to ask, "What?" when she continued.

"You might not have been involved in the incident, but you look as though you could use some downtime. Why don't you go home? Get some rest. We've got the debrief tomorrow morning anyway. I'd bet that both you and Logan will be in before it starts. You can see him then."

Rick felt the need to act. To *do* something. But what Shannon said was true. He probably looked like hell—and she was just showing her concern. He finished stuffing everything in his bag and slung it over his shoulder.

"You're right, and thanks," he said to Shannon, giving her shoulder a light pat as he walked by. "See you all tomorrow," he said.

DESPITE A RESTLESS NIGHT, Rick couldn't remember a single dream or nightmare, for which he was thankful. He'd believed the events of the day before would bring the nightmares back to haunt him, but he'd gotten a solid five hours of uninterrupted sleep. That wasn't bad under the circumstances. He'd woken twenty minutes before his alarm was set to go off. Since then, he'd been lying wide-awake, listening to Sniff snoring softly on his own bed.

Rick folded his arms under his head and stared up at the ceiling. Why his thoughts kept veering back to the new vet he couldn't say, especially when he had so much else to occupy him. Well, he supposed he *did* have an idea why. He was intrigued, and it was more than her looks. She'd gone toe-to-toe with him and in a manner of speaking had won. She'd gotten him out of the way, not backing down when he was at his belligerent worst. And she'd done her job. He thought of himself as a nice guy, a gentleman—thanks to the Stewarts and how they'd raised him—but he certainly hadn't left Madison with that impression.

He knew exactly what his mother, Hillary, would have to say about his behavior. He smiled ruefully. He was twenty-nine years old and just short of six-three, and it was his mother, maybe five-four and a hundred and fifteen pounds, who could put the fear of God into him.

As he climbed out of bed and turned off his alarm, he resolved two things. He'd apologize to the veterinarian. Maybe even surprise her, stopping by the clinic to bring her a bunch of flowers or make some other conciliatory gesture. Second, he was well overdue for a visit with his family. He wasn't shy about admitting that he missed his parents. He'd set that up today, too. Plan a get-together for the weekend, if Sophie and Daniel were available.

He didn't accomplish either of those goals over the course of the day. Jeff hadn't survived the night, and that had cast a pall over the debrief they had that morning.

Everyone was both grieving and fueled up to bring justice to those responsible. Rick had barely had time to take restroom breaks; it was insanely busy at the division. When he'd found a rare moment to check on Zeke's condition, Heather, the clinic's regular receptionist, advised him that Madison was unavailable but Zeke was doing well. She also informed him that Logan had already arranged for the unit's admin, Beth, to stay in touch with her for regular progress reports. Rick's opportunity to make casual contact with the veterinarian and attempt to redeem himself was lost.

The important thing was that Zeke was recovering, and the risk of infection was diminishing with the passage of time.

The division had set a plan in motion to track down the men responsible for killing Jeff, bring them to justice and, if everything worked out, take down the Los Zetas Cartel's operations in California. It was a bold plan, not without risk, and would require cooperation from a number of policing entities on both sides of the border. Rick had volunteered to co-lead it with the captain of the SDPD's Narcotics Task Force. That was the least he could do.

IT HAD BEEN one emergency after another at the clinic over the past three days since Zeke had arrived. Even her regular appointments had created challenges. Daisy was a perfect example, Madison thought, while she cleaned up after seeing the skittish little bull terrier. Daisy had been in for a routine checkup and her shots, but she'd been so nervous, she'd emptied her stomach *and* her bladder during the examination. Madison shook her head. She hadn't managed to get out of the way quickly enough. As a result, she'd had to change, and one of the techs had to do a cleanup in examination room three.

Despite days like this, Madison loved her job, and she loved the groundbreaking research she was doing at the San Diego Animal Rehabilitation Center.

She was very excited and confident about the progress she and the center's team were making in the area of platelet-rich plasma therapy. The opportunity to participate in the PRP research and what it would mean for tens of thousands of injured animals had been the key reason for her move to San Diego from El Paso, Texas, where she was raised and where her father still lived.

She'd done her homework before making

the move, of course. The San Diego rehab center was the best and most advanced in the country in her area of interest. They also had the necessary funding, an essential consideration since the research was costly. In addition, they gave her free rein with her secondary interest—advanced aqua therapy. The opportunity had been compelling enough for her to leave her father, the only family she had.

She took a moment to think of Patrick Long, Supreme Court judge and the best father anyone could hope for. He'd started his career as a crown prosecutor, had gone into private practice and had been ultimately called to the bench. Since her mother had died of ovarian cancer when Madison was a toddler, it was just the two of them. As a kid, she'd shadowed her father and spent many hours with him at his office and even in the courtroom.

She missed him. Much more than she'd expected.

But her career meant a lot to her. A professional drive and a desire to make a difference were values her father had instilled in her from an early age. And those factors had resulted in her move to San Diego and the Mission Bay Veterinary Clinic.

Through her father, she'd gained a tremendous respect for police officers, and the dangerous and often thankless work they did. She'd also had enough exposure to police dogs to know their jobs weren't any easier and often more dangerous than that of their handlers.

When she'd joined Mission Bay, Madison had learned that they provided care for the SDPD's canines, and she'd expressed keen interest in working with them. It hadn't taken long to prove herself to Jane and Don, the clinic's owners. She'd been thrilled when in addition to her other duties she'd been entrusted with the care of the SDPD's dogs.

Zeke was the first police dog she'd treated for an injury sustained in the line of duty. It had hit her hard emotionally, and she was gratified that she'd been able to help him.

She'd checked on Zeke first thing in the morning. He was still groggy from his medication, but she was pleased with his progress and had reduced his dosage. There was no sign of infection, which was a huge relief. If all went well, she thought he'd be an excellent candidate for a trial of the PRP therapy.

She put on a clean lab coat, brushed her hair and braided it. She wanted to have another quick look at Zeke before her next appointment to ensure that he was doing okay with the lower dosage. As she did, she thought of the cop—Rick—who'd brought Zeke in. Too bad he didn't have a personality. A guy like him probably got by on looks alone, and didn't care how rude and unfriendly he was. Well, that wasn't her type. She appreciated appearance as much as anyone, but what really mattered to her was a man's inner qualities—what was inside. Rick seemed to have more than his fair share on the outside, but a major deficit in the personality department.

In the months she'd been at Mission Bay, she'd met most of the K-9 Unit officers and their dogs. Being single, Madison accepted the amiable flirting from the officers. And being human, she wasn't immune to the attention from the mostly good-looking cops. She didn't take any of it seriously. If she allowed herself to be shallow for just a moment, she had to admit that Rick was the most attractive of the group. But based on what she'd seen of him, there wasn't going to be any flirting.

Which was probably for the best. He made her feel uneasy.

Then, why was she even thinking about him? And why Rick rather than one of the supernice cops who were gracious and pleasant? She knew a lot of women were attracted to a rogue. She'd always scoffed at that, but maybe she wasn't immune to it, either. She laughed at herself. She really needed to get more of a social life if her thoughts were turning in that direction.

Satisfied that Zeke was fine, she left the recovery area. Her next appointment was with one of the few SDPD K-9 cops she hadn't met yet, K-9 Unit sergeant Enrique Vasquez or Pitbull. She rolled her eyes at his alias. His canine partner's name was Sniff. She smiled at the cute name for a narcotics dog. The cop evidently had a sense of humor. Sniff hadn't come to the clinic for nearly seven months, certainly not during the time she'd been there.

Madison checked her watch. Of course she had to meet a new client on a day she was behind schedule. She happened to be a stickler for organization and effective time management. She didn't like to keep clients waiting, nor did she want to make a poor first impression, but she needed to review Sniff's patient file first.

Sniff was the only Labrador in the SDPD's K-9 Unit. If she wasn't mistaken, Sniff's handler, Enrique, was the cop Heather gushed about—classically tall, dark and handsome.

Madison remembered what Heather had told her about this particular cop. He and Sniff patrolled the most hazardous part of the border between San Diego and Tijuana to thwart the cartel-related drug trafficking that occurred there. Heather had gone on at some length about Enrique's looks and charm when she'd handed her the file, until finally Madison had laughingly told her to stop. Heather had claimed he was the best looking in the unit, which she considered unlikely after having met Zeke's handler, Rick. In any case, Enrique would *have* to be more pleasant and better mannered than Rick had been, she thought as she rounded the corner to the reception area.

And she came to an abrupt halt.

Enrique Vasquez might have had his back to her, talking to one of the techs, but from what she could see, Heather had *not* been exaggerating about his looks. He was tall, with broad shoulders that narrowed to a lean waist and a trim backside. Realizing where her gaze—and her thoughts—had drifted, she pulled both away. He wore a baseball cap and must've been off duty, as he was wearing street clothes. He rested one hand comfortably on his dog's head, which showed a caring that appealed to her soft heart. When the cop raised his other hand to push back his ball cap, impressive biceps bunched under his short-sleeved shirt. "Wow," she breathed before she could catch herself. When he did it again, she focused on the way he moved rather than his physique. There was something familiar about him.

She felt a gentle nudge on her shoulder and heard a soft voice next to her ear. "I *told* you!"

It was just Madison's luck that she'd let her guard down when Heather was coming out of the back storage area.

"Yeah, well, I'm late and I'd better get going."

Heather placed a hand on her arm. "I'll let him know you'll be with him in a minute. Come join us when you're ready."

Madison was about to protest, but recognized that a minute or two to get herself in a more professional frame of mind wouldn't make much of a difference, time-wise. She was already worried about her first impression on a new client because of being late. A little later wouldn't matter, but if she was tongue-tied and scatterbrained when she met him, she'd embarrass herself. So she let Heather precede her.

"HEY, ENRIQUE," HEATHER greeted Rick in a pleasant singsong voice.

He waved goodbye to the tech, who'd been grilling him about his chances of becoming a police officer, and turned his attention to the receptionist. He generally didn't like to be called by his full given name—it reminded him too much of his childhood in Mexico—but Heather preferred it, and he'd stopped trying to dissuade her.

"I'm sorry we've kept you waiting. Madison had a bit of a…an incident with a patient and had to clean up. She'll see you and Sniff any minute now." Her face sobered. "I'm so very sorry to hear about Jeff. Please give his family our condolences."

"Yeah. Thanks." It hadn't gotten easier to deal with Jeff's death, despite the passage of several days.

"What have you got there?" She gestured

to the duffel he'd rested on the floor beside his feet.

Rick felt the heat rise to his face. "Just stuff," he mumbled. "So I understand Madison's taking over from Jane for our dogs."

"Uh-huh," Heather responded. She walked around the reception desk to return to her station.

Rick leaned on the counter. He wasn't at all perturbed about Madison's being late. It gave him a chance to question Heather about the new vet. Heather obviously didn't realize he and Madison had already met. There was no reason she would have, he reminded himself. Unless the part-time receptionist had told Heather he'd been in, she'd have no way of knowing that he was the one who'd brought Zeke. Even though he'd called about Zeke a few times, Heather must have assumed he was checking up on one of the unit's dogs. Her not knowing gave him the advantage. "Has Madison worked with police dogs before?" he began.

Heather sat down behind her desk. "You know, I'm not sure. She moved here a few months ago from Texas. She must have some experience. They wouldn't have assigned her to care for the SDPD's canines if she wasn't qualified. Logan wouldn't have approved, either," she added. "You'd have to ask Madison about her experience."

"Is she good?" He'd concluded that she was, based on what she'd done for Zeke, but he was curious about what Heather had to say. Working with Madison would give her a different point of view. The more he'd thought about it, the more he recognized the skill and calm resolve it must have taken to save Zeke. He was anxious to see him, after Sniff's examination.

Before Heather had a chance to answer, he heard soft footsteps behind him.

"I'll let you be the judge of that." Heather motioned toward the hallway. "Here's Madison now."

"Great. Thank…" Rick looked over his shoulder, and whatever else he was going to say escaped him. He felt his mouth go dry. Sure, he'd met her before, but he must not have been seeing clearly at the time. He certainly hadn't been *thinking* clearly. He'd remembered her as attractive but not dropdead gorgeous. She was wearing a lab coat again, a blue one this time, yet her curves were evident. Today, she had her hair in a thick braid, hanging over one shoulder. Even braided, the mass of it hung well down toward her waist. Instead of greeting him, she stood still, her lips slightly parted, shock on her face. It was almost as if she hadn't been expecting him—or had forgotten that she'd met him.

He took a step forward, Sniff trailing him, and smiled. "Are you ready for us?"

She gave a slight shake of her head, not so much to indicate *no*, but almost as if clearing her mind of whatever had preoccupied her. Before she could say anything, Heather filled the silence.

"Madison, this is Sergeant Enrique Vasquez, aka Pitbull, and his canine partner, Sniff."

"Officer Rick," Madison said with frost in her voice, and Rick's smile faded. Apparently, she wasn't inclined to let bygones be bygones.

"You've met?" Heather asked, obviously confused.

"Yes," they responded in unison.

Heather glanced from one stern face to the other and backed up. "Okay, then. I'll just get back to work."

Madison gave Rick one more long, hard look before stepping forward and bending down to greet Sniff. Her features softened; the dog's good nature must have won her over. By the time she straightened and extended a hand to Rick, the reserve had returned.

"As you *know*, I'm Madison Long," she said in a perfunctory manner, putting the emphasis on *know*, and flipped her braid over her shoulder. "Follow me, please."

Rick tapped his thigh, and had Sniff heeling next to him as he followed her. Madison's braid swung across her back with each step she took. Glancing at Heather, he saw her bemused expression and wondered what had caused it. Then he noticed the duffel he'd forgotten and rushed back to grab it before joining Madison.

"How's Zeke?" was the first thing he asked when they were in the examination room.

"He's coming along nicely."

"That's terrific. Can I see him when we're done here?"

"Of course," she said, gathering everything she needed for Sniff's exam.

She was being professional and courteous, but there was a distinct remoteness in her voice and demeanor. Conscious of the duffel in his right hand, he wondered how smart an idea that was. "The unit's retiring Zeke," he offered as an olive branch.

Her hands stilled and she gave him a contemplative look before nodding, but her cool formality remained as she opened a cabinet to get additional supplies. There was something...out of character about her expression. The lines bracketing her mouth were a dead giveaway that she laughed more than she frowned. He shifted the duffel from one hand to the other, then placed it on a chair in the corner of the room. "Look, I'm sorry for the way I acted when we first met."

She turned back to him, and he saw the surprise on her face.

"It was a hell of a day. Zeke being hurt wasn't all of it."

"I heard on the news that an officer was shot...and that he passed away... I'm sorry..." Her voice rang with sincerity and compassion.

"Yeah. Jeff didn't make it." Rick broke eye contact, reached down and stroked Sniff's back. The grief was still too raw. The dog raised his head, tongue lolling, adoration in his eyes that never failed to melt Rick's heart.

"What will happen to Zeke?" Madison interrupted his thoughts.

Rick's eyes lifted to hers and he could see she was moved, too. The fact that she seemed to care about Jeff and about Zeke said a lot about her. "Jeff's family—his wife and son—want to keep Zeke. Zeke mattered to Jeff and is therefore important to his family." He cleared his throat with a small cough and changed the subject to a more practical matter. "SDPD will pick up the cost of Zeke's treatment and rehabilitation. Whatever it takes, just do what's best for him. We'll help the family with some retraining so Zeke can adapt to being a pet. Jeff was a good cop...a good man. He'll be missed and not just by his family."

"I'm so sorry," Madison repeated in a whisper, and briefly rested a hand on his forearm.

"Thanks." The sense of loss and futility, the sudden rush of emotion, was threatening to strangle Rick. He coughed again to try to cover up his feelings, but the sorrow was backing up in his throat. He grabbed his duffel and held it out to her. "We got off on the wrong foot the other day. I brought you something. Sort of a peace offering."

Her gaze slid from his eyes to the black,

well-worn bag and back. "You're giving me a used gym bag?"

His nervous, amused laughter burst forth. He wasn't usually this awkward around women. But then he generally didn't start out from such a deficit. "No. Of course not!" He chuckled and fumbled with the zipper before placing the bag on the chair and un-zipping it. He reached in and handed her a brightly wrapped bunch of flowers. "These are for you."

Her eyebrows seemed to be stuck under her bangs, but at least the corners of her mouth had turned up. She took the bouquet from him. "You brought me flowers?"

He shoved his hands into the pockets of his cargo pants. "Yeah. It's a small token of apology. I was a jerk and I'm sorry."

"Thank you." She raised the bouquet to her nose and took a deep breath. "I love freesia. They smell heavenly."

He had no idea which of the colorful flow-ers was freesia, but he'd have to remember the name. It had evidently done the trick. He was surprised by and appreciative of the ease with which she'd put their awkward be-ginning behind her. No stalling. No making him grovel.

She retrieved a jug from the cabinets and filled it with water. When she'd placed the flowers in it, she lifted them to her nose again, closing her eyes as she inhaled. She opened her eyes again, and her gaze locked with his. He could have sworn he heard the clock on the wall ticking the seconds away as they stared at each other. There was something unfathomable in the depths of her eyes. "Sniff…" he finally said.

Madison smiled, took a treat out of her lab coat pocket and offered it to the dog.

Sniff accepted it politely. She lowered to one knee beside the dog. "What brings you here today, my friend?" she asked while she checked Sniff's eyes and heart rate.

Rick noted the tender, caring way Madison touched and manipulated Sniff's joints. She immediately eased up when he flinched as she moved his hind left leg. She raised her eyes, a hand on Sniff's back. "Cruciate ligament acting up?"

Rick nodded. She'd obviously checked the file. "I know he's not that old, but I want his policing days behind him soon."

Madison had a thoughtful expression on her face. "He's more than a tool to you, isn't he?"

Through her work, she must have discovered that very few handlers were able to maintain the detachment from their dogs to consider them "tools." Rick and Sniff were a team. He cared about Sniff as much as he cared about his two-legged colleagues. He nodded again, slowly.

As he watched Madison continue her exam, he felt a peculiar churning in his gut. Yeah, he'd had breakfast at six, grabbed a quick sandwich for lunch and it was almost five now, but he didn't think the sensation had anything to do with being hungry.

Rick shifted his weight from one foot to the other. He thrust his hands back into his pants pockets. He didn't want to dwell on the reason he'd done it—the fact that all of a sudden he was tempted to reach out and discover the texture of Madison's springy red hair or how smooth her complexion really was. He liked women. Sure. Too much sometimes. But this felt *different* somehow, and he'd just met her. He considered how gentle she was with his dog.

That's it! It was Sniff, he rationalized. Anyone who loved his dog was okay by him. That was all. He cleared his throat, wondering if he was coming down with a bug, and tried to ignore the strange sensation in his stomach.

Madison cocked her head slightly and shone a light into Sniff's right ear. "You would've initiated the process to retire Zeke, even if I hadn't bullied you into it," she said, switching the light to the dog's other ear.

Rick laughed. The thought that she'd be able to bully him into anything struck him as ludicrous—but judging by the look on her face, she wasn't amused. "Yeah," he said, sobering. "Of course. Zeke's earned retirement." Seeing that she was about to give Sniff a cortisone injection for the pain in his leg, he bent down to soothe and distract his dog.

Rick's head was only a foot or so from hers, and her scent swirled around him. It was something subtle and musky. It caused an uncomfortable itch at the back of his neck. He reached behind him to scratch at it. "So has Sniff," he went on. "And I don't want him getting injured to earn it."

Madison looked up at him again, and he noticed that her green eyes were specked with gold, the irises rimmed with it. "Sorry," he murmured, "what was that?" He'd entirely missed what she'd said.

She smiled again. "I asked what the SDPD usually does with service dogs when they retire. You told me what's going to happen with Zeke. Is that typical? And what'll happen to Sniff once he retires?" she asked while uncapping the hypodermic needle.

He shrugged. "In most cases, if a dog's handler is able to, he or she will generally keep the dog. Sniff will live out his life with me."

Madison gave Sniff his shot, the dog barely noticing the pinprick sensation. Seeing the look of understanding and concern in her eyes, Rick felt even more drawn to her.

"Jagger—our captain—he's having a barbecue for the unit this weekend. On Sunday." The words tumbled out before he realized he'd said them. Her eyes were questioning. She was no doubt trying to figure out what his declaration had to do with her. Before he could question his own sanity, he barreled on. "You've met Jagger and most of the unit already?"

She nodded, uncertainty still evident on her face.

"Why don't you come with me?" he suggested. They both rose, and Sniff danced between them, knowing the routine well enough that he expected a dog treat after an exam. Madison didn't disappoint him and offered him a biscuit she extracted from a glass jar on the counter, slipping some extras in her pocket.

"Why?" she asked.

"Why what?" He must have missed part of the conversation again. He didn't understand the question.

"Why are you asking me to go with you?"

What was she expecting? It was just a spontaneous thing. Did she have to analyze it?

She must have sensed his confusion and clarified. "Are you inviting me so you can introduce me to the whole unit? To help me fit in?"

He laughed. "No. I'm asking you as…as my date." He grinned, hoping it would seal the deal. He really wanted to get to know her better. The more he saw of her, the more he liked her.

Madison bent down to scratch Sniff behind the ears, pulling out another treat from her pocket and presenting it to him.

The fact that she seemed to be thinking about his invitation wasn't a good sign. At least she hadn't given him an outright no. But the "no" was coming. Rick could feel it. He was seldom wrong about women's re-actions to him. He supposed it would be un-derstandable if she declined. They hadn't had the smoothest of introductions, and he had to accept responsibility for that. He assumed his customary stance of hands in pockets, anticipating rejection.

Madison held his gaze for a long moment, until a smile spread across her face. "Sure. Why not?"

"Great. That's great. Are we done here with Sniff?" It seemed he'd been wrong this time, and he was glad of it.

"Yes. Other than the cruciate, he's in good health and obviously happy, but I agree that you should think about retiring him. His hind legs will only get worse with age and stren-uous use. You want him home as a pet, en-joying a well-deserved retirement, before he injures himself and perhaps does permanent damage."

"That's the plan. Can I see Zeke now?"

Madison nodded and took him to the re-covery area.

Zeke looked good, considering everything he'd been through. Madison explained that he was coming along nicely and could go to Jeff's family in a few days.

When they'd finished with Zeke, Rick paused by the door. "I'll pick you up at five on Sunday. Does that work for you?"

She nodded. "Yes, that's fine."

"All right." He was about to exit when he saw her grin. "I guess I'd better get your home address, right?"

"I guess." She took a pen out of her pocket, scribbled an address and phone number on a sheet of paper and handed it to him. "See you Sunday."

He folded the paper and tucked it in his shirt pocket, then gave her a jaunty little salute. "Yeah. I'm looking forward to it. Grab your leash," he instructed Sniff. Tapping the side of his thigh, he had Sniff heeling again as he walked through the reception area.

"Everything okay?" Heather asked when he passed the reception counter.

Rick raised his eyes to the ceiling, and his expression made Heather giggle.

"Don't worry about it. You're not the first man and you certainly won't be the last to come in here and react to Madison like that."

MADISON CLEANED UP the exam room. Since there were no patients waiting for her, she walked over to Heather and leaned on the reception counter.

"How'd it go with Enrique?" Heather asked with a smirk.

"Fine. Why do you call him that?"

"What? Enrique?"

"Uh-huh."

Heather shrugged. "I think Enrique suits him better than Rick—too common. So does Pitbull."

"What kind of alias is Pitbull anyway? Why do they call him that?"

"Logan told me it's because he's tenacious. About his work. About what matters to him."

Oh, yes, Madison could see that. She could see him being very determined and stubborn, depending on the circumstances.

"You two met before?" Heather interrupted her thoughts. "And you didn't remember him?"

"Oh, I remembered, all right," Madison said.

"But you let me go on about him..."

"First, I didn't know he was the sergeant. I thought his dog was Zeke, not Sniff. Also, you called him Enrique. I was introduced to him by Angela as Rick. No last name."

Heather grinned. "Well, I really do think

Enrique suits him better. He's not keen on it... *I* like it, though. I think it actually amuses him when I call him that. The aka suits him, too, but in a different way. Pitbull fits his personality. Enrique... Well, he's got that whole sexy Latino thing going for him, and that appeals to me!"

Madison chuckled.

"What can I say? I'm attracted to tall, dark, good-looking men."

Madison felt her eyes widen. It occurred to her that she might be treading on Heather's territory by having accepted a date with Rick. "Are you...together?"

Heather laughed, as well. "No! We're not." She got up and walked to the printer. Flicking her hair over her shoulder, she retorted, "But a girl can dream, can't she?" She grabbed a printout and left the reception area, her laughter drifting over to Madison.

Madison watched Heather walk away, but her thoughts were on a tall, dark and decidedly handsome cop. Yeah, a girl could dream.

CHAPTER FOUR

RICK RODE HIS Harley-Davidson Electra Glide onto the narrow driveway at Madison's house. He shut off the engine and removed his helmet. The small cottage-like house wasn't what he'd expected. As structured, organized, practical as Madison seemed to be, he'd expected something a little more... well, a little *less* fanciful. *Whimsical* was a word he couldn't remember ever using, but that was what popped into his mind. It made him think of the houses the hobbits occupied in the *Lord of the Rings* movies.

He remembered his parents taking him to all three films in the series when he'd first lived with them. He smiled at the memory of how they'd tried to translate, in their broken Spanish, some of the finer points related to Middle Earth that he hadn't understood, despite the fact that he'd spoken English reasonably well as a kid.

Just thinking about it gave him a warm

feeling he'd never experienced prior to being part of the Stewart clan. Madison's place made a similar impression on him.

Her house was well maintained, neat and orderly, if on a small scale. From what he'd seen, *neat and orderly* defined Madison. He dismounted and grabbed the spare helmet that had been strapped to the back carrier of his bike, then made his way to the front door.

He knocked and glanced at the planter next to him. It didn't surprise him that he couldn't see a single dead petal or leaf on the colorful, sweet-smelling plants or in the container. The flowers were so perfect he was tempted to touch them, to make sure they were real. He was a stickler for cleanliness, but he couldn't consider himself particularly neat. It was almost impossible, living with a police dog.

When the door opened, he felt like a teenager experiencing his first high-school crush.

Madison was wearing a flowing, frilly, multihued summer dress that might have looked fussy on someone else. On her it looked... He couldn't find the word for it, other than *right*. Her hair was in some fancy updo, little ringlets teasing the sides of her face. She wore dangly earrings. And her lips, with that beguiling smile, glistened with some sort of shiny stuff as if…well, as if she'd just been kissed and her lips were still moist from it.

He rubbed a hand over his stomach where a knot was forming because the thought of kissing her was all too tempting. Watching those lips, he saw her smile fade. He shifted his gaze to her eyes and noticed her staring at his motorcycle. He glanced over his shoulder at his bright blue bike—his pride and joy—wondering what had put the look of consternation on her face. There wasn't anything wrong with his bike. He'd polished it to a gleam that morning. He glanced back at her. "Is something wrong?"

She motioned toward the Harley. "You brought a motorcycle."

"Yes."

"Look at me." She gestured with a hand from her torso to her feet. "How am I supposed to ride on that thing in *this*?"

Rick did look at her. The light material fluttered in the gentle breeze, accentuating the curves he admired so much, the hem ending just above slim, shapely ankles. And he looked down at her feet, virtually naked in the high-heeled, delicate, almost nonexistent sandals she wore. He understood her dilemma, and felt a little foolish. "It's a *barbecue* we're going to," he said in self-defense. He indicated his own faded jeans and white T-shirt. "You know, burgers, fries, apple pie and beer."

Madison's eyebrows furrowed. Obviously, he'd said the wrong thing.

Rick tucked the spare helmet under his arm. "I'm sorry I didn't let you know I'd be bringing my bike. It didn't occur to me that it would be a problem." He dropped his gaze to her feet again, those darn sexy feet with the orangey polish on the toenails. "You can't ride in those shoes. Do you have some sneakers or something?" He almost groaned at the look she gave him. He'd managed to put his foot in his mouth again.

"Do you really expect me to get on that thing with you? As far as my outfit goes, you're taking me to meet your boss and your colleagues. My *clients*. I know I've already met most of them at the clinic. But that was work and I was in work clothes. Did you expect me to wear jeans?"

Rick felt frazzled and was starting to think this was a big mistake. He wasn't usually an impulsive person, and this seemed to be a perfect example of why he shouldn't be.

"Well, yeah. That's what they'll all be wearing."

"And their wives or girlfriends?"

"Much the same. But you look great!" he added hastily, forcing a too-wide smile and trying to appease her or at least recover some of the ground he seemed to be losing fast. "*Really* beautiful."

Her frown was more pronounced as she eyed his bike again. "I'll get my keys and we can take my Cayenne instead," she decided.

He waited until she'd turned her back, then rolled his eyes. She disappeared inside her house but left the door ajar. Before Rick had a chance to wonder why she hadn't invited him in, a big silver-gray dog, a beautiful Alaskan malamute, sauntered into the doorway. Rick wasn't afraid of dogs—obviously not with his profession—but he knew all dogs could be protective of their handlers, uh, owners. And their territories. In this case, the dog seemed relaxed, even friendly, although he had to weigh at least a hundred and twenty pounds. There'd be a lot of power in the dog's broad jaw. Madison hadn't mentioned anything about having a dog, but he shouldn't have been surprised. He wouldn't have expected one quite so large, though. Rick tucked his hands in his pockets and smiled. "How's it going?"

The dog plopped down right in the middle of the doorway, raised his snout and let out a woo-hoo sound.

He didn't look menacing. Rick held out a hand for the dog to sniff. When that went well, he crouched down and scratched him behind the ears, all the while wondering what was taking Madison so long to find her keys. He might not have known her well, but one thing he'd gathered from her office and her house—she was organized and neat, meticulously so. He would've thought she'd know exactly where her keys were. She should have been back already.

To pass the time, Rick ran a hand along the dog's silky coat.

He caught a whiff of that alluring musky scent of Madison's before he saw her enter the vestibule from a hallway to the left.

"Oh, I'm glad you met Owen. I'm sorry to have kept you waiting."

Seeing her, he nearly toppled over. He steadied himself with a hand on the railing.

He'd been disappointed that she was averse to riding a motorcycle, something he had a zeal for. He'd also been a bit baffled by her apparent lack of spontaneity. But now, seeing her... *Wow!*

She didn't seem to be holding keys. Instead, she'd reappeared wearing dark skinny jeans, a snug long-sleeved T-shirt and—biggest surprise of all—low-heeled biker boots. She'd undone the arrangement of her hair, and all that springy red now rioted around her face and shoulders, nearly down to her waist.

"You changed?" Rick immediately felt ridiculous about stating the obvious, but his brain cells must have gone into a coma. He couldn't think straight, staring at her looking so undeniably *hot*.

He rose, and she gave him a flirty smile. If she'd appealed to him before, what he saw now could drive him crazy. It wasn't about the clothes or how sexy she looked. Okay, that didn't hurt, he corrected himself. But it was about her spontaneity and her willingness to change her plans—and her clothes. *This* woman was someone he could really fall for.

"Yes," she said, her eyes sparkling. "You'd made your point."

"Sorry? What?" He'd been so distracted again he'd lost the train of their conversation.

She smiled, showing even, white teeth between sexy, full lips. "I had to change to be able to ride on your motorcycle." She slid an elastic off her wrist and reached up to tie her hair in a ponytail. "I'm glad Owen kept you company while I was gone," she said, and gave the dog an affectionate hug before sending him out into the yard.

"Great dog. *Big* dog!" Rick said as they watched him find the perfect spot on the grass. When Owen sauntered back, Madison placed a kiss on his snout, signaled him to go inside and closed the door behind her.

"Ready?" he asked, holding out the helmet he brought for her.

"Ready," she said, accepting the helmet and putting it on as she preceded him down the steps.

Rick theatrically patted a hand over his heart.

SINCE IT WAS SUNDAY, they made good time to the captain's house in Poway just off I-15, where the barbecue was being held. Logan O'Connor's place was a sprawling bungalow with an ample backyard. That was handy, since there were a *lot* of people there.

Taking in the throng, Madison was glad she'd changed. As Rick had predicted, all the men wore jeans or shorts, and there wasn't a single woman wearing a dress.

Shortly after their arrival, Logan asked for everyone's attention and made a toast to Jeff Bradford, their fallen colleague. Logan said that Jeff's widow had declined to attend; her loss was too recent, her pain too raw. One by one, all the cops present shared their most memorable story about Jeff. Then they all agreed to put aside the sadness and use the occasion to celebrate Jeff's life.

Rick introduced Madison to everyone she didn't know. It was nice to see the cops she'd already met through work outside the clinic environment. See them relaxed. Having fun. They were welcoming and friendly, even if a few reacted with raised eyebrows or mean-ingful looks cast toward Rick. A couple of the single cops—the ones who'd flirted with her the most outrageously at the clinic—jokingly pretended to be heartbroken that she'd chosen Rick over them. Mostly they did it out of earshot of their dates, but the few women who heard didn't seem to take offense.

It felt like a big, boisterous extended family, and everyone appeared to get along. Madison noticed only one person who appeared not to fit in. He sat by himself in a corner of the yard, a bottle of beer clasped in his hand. At first, she didn't think he was a cop. He didn't look like one. He was heavy and out of shape. She hid her surprise when Rick introduced him as Tom Brody, a K-9 Unit officer. She hadn't met him at the clinic yet, which was fine with her. There was something about him that made her uncomfortable. In a group where everyone was having a great time, he seemed sullen.

Madison was glad when Rick moved her along toward the two police dogs that were present. He introduced her to Boomer, Logan's explosives-detection dog. The other dog, Sawyer, was one of the newest dogs in the unit. He was still in training to be a cadaver dog.

Once she'd met everyone, they circled back to join Logan, who was standing by his barbecue.

"Can I get you a drink?" Rick asked her.

"That would be nice."

He excused himself to move to where the coolers were, returning a short while later. He held a well-chilled bottle of beer and a can of Coke. He offered her the beer.

Madison wasn't a big fan of beer. In fact,

she'd never had a full bottle in her life. She didn't want to be rude to their host or offend Rick, but she couldn't stomach the stuff. "Why don't you have the beer, and I'll take the Coke?" she suggested, reaching for the soda instead.

"Sorry, but that's mine. When I ride the bike, I don't drink."

Logan snatched the opened beer bottle from Rick. "Thanks," he said to Rick, and tapped the bottle against the can of Coke Rick held in his hand. "Since this is my place, I'm not driving anywhere. How'd you know I wanted a cold one?" Before Rick could reply, Logan turned to Madison. "Presumptuous of him. Thinking you'd want a beer without asking you. And not even bringing you a glass!" He made a tsking sound. "Personally, I picture you more of a wine drinker." He took a sip of the beer. "I'm thinking white wine. A well-oaked chardonnay?"

She laughed and he smiled in return. "I take it that means I'm correct?"

"It sure does. And I'd love a glass of chardonnay."

Logan grinned at Rick, handed him his bottle and smacked him on the back. "Hold this for me, will you, while I get Madison a drink?"

Madison watched Rick for some adverse reaction, but he didn't seem to mind. She liked a confident man who wasn't easily offended and wasn't unreasonably jealous.

They watched Logan's retreating back, saw him stop occasionally to chat with a guest or two, then disappear into his kitchen through a set of sliding doors.

Rick motioned with his Coke bottle toward the doors. "You just experienced firsthand why he's called Jagger."

"Jagger?"

"You know the Rolling Stones?"

"Of course." She was perplexed and amused. "What are you getting at?"

"Well, let's just say that the captain has moves like Jagger."

Madison laughed. "I assume you don't mean on the dance floor, like in the song by Maroon 5? 'Moves Like Jagger'?"

Rick raised his soda bottle to her in salute and took a sip. "I'll let you be the judge of that. And speaking of…" His words trailed off when Logan rejoined them and handed Madison a glass of wine.

"So, Madison," Logan began. "You're from El Paso."

She wondered how he'd known that. She hadn't shared much about herself with the cops who came to the clinic. But people talked. Including Heather, the clinic's receptionist. It occurred to her that being the captain of the unit, he might have done a background check on her when she'd been assigned to take care of the SDPD dogs. She wasn't sure that was acceptable procedure, but realized it happened.

"And your father is Patrick Long, Supreme Court judge, correct?" he continued.

"That's right."

"My father used to be a police chief. He had some dealings with your father concerning matters that had fallen under your father's jurisdiction. He held him in high regard," Logan added.

That answered her question about how he'd known where she was from.

Rick let out a low whistle. "Your father's a judge?"

Madison nodded. A lot of men were intimidated by what her father did for a living. She expected a cop wouldn't be, but you never knew.

"Impressive," was Rick's reply.

He didn't seem daunted. That was positive—and refreshing.

"With your family in El Paso, what brought you to our fair city?" Logan asked.

She was a private person, but one thing she didn't mind talking about was the reason she'd moved to San Diego—her research. Still, it was a hefty subject to get into, and she had a tendency to bore people with it. Rick must have picked up on her hesitation, because he interjected smoothly. "C'mon, Jagger. Save the interrogation for business hours."

Logan didn't seem disturbed in the least. Madison sensed there was more than a professional relationship between these two cops based on the way they bantered back and forth; they were friends, too.

"You've got a point." He smiled at Madison. "I didn't mean to pry. I'm glad Rick brought you, and I hope you enjoy yourself."

Logan excused himself to play host to his guests, and soon he started preparing dinner. Madison knew he wasn't married and she surmised he didn't have a date. She did, however, see exactly how attentive and smooth he was with his female guests.

She watched him with amusement. He manned the barbecue expertly while carrying on a conversation with one of the women. Suddenly Madison was distracted by a disturbance she caught in her peripheral vision. "No. Oh, no!" she whispered.

Rick, who'd been chatting with one of his colleagues, turned to her with a questioning look. She shifted her gaze back to Logan and the barbecue just as one of the dogs, Sawyer, with a near-effortless leap, snagged a steak right off the grill. Boomer, not far behind, started to bark furiously, getting everyone's attention. Logan, closest to Sawyer, gave him an "Out!" command, to no effect. He tried again, but Sawyer ignored him, and cavorted with the piece of meat dangling from his mouth.

"Jackson!" Logan bellowed for the officer who must have been Sawyer's handler. "Get your dog under control and get that piece of rib eye away from him."

Jackson rushed over, but it was obvious he was having a hard time containing his hilarity, which only incited Sawyer, who proceeded to engage in a spirited game of chase with his handler. Boomer joined in, until

Logan ordered him down, and he dropped where he was.

Madison tried not to laugh, watching Sawyer frolic around the yard. When the dog pranced in front of Brody, still sitting in the corner by himself, her eyes connected with his. Even from a distance, she could see something disconcerting in their depths. Her smile dimmed and she quickly looked away.

"Should we worry about your cooking, Jagger?" someone called out, drawing her attention back to the dog's antics. "Sawyer's a cadaver dog. He usually goes after rotting things!" There was another ripple of good-natured laughter as Sawyer continued to elude his handler, the steak hanging from his mouth. Another cop made a grab for the meat but ended up sprawled on the grass with only a piece of gristle that had torn loose in his hand to show for his effort.

By the time Jackson finally got hold of Sawyer, he was red-faced both from exertion and embarrassment. Everyone laughed uproariously at his expense. Jackson did his best, without success, to get the dog to release his prize.

"Might as well let him have it now," Logan

suggested. "No one's going to want to eat that steak."

"Sorry, Jagger," Jackson said self-consciously. "Can I put Sawyer in Boomer's kennel for a time-out?"

"Sure." Logan pointed to the side yard. "But since I only had enough steak for my two-legged guests, you, my friend, are going to be eating a hot dog."

That made all the cops laugh even harder. A few catcalls could also be heard. Madison couldn't help laughing along with everyone else.

Rick excused himself, explaining that he'd been involved in Sawyer's training and wanted to check on the dog and his handler, and loped after Jackson and his dog.

"Enjoying yourself?" Madison heard a slurred voice by her ear and was assailed by the scent of sour breath. She stepped back. It was Brody. He must have left his perch after they'd made eye contact. She took another step back.

"Yes, I am. Thank you."

She was about to walk away, but Brody grasped her upper arm with a clammy hand. "Where you going?" he asked.

There was no doubt in Madison's mind that

he'd had too much to drink. She wondered how he could get away with it at a party with a bunch of cops, including his boss. Then she realized that the whole time she'd been there, she hadn't seen him talk to a single person other than her when Rick had introduced them. Whenever she'd noticed him, he'd been sitting by himself in the same spot at the far end of the yard, drinking beer. She looked down to where he held her arm, hoping he'd get the hint and back off. When that didn't work, she tried to pull free, only to feel his grip tighten on her biceps. He had more strength than she would've given him credit for. She wasn't worried, though, not with a yard full of cops, but she was annoyed and uncomfortable. She didn't want to cause a scene.

"Look," she began. Before she could say more, the hand was off her arm, and a flailing Brody landed on his backside on the grass, the bottle of beer spilling on the soft ground.

Madison rubbed her upper arm where Brody's fingers had been digging, trying to ease the dull ache. For a second time, everyone stopped to look at the commotion. This time she wasn't on the periphery but central to the incident.

Rick towered over Brody, a menacing look on his face. He extended a hand. "Gotta be more careful there, Brody. Uneven ground here," he said, speaking loudly enough that anyone who was paying attention could hear. She was grateful that Rick was trying to defuse the situation to avoid causing a scene. But Madison was closest and heard him continue in an undertone as he helped the other man up, "Touch her like that again, and you and I are going to have a problem."

Madison glanced around quickly to see if anyone else had heard, but it seemed that they'd all gone back to what they'd been doing. Except Logan. The charm was gone as he watched the interplay with narrowed eyes. He obviously knew there was more to the incident than Rick had let on.

Brody grumbled something under his breath, then dusted off his jeans and moved away. She assumed he'd gone home, because she didn't see him again the rest of the evening. A couple of people mentioned that they'd seen him get into a cab. A smart move, in her opinion.

She saw Rick and Logan huddled together

shortly after the incident, with long faces and intent eyes. She was certain it had to do with what had happened with Brody, but when Rick returned, he was all smiles and easy manner.

He hardly left her side for the rest of the evening. The altercation with Brody aside, Madison had enjoyed herself. She was sad to see the evening end, but she had an early start at the clinic Monday morning.

At Madison's house, Rick placed both helmets on his seat and walked her to her front door. She hadn't thought to turn on the outside light, so they stood in the silvery glow of the moon.

"Thank you for coming with me today," Rick said.

"I had a nice time. You work with great people."

"I hope those *great people* will stop flirting with you now when they bring their dogs to the clinic!" he joked.

"And take all the fun out of my job?" she retorted.

He laughed and reached out to tuck a strand of her hair that had come loose behind her ear. His fingers lingered on it, and when he took a step closer and lowered his head, she let her eyes flutter closed. She didn't have to see him to know he was only inches away. She could feel his warmth, the caress of his breath. She didn't exhale, anticipating the brush of his lips across hers.

At the loud woo-hoo from behind the door, they both stepped back. Madison gave a nervous laugh.

"Your chaperone?" Rick asked, his voice a little hoarse.

"So it would seem." Madison might not have been accustomed to good-night kisses on a first date, but she was disappointed that the opportunity with Rick had slipped away. There was something she really liked about him. A number of things, actually. "I had a nice time," she repeated to fill the silence. "Thanks for inviting me."

Rick hesitated, then took her hand and lifted it to his lips. "Have a good night, Madison. I hope I'll see you again, soon."

Before Madison could say anything, he jogged down the steps, put on his helmet and placed the other inside the back carrier. Then, with a roar of the powerful engine, he rode out of sight.

CHAPTER FIVE

"HEATHER, PLEASE APPLY a discount of ten percent to Mrs. Singer's bill," Madison instructed the Mission Bay Veterinary Clinic's receptionist.

"Sure, but why?" Heather asked in a whisper.

"Mrs. Singer is elderly, and Maple," Madison said, referring to the woman's Labradoodle, "isn't getting any younger, either. We'll be seeing them on a regular basis."

"That's so—"

Before she could finish, the door to the clinic swung open and both women glanced at the blonde who rushed in. She was... *striking* was the word that came to Madison's mind. She was tall. On the slim side. Her face was longish, not classically beautiful, but...striking.

Madison looked at the dog by her side. Him she recognized. "Hey, Scout," she called to the German shepherd, and bent down to greet him. Then she looked up at the woman and met wide-set, intelligent but appraising eyes. "I'm Madison Long," she said. "Is there something wrong with Scout?"

"Madison's assigned to take care of the SDPD dogs." Heather joined them. "Madison, meet Jessica Palmer, Officer Calen Palmer's wife."

"Nice to meet you, Dr. Long. Do you have time to see Scout?" Jessica asked.

"I just finished my last appointment for the day, so yes. Of course." She led Jessica and Scout to examination room one.

"What's the problem?" she asked. Scout seemed fine to her. Energetic and happy. She crouched down to check his eyes, ears, teeth and gums.

"Scout ate a sock."

Madison glanced up at Jessica and noted the flush on her cheeks. "Believe me, it's not the first time a dog has done that." She proceeded to palpate Scout's abdomen.

"Maybe not, but it's the first time for me with Scout. I'm a doctor. I understand the risks. If it comes back out before it makes its way into his intestine, it's not dangerous," she went on hurriedly. "I know dogs usually eliminate small objects like this on their own, but…Scout is much more than a partner to my husband. He's part of our family. Cal risked his own life to save Scout. I don't want to take any chances."

Madison stood up and placed a reassuring hand on Jessica's arm. "Don't worry. He'll be fine." She removed a jar from a cupboard and a syringe from a drawer.

"What are you doing?" Jessica asked.

"Administering a small dose of hydrogen peroxide. I don't believe the sock's made it into his intestine yet, so it should be a simple matter of getting him to bring it back up."

"Oh, good."

"You and your husband weren't at the K-9 Unit captain's barbecue," Madison said conversationally, trying to ease Jessica's anxiety.

"No. We were out of town with our girls for the weekend. We were sorry to miss it." Jessica tilted her head and gave Madison a considering look. "You were there?"

Madison nodded. "Yes. It was fun."

"So…you went in an official capacity to meet the members of the K-9 Unit?"

Madison detected the curiosity in Jessica's voice. "No, I didn't. I went with Rick Vasquez."

"You *did*?"

Madison cast a quick glance at Jessica as

she extracted a syringe full of liquid from the jar. Jessica's mouth was all but hanging open.

"Yes. Is that a problem?"

"No. Yes. I mean, no… It's just… Rick? He doesn't usually…"

Madison wasn't sure she wanted to find out what Jessica was thinking. She'd enjoyed herself at the barbecue, liked Rick and was looking forward to getting to know him. She didn't want her judgment clouded. She changed the topic. "You said you're a doctor?"

"Yes."

"Where do you practice?"

Jessica flushed again. "Oh, I don't anymore. I run Care Across Continents. We're a charitable organization. We send doctors to developing countries in need. Have you heard of us?"

"Yes, of course. Your organization has an excellent reputation."

Jessica beamed with pride. "Thank you. We have a terrific team, and they really do good and meaningful work."

Scout started to emit dry, heaving sounds, drawing their attention back to him. His eyes were shut tight and his face looked as if he had a big, toothy grin spread across it. He was obviously trying to hold back from vomiting. The hydrogen peroxide was working.

Jessica immediately squatted down to comfort Scout, while Madison held a stainless steel bowl in front of him and stroked him gently. Within seconds, the dog could no longer control the heaving and he retched into the bowl.

Madison angled the bowl so Jessica could see its contents. "Mission accomplished. It looks like a tennis sock to me. One of yours?"

Pink cheeked, Jessica nodded.

"Safe to say, you don't want it back?"

Jessica laughed sheepishly. "Oh, no, thank you. I'm just going to have to find its mate before Scout does." She gave an embarrassed shrug. "I'm not the most orderly person, and Scout, being a search and rescue dog, is very good at finding articles I misplace. Usually I get them back…" She waved a hand toward the bowl. "And not in *that* manner."

"No, this wouldn't be the preferred method," Madison agreed with a smile, and emptied the contents of the bowl into a waste receptacle.

"You're new to the clinic?" Jessica asked while Madison cleaned up.

"I've been here a few months now. I'm not just new to the practice, but to San Diego."

"Oh, welcome! Do you like it?"

Madison dried her hands on a paper towel. "For the most part, I love it." She tossed the towel in the garbage and offered Scout a treat. "I miss my family and my friends, though." It surprised her that she'd confided in Jessica. What she'd said was true, but she didn't like to complain.

Jessica looked sympathetic. "I can imagine that would be difficult. I don't know what I'd do if I couldn't drop by my parents' house for a cup of tea and a chat. There's always the phone, but it's not the same, is it?"

Madison shook her head. "No, it isn't."

"I have to get Scout back, but how about having a coffee or a glass of wine one day after work in the next week or two?"

Madison ruffled Scout's fur, then opened the door to the examination room. "That would be nice."

Jessica shook Madison's hand on the way out. "Good. I'll give you a call to set it up. Thanks for your help with Scout."

"No problem. I look forward to getting to-gether." Madison meant it. She felt a connection with Jessica, one that was based on more than the similarities in their professions.

IT WAS ONLY MIDAFTERNOON, but the day had already been a grueling one for Rick. Despite its being a scheduled day off for him, he'd been at the division since six that morning. He and Logan and a couple of the other guys from the unit had met with SDPD Chief Cohn, and the heads of the SWAT team and Narcotics Task Force. They'd kicked around their strategy for taking down the Los Zetas Cartel. Through their intelligence sources, they'd been able to ascertain that it *was* Los Zetas behind Jeff's murder.

They'd considered every opportunity, every known risk and potential flaw, until they'd exhausted themselves. They'd been working on the plan all day, refining it as much as they could. In their line of work, there was never such a thing as a perfect plan.

They figured they'd have one shot at it; they were taking it and they'd better make it work. They didn't want any cops or innocent civilians sustaining any injuries, and certainly didn't want to risk the loss of another life. There was more at stake here than curtailing the cartel's operations. No one could ignore what had happened to Jeff. And if they could stem the flow of narcotics into San Diego by shutting down one of the most active Mexican cartels—even for a limited period of time before they regrouped—they'd accomplish something significant. They had to believe there were kids who wouldn't be lured into a life of drug abuse or trafficking if the SDPD could eliminate the enticement.

Rick thought of Madison often throughout the day and had wanted to call her. But the day had brought back memories of Jeff's murder, and Rick just couldn't force himself to sound cheerful. It was with the gloomy cloud of loss and grief hanging over him that Rick entered his parents' house that evening. This house had been his home from the time he was thirteen, the home in which the Stewarts had raised him to become the man he was.

Countless times he'd thanked the powers that be that his mother, Hillary Stewart, had been volunteering at Child Services the day he'd dragged his sorry butt in, and that she'd seen something in him that he hadn't seen in himself. The Stewarts had fostered him, adopted him and in the process more than likely saved him.

He hated the idea of bringing sadness to his parents' home, not to mention worry. He fully appreciated that his family's concern about his safety would be heightened by the recent events.

But merely walking through the cheery living room and into the bright, sunshine-yellow kitchen lifted his spirits—which rose even more when he saw his mother standing at the kitchen sink, washing vegetables.

She was humming some jaunty tune. With the water running she must not have heard him approach because she jumped when he wrapped his arms around her waist.

"Oh, Rick! You took ten years off my life!" Hillary exclaimed, turning and placing a hand over her heart.

He enfolded the petite, blonde woman—his polar opposite—in a bear hug. "Hey, Mom!" He dropped a kiss on the top of her head and inhaled the scent he'd grown up with—sweet alyssum and lily of the valley. He knew what it was because he'd been so fascinated by it when he was a kid, and she'd told him more times than he could count.

When Hillary tried to step away, he held tight. "One more minute, Mom. I need this."

She hugged him back, and he wondered

how he'd been so lucky as to end up with these people as his family. "Where's Dad?" he asked as he released her.

Hillary laughed. "Where do you think? He's in the garage puttering away on something or other. He's expecting you. I'm sure he'll be in soon." She slid her arm through the crook of his. "But it's just us for now, so we'll have a chance to catch up." She steered him to the kitchen table, then set about brewing a fresh pot of coffee.

Rick pulled out a chair, turned it around and sat with his arms crossed on its back. He took pleasure—as he always did—in watching his mother's efficient and graceful movements. Yet today, he could sense the nerves below the surface. "You want to talk about it?" He didn't have to clarify that he meant Jeff's murder. He understood his mother well enough to know it had been troubling her since she'd heard about it.

She glanced over her shoulder, worry etched on her brow, the sheen of moisture in her eyes. "I don't know what there is to say, other than my heart is broken for his family. We met him, didn't we? At your birthday celebration last year? Him, his wife and their little boy."

Rick nodded.

She turned to the coffeemaker, but he could hear the raw emotion in her voice. "It could've been you."

"Yes, it could've. But it wasn't."

With her back to him, she nodded rapidly. "That's good, yes, but it's selfish, too. Oh, that poor man and his family…"

Rick had spoken to Jeff's wife and mother. He knew them both personally. Although he hadn't been the one to impart the heart-wrenching news, he'd had to talk to them. Extend his condolences and whatever support he could. He had no words of comfort to offer his mother. He knew perfectly well that cops' families lived each and every day with the possibility that their loved one might not come home that night. Not prevalent, but it happened. Whenever a cop lost his or her life, the apprehension grew more intense. How could he bolster his mother's spirits when he himself felt so down? Then it occurred to him that he had a way to distract her. "I met a woman."

Hillary spun around. "Oh?"

He hadn't intended to raise the subject, but it seemed to have been the right thing to do. Through the remnants of tears, he could see the bright curiosity in her eyes. Oddly he found he *wanted* to talk about Madison.

"I thought that would get your attention."

She finished pouring the second coffee and brought both mugs to the kitchen table. "This is major," she said with a raised brow.

Rick took a sip of his coffee. "C'mon. It's not that big a deal. It's not as if I don't date."

"Oh, you date," she said. "*That's* not news."

"Then, why are you looking at me as if I've grown horns or something?"

She chuckled and patted his hand. "Don't you realize what you've done?"

Baffled, he shook his head.

Her grin widened, and she cupped his cheek. "Rick, my dear son, this is the first time *you* started a conversation about a woman you're seeing."

"I'm not seeing her. Not exactly...yet."

She dismissed his comment with a wave of her hand. "That might be. But think back. Do you remember a time when Sophie, Daniel or I didn't have to pry it out of you if you were seeing someone?"

Was that true? If his mother said so, it must have been. "Huh" was all he said.

"Well, then. Tell me about this woman before we're interrupted."

"Too late for that," his sister, Sophie, said, walking into the kitchen with baby Emma balanced on her hip. She leaned down to give Rick a kiss, and handed the baby to her mother with a hug and a kiss before sitting on the chair opposite Rick. She leaned her elbows on the table, rested her chin in her hands and fluttered her lashes. "So do tell, dear brother. Who *is* this woman, what makes her so special and when do we get to meet her?"

Although Rick gave his mother a mock exasperated look, she was oblivious to it. She was preoccupied with bouncing his adorable blonde niece on her lap, while the little girl finished off a chocolate-chip cookie she'd snagged from a jar his mother kept on the table.

Emma noticed him watching her, and stretched her pudgy arms out toward him. "Wick. Wick!" she called.

He was a marshmallow when it came to Emma. There was no way he could resist her. He leaned forward to take her from his mother, despite the chocolate smudged on her fingers and face. "Rick," he enunciated for her. "It's Rrrick."

"Wick. Wwwick!" she exclaimed, and

planted noisy kisses on his cheek. From the way his mother and sister smirked, he presumed he now had chocolate smeared all over his face.

"Here, let me take her," Sophie offered.

"Not on your life." Rick settled Emma more comfortably on his lap, handing her another cookie from the jar.

Sophie shrugged. "Have it your way, but tell us about your new girlfriend."

"I think that's where you walked in. I was just explaining to Mom that she's *not* my girlfriend. I've only taken her out once."

"Hmm," both women said in response.

When he gave them another frustrated look, his mother rubbed his forearm. "And as I was pointing out, you started this conversation. You might as well finish it."

Rick took a deep breath and dived in. He told them about Madison and how they'd met. He felt pride in talking about her work and her accomplishments.

"Educated, beautiful and no pushover. I don't think you could respect someone—at least, not in the long run—who wasn't capable of standing up to you," his mother said.

He chuckled. "Oh, there's no risk of her *not* being able to stand up to me."

"So where did you take her on your first date?" Sophie asked, wiggling her eyebrows as she rose to get herself a cup of coffee.

"To Logan's for a barbecue."

The two women exchanged meaningful glances. "You took her to meet your boss?" Sophie asked. "On a first date?"

"It wasn't like that. Logan was having a barbecue for the unit and I asked her to come with me. Besides, she's met most of the guys already through her work. She fit right in."

"So you took her to meet your boss *and* your coworkers?" his mother asked, before she and his sister traded looks again.

"Hey, it's not the first time I've done that."

"But it's the first time on a first date!"

"Okay, that's enough teasing for now, Sophie. Let him be," his mother admonished, without heat in her voice. "When do we get to meet Madison?"

Emma started to fuss, obviously frustrated by not having Rick's undivided attention. He bounced her on his knee until she quieted again. "Well, it's been too long since we've had a complete family get-together. Why don't we plan something soon when you're all available? Daniel, too," he said. "I'll bring Madison."

"How about that? We didn't even have to prod," Sophie noted.

Hillary laid a hand on her arm. Rick could tell the difference between an encouraging touch, like the one his mother had given him a few minutes ago, and the restraining one she had on Sophie's arm now. "That would be nice, dear. Why don't you let us know what works for you?"

"Let me have another date or two with her first. Make sure we're compatible."

"You do that and give us a call when you're ready." Hillary smiled mischievously. "So let me sum this up. You're telling us about a woman you met at a difficult time. A woman you irritated on your first meeting. But you managed to turn it around so she'd go on a date with you. You're willing to introduce her to us, but you're not certain yet if you're compatible? Have I got that right?"

He'd just taken a sip of his coffee, and nearly spit it back out with his laughter. "I never said I was the smartest of your kids," he told her with a grin.

She patted his hand. "It's never been a competition. You're all smart and, more important, good people. I hope—"

Whatever she was going to say was forestalled when the outside door opened and Rick's father, Harold, strode in. He was a tall, slim man, with light-colored hair starting to show some thinning at the crown, but he had the sharpest gray eyes Rick had ever seen. He had their little shih tzu at his heels.

Seeing his son, Harold strode over. Rick was barely out of the chair when his father embraced him and Emma at the same time. "Good to see you, son. Real good."

He hugged his daughter next, then his eyes landed on his wife of forty-two years. Rick knew those gray eyes of his father's never missed a thing—to Rick's chagrin when he was a kid.

"Hey, Toby," Rick greeted his parents' dog.

Showing none of the distress she had earlier, Hillary beamed up at her husband. "Your son says he's met a woman!"

His father's laugh was immediate. "When *doesn't* he meet women?"

Hillary poked her husband's side. "I think this is different." She looked to Rick for confirmation.

"I don't know yet. Let's see where it goes," he said noncommittally.

MADISON WAS OUT with Owen for his last walk of the day when her cell phone rang. With a sense of anticipation, she took it out of her pocket. She felt mildly disappointed realizing it wasn't Rick, but consoled herself that it was the next best person—her father.

"Hey, Dad!"

"How are you, honey?"

She let Owen off the leash in the deserted park, knowing he wouldn't go far, and sat on a bench.

"Good, thanks."

He asked about her research project and her work, and she gladly told him. He was such a huge supporter she doubted she would've been able to accomplish half of what she had without his encouragement and belief in her. "And what about you, Dad? How's that case you mentioned when we last spoke?"

She heard him sigh. "Jury trials can be the bane of my existence."

"It didn't go the way you thought it should?"

His laugh was without humor. "I just don't understand jurors sometimes. The facts are irrefutable, and a group of intelligent people can't come to the right and obvious conclusion."

Madison kept an eye on Owen while her

father ran through the case and its outcome. When Owen returned, she held the phone to her ear with her shoulder and snapped on his leash for their walk home. She smiled at her father's categorical statement about there being a "right" decision. To him, the law was everything. His work energized him, but she was well aware that this wasn't the first time he'd been frustrated with the outcome of a jury's deliberations.

"Isn't the jury's role to make a decision beyond a reasonable doubt?"

"Well, *of course*, and that's my point. You'd think they could see the right and wrong of it, when it's plain as day and directly in front of their faces!"

Madison chuckled. She respected her father greatly. He was the most principled, honest and ethical person she knew. But sometimes he could be a little unyielding. She'd learned that early in her life, even before he became a judge. With Patrick Long, there wasn't a lot of gray. Not much stretching the line. That was probably what made him such a good judge—he didn't let compassion outweigh the letter of the law; however, it caused him no end of frustration on the rare occasions a jury put feelings ahead of facts. From what she understood of this case, that was what could have happened. The evidence that the accused had murdered his own brother seemed unambiguous, but the jury must have factored in the hard upbringing he'd had and been lenient.

"I know I can't enter a judgment, notwithstanding the guilty verdict, since it's a criminal case and the jury acquitted. Still, I'm seriously thinking about granting a motion to set aside the judgment on the basis that no reasonable jury could've reached the verdict they had if they'd correctly applied the law. I've never taken such a drastic step in my career, but in this case, there may be…well, let's say extenuating circumstances for me to consider it."

That statement surprised Madison. She understood the law sufficiently to realize what a drastic step that would be. She wondered about the "extenuating circumstances" comment. Was it bribery or intimidation of a juror that had swayed the decision? She didn't ask him about it. If he could've told her, he would have. He'd said the accused had an association with organized crime; she concluded that attempted intimidation of jurors was a distinct possibility. She hoped *he* wouldn't be at risk if he did take the step he mentioned.

They chatted about more mundane topics as Madison made her way home and said good-night as she let herself into her house.

Standing in the hallway of her dark house, she tried to put concern for her father out of her mind. She trusted him to be careful.

Instead, she turned her thoughts to Rick. She wondered why she hadn't heard from him since their date. He must be busy, she rationalized. If he was, she didn't want to bother him. She'd give it another day or two. If he didn't call her, she'd take the initiative and call him.

CHAPTER SIX

RICK WOKE BEFORE his alarm went off, but he felt rested. Remarkable how invigorating it was to spend time with his family. Seeing his parents, like he had the evening before, always put him in a good mood, no matter what was weighing on his mind. Add to that, his sister, Sophie, had been there with his favorite girl, Emma, and spending time with his folks went a long way to dispelling the anger, guilt and just plain mad that had been plaguing him since Jeff's shooting.

As he went into the kitchen to fix breakfast, Sniff trailing behind him, he thought he understood what people meant about having a spring in their step.

He still felt terrible about Jeff, but he took comfort in the fact that the SDPD had a plan to take down the cartel, and he'd be integral to its execution. They had the buy-in and cooperation of the other relevant authorities.

Rick let Sniff out into the backyard, then

pushed the button for his coffeemaker to start the brew cycle. He wasn't particular about much, but he loved his coffee—especially that first cup in the morning—and he loved it strong. While waiting for the coffee to brew, he wandered around the kitchen and living room, picking up the odds and ends Sniff had "displaced" in his efforts to amuse himself while Rick had been out the evening before. It was just one of those behavioral idiosyncrasies some police dogs had. He'd become accustomed to it a long time ago, and considered himself fortunate that Sniff wasn't a search and rescue dog. They could be brutal to a place if they caught a scent they wanted to follow.

As he stood by the window, coffee mug in hand, watching Sniff, he thought of the other reason he was feeling pretty darn good this morning. Madison. It felt great to have met a woman who interested and intrigued him. He wanted to see her again.

Sniff ambled to the door and pressed his nose against the glass, his breath fogging it. With a laugh, he let the dog back in and scooped kibble into his dish. While Rick quickly had a bowl of cereal and a large glass of orange juice, he watched Sniff transfer his weight from one hind leg to the other as he inhaled his own breakfast. Clearly, his cruciate ligaments were bothering him again this morning.

Rick had the evening shift, but he was headed to the division anyway, for a workout. He'd have a word with Logan before he went to the gym. He wanted to begin the conversation about Sniff's retirement. He knew there'd be the additional challenge of getting approval for the unbudgeted cost to acquire and train another dog in addition to Zeke's replacement, but Logan cared about dogs, too, and Rick trusted he'd be receptive. None of them wanted to see a dog hurt on the job, and Sniff's mobility impairment put him at risk.

Finding the right dog to be Sniff's replacement and training him would determine the timing, but his four-legged pal had earned an early retirement. Sniff would also have the benefit of companionship in his old age with Rick's new canine partner around.

He thought about Madison again while he drove to the division. He'd give her a call and arrange another date. Sophie had made a good point. Just the two of them this time. An opportunity to get to know her better...

and be alone with her, without other cops hanging around and vying for her attention.

He parked his vehicle in his designated spot, and brought Sniff into one of the holding pens adjacent to the training yard.

Logan was in his office but clearly preoccupied with something, so Rick took only a few minutes of his time. Mentioning Sniff's health challenges and the idea of retirement was enough to get the captain thinking. After leaving Logan's office, he headed to the gym.

"Hey, Brody. You're looking a little rough this morning," Rick commented, seeing the other cop enter the squad room as he was exiting. Rick squatted to give Brody's dog, Nitro, some attention.

"Leave him alone," Tom Brody snapped.

Rick kept his hand steady on the dog's head. Because of that, he felt the dog's immediate tensing at the harsh tone of his handler's voice. He gave the dog a final, calming stroke before rising.

Rick noted Brody's disheveled appearance—the greasy hair, the shirt with one button undone, the scuffed and dusty shoes. "Do we have a problem, Brody?" Rick's voice was unruffled on the surface, but anyone who knew him would have recognized the no-nonsense resolve beneath.

"This damn dog." Brody gave the leash a hard tug, despite the fact that the beautiful near-black Malinois–Dutch shepherd cross was sitting sedately. "He acted up in training again. He wouldn't focus and indicate when I deployed him, and he wouldn't 'out' his damn toy."

Rick's simmering anger threatened to boil over, something he seldom allowed. He took a step forward, intentionally forcing the other cop to look up at him. "Brody, go get yourself a coffee, huh? I'll watch Nitro while you take a break. Sounds like you guys could use a time-out. I'll take him to the yard for a bit." His words weren't antagonistic, but they still carried the authority he knew few would argue with.

"Fine." Brody took a step back. He passed the end of the leash to Rick. "Go knock yourself out," he added before stomping off, mumbling something under his breath. Rick knew it was directed at him and not complimentary. He shook his head watching Brody, and wondered why the guy didn't participate in at least the basic fitness programs. That cop hadn't seen the inside of the gym for years. Rick might've been a sergeant, but Brody didn't report to him. Brody wasn't his problem.

He ran a hand along Nitro's back and was gratified to feel the dog's tension subside. Handlers had to be alpha to their dogs, but it was a bad situation when a dog was stressed just being in the vicinity of his handler. He knew a good canine with an ineffective handler made a poor team and could be a recipe for disaster. It also frustrated him that, more often than not, the dog was blamed when it was the handler's fault.

Rick left Nitro's leash slack and signaled him to heel.

Nitro had come to them with an excellent pedigree when he was fourteen months old. He had all the qualities they looked for in a detection dog—initiative, intensity, speed, agility and intelligence. He had high prey drive, combined with moderate rank drive, making him an ideal police dog. Nitro also possessed an elevated level of independence, which was better suited for narcotics dogs, allowing them to cover large areas more quickly. For explosives dogs it could be a hindrance since the dog might not readily perform directed searches of the type needed for explosives. However, they'd needed an explosives-detection dog at the time, and they'd found that Nitro was not just intelligent but adaptable. His independence wasn't a deterrent. But Rick suspected that Nitro might have been a bit *too* independent and strong-willed for the spineless Brody.

Rick had some experience with explosives detection, too, so he'd worked with Nitro for some of his training and felt the dog had excellent potential. Unlike what Brody had claimed, Nitro had performed very well from an obedience standpoint and never demonstrated problems with "outing," or releasing, his toys.

But an out-of-shape handler with an intense, fast-moving, purely instinctive animal was not a good pairing. Rick shook his head in disgust. Not the dog's fault, he thought again. He draped Nitro's leash across the dog's back as they walked outside. He knew Nitro didn't need to be led. He had the dog follow him into the kennel area, where he'd left Sniff. He put Nitro into a kennel briefly, too, while he went into the yard to set up the training exercise. Once he was done, he released both dogs and called them to follow him to the yard.

When he reached down to unclip Nitro's leash, the dog flinched. Rick narrowed his eyes and felt his temper rise again. In his experience, dogs flinched when you reached toward them only if they expected to be struck. That meant it had happened to Nitro on more than one occasion. Although Rick had no fondness for Brody, he hadn't planned to make an issue of what had happened that morning. But if Brody was abusing Nitro, Rick couldn't ignore that. He had to tell Logan what he suspected.

Rick instructed the dog to sit-stay. With quiet, soothing words, he allowed Nitro to sniff his hand, then slowly reached from below his head and around to unclip the leash. He hung it up near the entry gate and let the dogs run around to blow off some steam. Ordering Sniff to down-stay, he motioned for Nitro to follow him.

Rick had set up a training cylinder containing trace amounts of explosive residue in a wooden storage box, and he'd placed several decoy cylinders and various other scented decoys around the yard while the dogs had been in the kennels.

When he gave the order for Nitro to search, he observed him carefully. Rick purposely didn't direct or encourage the dog, yet Nitro quickly found the training cylinder. He did the appropriate passive indication, sitting and staring at the storage box containing the cylinder. The dog was a perfect detection dog—if properly handled. Rick followed the training exercise with some basic agility and environmental drills, then released Sniff and allowed the dogs to play for a few more minutes.

When he reached over to affix Nitro's leash to his collar, he watched the dog carefully—and was revolted to see him flinch again.

He'd have to speak to Jagger about this, no question. He checked his watch. He was anxious to do it, but it would have to wait, or he'd be late for his and Sniff's drug-abuse awareness session with the teens at La Valencia High School. It was the session he'd had to cancel the day of the shooting. He'd rescheduled and didn't want to be late.

On his way he'd give Madison a call.

But when he got into his SDPD Explorer, his personal cell phone rang. He glanced at the display and saw it was Sophie. He knew that if he answered, he'd be on the phone with her until he got to the school. But he loved his sister and couldn't ignore her call.

Sure enough, he finally had to force her to let him go when he arrived.

Rick parked his SUV in the lot at La Valencia High and ordered Sniff to hop out. In addition to his collar and police badge, he put the SDPD jacket he'd had specially made for Sniff on him. Sniff preened and did a little dance, despite his sore hind legs. Sniff loved the kids, always had, and was eager to get started.

Rick stopped at the administrative office to check in. The office manager greeted him warmly. Rick liked Nina, had even taken her out a couple of times. Nothing serious, but they'd had fun. He'd realized she was more interested in him than he was in her; it had never been much of an issue for him. But today, seeing her lean toward him in a suggestive manner, he thought of Madison.

One date with Madison and he felt it was wrong to flirt with someone else? That was new for him, too. Not that he'd ever *cheated* on a woman he was dating. He'd never do that. But most of his relationships had been casual, and harmless flirting with an attractive woman had never been out of question. Until now.

He gave Nina a quick wave and backed

out before she could engage him, and maybe suggest getting together.

With Sniff at his side, he hurried to the auditorium, where he knew the kids would be gathered. The murmurs died down when they entered. It never failed. Whatever other issues these kids might have, it was good to see that at this age they still had a healthy respect for the law. Rick regretted that would change for too many of them. He knew the sobering statistics about the percentage of kids in the room who'd become involved with drugs—whether dealing or using—and then there were those who'd be drawn into other illegal activities.

He waited for the teacher to make the usual introductory remarks, then he and Sniff took over. They did their normal presentation. At its conclusion, the kids giggled while Sniff did a search for drugs, snuffling each of them in the process. Watching Sniff, Rick let his mind wander to Madison again. He needed to find the time to give her a call when he was done and ask her out to dinner. He really wanted to see her.

MADISON TIGHTENED OWEN's leash when she approached the front doors of Ocean Crest

Hospital. Not because Owen needed it, but more to reassure anyone who might feel intimidated by the large silver-and-white dog. Owen wore his snappy red therapy-dog jacket, which helped with the intimidation factor, but also made clear why there was a dog in the hospital.

Owen loved to interact with people and enjoyed their visits to Ocean Crest. His tail was wagging as they entered the building.

"How are you, Lydia?" Madison called to the brunette behind the reception counter when she and Owen walked by.

"Good. Wait, wait!" Lydia scooted out of her chair and rushed around the counter to see Owen. "You're such a sweet boy. Yes, you are," she cooed to the dog.

Owen simply sat and accepted the attention as if it was his due.

"Do you know where they'd like us today?" Madison asked.

"Oh, I think they have you scheduled for the palliative-care ward."

"Okay. I'll see you later."

Madison made her way to the elevators. She and Owen entered last, and she had him sit while the elevator stopped at various floors, and people got on and off. On the sixth floor, they exited and turned right. Her cell phone vibrated with an incoming call just as she entered the ward's recreation room. She let it go to voice mail.

She was always gratified to observe the look of joy on patients' faces when they spotted Owen. A few rose and came to greet them, while others waited expectantly, knowing that she and Owen would walk around to see everyone. Many of the patients had been there for some time. Over the months she and Owen had been visiting, she'd come to recognize their preferences—the ones who liked to hug Owen and thrived on the physical contact, the ones who preferred to have him sit patiently while they talked and the ones who liked to watch him do tricks for them. The few patients who seemed uneasy, she approached slowly and asked if they'd like to say hello to him.

When Stanley, an elderly gentleman with advanced Alzheimer's, hesitantly said he thought he was ready to pet Owen, she smiled. It wasn't the first time, but he didn't always remember. They'd done it often enough that she knew it would bring him pleasure.

She told Owen to lie down. That way he was less imposing. She instructed him to inch toward Stanley. The large dog crawling forward on his belly caused Stanley and a few of the other patients to laugh, something that didn't happen often enough in this ward. When Stanley leaned down to pat Owen's head and chuckled with delight, that made the trip completely worth it for Madison. She spent another hour with the patients, and then said her goodbyes with a promise to see them again the following week.

In the parking lot, while Owen jumped in the back of her Porsche SUV, she checked her iPhone for the call she'd missed. There was a message. She prompted her voice mail and felt warmth spread through her when she heard Rick's deep, sexy voice. She called the number he'd left and smiled when he picked up on the third ring.

They exchanged pleasantries and talked about their days while she climbed into her vehicle and activated her Bluetooth. He apologized for not having called her sooner, and she was comforted knowing it wasn't from lack of interest.

She drove out of the parking lot and tapped her fingers lightly on the steering wheel as she listened.

"I want to see you again, Madison. Would you have dinner with me?" he asked.

"I'd like that. Very much," she added. "What do you have in mind?"

"I thought I'd leave that to you."

Madison hadn't gone out much since she'd moved to San Diego. She'd spent most of her time at the clinic, the rehab center or with Owen at the hospital. She didn't consider any of the restaurants she'd gone to with Heather or one of her other colleagues as suitable for a dinner date with Rick. "I don't really know too many places here."

"Okay, then how about you tell me what kind of food you enjoy and I'll pick."

She laughed. "It would probably be easier to tell you what I *don't* enjoy! I have a pretty healthy appetite. I'm sure you concluded that from Logan's barbecue."

"You're not being very helpful," he teased.

She considered the elegant, candlelit restaurants most guys had taken her to on early dates, and decided that wasn't what she wanted with Rick. Not because she didn't want the romance of it. She loved romance. But she didn't want something predictable, either. Something she'd done many times. Suddenly she realized that she wanted it to be *different* with Rick. So she said what was on her mind. "Different. I'd like something fun and different. Show me what you're made of, Vasquez," she said with a laugh.

"All right. If that's what you want. How's Thursday?"

Madison did a quick mental check of her work schedule and was fairly certain that she wasn't at the clinic or the rehab center that evening. "Sounds good."

"What if I pick you up at seven?"

"Sure."

"Oh, Madison?" he said, just as she was about to hang up. "Wear something casual."

They said their goodbyes, and she disconnected. She recalled how she'd missed the mark in proper attire for his captain's barbecue and was glad he'd offered the clarification. She hadn't considered casual, but she probably should have with Rick. He didn't seem the suit-and-tie type she was accustomed to. But hadn't she asked for something different?

CHAPTER SEVEN

BY THE TIME Thursday came around, Rick was impatient to see Madison. He couldn't get the woman out of his mind. At work, his primary focus had been the preparation for taking down the Los Zetas Cartel. Fortunately, his preoccupation with it made the days pass quickly and kept him from picking up the phone to call Madison a hundred times. But every spare moment he had, and in the evenings when he was at home and alone, he found his thoughts repeatedly drifting back to her.

He liked the place he'd come up with for dinner and figured it might be a true test of their compatibility, not unlike the ride on his Harley had been. There was a part of him that worried she wouldn't enjoy it and that would be the end. That thought made him realize he very much wanted this to be a *beginning*.

He considered changing the reservation

to a more traditional restaurant. Less risky. Something with white linen, silver and crystal, subdued lighting and muted classical music. That was probably more her style, he mused, knowing what he did about her background. He was reaching for the phone to make another reservation, then decided the heck with it. O Touro was one of his favorite restaurants, so he'd better find out now if she liked that sort of thing. Besides, she'd wanted something different. She was going to get what she'd asked for. He'd gone with his instincts and now he'd just have to see…

He shook his head. He was behaving like a high-school kid going on his first date. Madison was having an effect on him. He'd begun second-guessing himself. And when had he felt nervous about going out with a woman? Never in his recollection. Sitting at his desk, he checked his watch for the hundredth time that morning. Just a few more hours now.

He watched Brody walk past his work space, holding Nitro's leash choked up too much for comfort, and remembered he was going to speak to Logan about what he suspected. He waited until Brody had left, then rose and grabbed a couple of coffees from the pot in the unit's small kitchenette on his way to the captain's office. The coffee was always vile, but it was better than none at all.

"Jagger, got a minute?" Rick asked from the doorway of Logan's office.

Logan glanced up. "Yeah, sure."

Rick closed the door behind him, eliciting a raised-eyebrow look from his captain. He handed him one of the coffees and sat in the visitor chair.

"What's this about?" Logan asked.

"Brody," Rick replied.

Logan exhaled. "He's not on your team. What about him?"

"Other than that the guy needs to get some exercise?" His tone grew serious. "I suspect he's hitting his dog."

"What makes you say that?" Logan had straightened in his seat and his eyes had an intense gleam to them.

Rick never brought issues forward that weren't substantiated, and Logan would know that. He wasn't a whiner, nor did he like to tattle on his colleagues. So Rick wasn't surprised at Logan's immediate and serious reaction to his statement. Logan wasn't questioning what he'd said. He simply wanted to understand the circumstances, in case he needed to act.

Rick outlined the reasons for his suspicion.

Logan slammed his fist on the desk. "Damn it! I don't condone that and everyone *knows* it!"

"Yeah. That's why I told you."

"Appreciate it" was Logan's curt response.

"Any update on getting a replacement for Sniff?" Rick asked, changing the subject.

"Nothing yet, but I'm working on it."

Rick left Logan's office shortly after. The discussion had put him in a foul mood. He was angry at Brody; he was no happier with himself for having to snitch on another cop. But Brody'd had it coming. His dog couldn't speak up for himself. Rick had also hoped there'd been some progress with Sniff's retirement.

"Didn't go well?" Shannon asked when he walked past her desk on his way to his own.

"Huh?"

She motioned with her head toward Logan's office. "The meeting. It didn't go well?"

Rick glanced over his shoulder, noted that Logan was on his phone, and the captain didn't look any happier than Rick felt. "Nah. It'll get worked out."

"The woman you brought to the captain's barbecue. How's your relationship with her going?" Shannon asked as Rick was about to leave again.

He must have given her a "what business is it of yours?" look, because she shrugged and smiled. "Just asking. I like her."

From the corner of his eye, he saw Brody walk back in, minus Nitro, and some of his anger fled. He was doing the right thing. He was sure Brody was mistreating his dog, and he couldn't allow that to happen. "Sorry. What?" he said to Shannon.

"I said I like Madison."

Rick felt his mood lighten. "Yeah, so do I. In fact, I'm having dinner with her tonight."

"Glad to hear it!" Shannon nodded to Brody as he walked by, but her smile dimmed, and Rick wondered if *anyone* liked Brody. Brody, for his part, ignored Shannon but gave Rick a hostile stare. He shrugged it off, although he suspected Brody knew he'd spoken to the captain about him. So be it. This wasn't a popularity contest. Apart from how Brody treated his dog, Rick had a generally bad feeling about the guy.

Shannon's phone rang and he looked back at her. "Have a nice dinner, and say hi to Madison for me," she said as she reached to answer it.

Rick remained in the office for the rest of his shift, and for once he left on time. At home he changed his shirt twice before deciding on the one he wanted to wear. Foolish, he thought with amusement.

He couldn't remember looking forward to seeing a woman this much in a while, if ever. Now, if only his choice of restaurant didn't backfire on him.

MADISON GLANCED AROUND her as the hostess escorted her and Rick to a corner table in the restaurant. Rick had brought her to a genuine Brazilian churrascaria. She hadn't known what a churrascaria was until he'd explained it on their way to the restaurant. It was an all-you-can-eat place with Brazilian meat served tableside from huge skewers. He'd given her the option of going somewhere else, if she preferred, but she'd told him she was game. When he'd explained the concept to her, she'd expected something more...rustic. Less refined. They walked by an ample salad bar, and through a couple of busy rooms to the section where they were seated.

Madison smiled, seeing the waiters dressed in traditional Brazilian gaucho attire circulating around the room with their huge skewers of meat and sharp knives.

When she'd told their waitress that it was her first time in a churrascaria, the woman described the use of the colored disks on their table that, depending on which side was up, meant either that she was still hungry and the gauchos should keep the meat coming or that she was full and they should bypass her as they moved around the room.

She watched Rick as he ordered their wine and gave the waitress a pleasant smile. That smile alone, the even white teeth contrasting with his dark complexion, could have accounted for the little thrill she felt, but it was the whole package that attracted her.

If she hadn't known he was a cop, she might have assumed he was an athlete. Perhaps a mixed martial arts fighter, she thought as he handed the wine list back to the waitress and the sleeve of his golf shirt tightened across his biceps. Yes, an MMA fighter. He had the shoulders and the arms for it.

She'd found him physically attractive from the moment she'd seen him, but what appealed to her even more was evident in his interaction with the waitress.

He was friendly but respectful. The easy

smile and the words of appreciation. Engaging yet not flirtatious. She knew how often people dismissed servers, but Rick wasn't the type. That mattered to her.

When the waitress left, Rick turned that smile on her, but now there *was* a hint of flirtatiousness. That and the slight crinkles around his eyes when he smiled were very sexy, and she felt a flutter in her belly.

"What do you think?" he asked. "Does it meet with your approval?"

"I asked for fun and different, and you delivered!"

"I think you'll approve of the food, too."

Madison couldn't help laughing when server after server, all dressed like gauchos, brought huge hunks of meat to their table. They would slice it to her preference right there and she would grab the slices with small tongs. "You're right! The meat *is* delicious," she said after sampling another tender piece of beef.

Her smile faded when Rick reached out with his napkin and dabbed at her chin.

He showed her the white cloth with barbecue sauce on it.

"Thanks," she said, but had a strong urge

to raise a hand to her chin, which still tingled from his touch.

Rick savored a piece of grilled chicken and wiped his own mouth. "What brought you here? To San Diego?" he asked. "I trust it's okay for me to ask?" he amended, referring to the fact that he'd stopped Logan from doing so at the barbecue.

Madison nodded. "I had an opportunity here, career-wise, that I couldn't get at home."

Rick leaned back in his chair, watching her attentively. He took a sip from his glass. "Not that I'm complaining, but aren't there opportunities for veterinarians in El Paso?"

"About the same as anywhere else, I suppose."

"Then, why did you leave?"

"Research and rehabilitation. There's groundbreaking work being done here, at the San Diego Animal Rehabilitation Center." She tasted another chunk of meat. "Mmm. Very tasty."

"I'm glad you like it. What type of research?"

Surprised, she glanced up at him. She hadn't expected him to ask for elaboration. In her experience, most people's eyes glazed over when she tried to explain. "The term is platelet-rich plasma or PRP therapy. It's a way of treating injuries with a concentration of the patient's own blood. The treatment was originally used for sports medicine, for spinal cord rehabilitation, even for cosmetic surgery in some cases. It's been found to be highly effective for nerve, cardiac muscle and bone rehab, and for facilitating soft-tissue repair and wound healing."

Rick sat silently and looked attentive, so she continued.

"The San Diego Animal Rehab Center also has some of the highest success rates with aqua therapy. Rehabilitation is my area of specialization, and I'm very keen on research." She looked down at her plate, and added softly, "I can't stand to see animals suffer, or to be put down if there's any chance of helping them."

"Must make it hard to be a veterinarian," he said gently. "You see animals suffer all the time."

He was probably thinking that she also had to euthanize them on occasion, but was glad he hadn't raised it. She didn't like to dwell on that aspect of her work.

"And the police dogs? Why the interest in them?"

She smiled. "It's actually related. I worked with police dogs when I was going through school. I know they have a job to do, but they work hard and it broke my heart when they were in pain, whether just from the everyday demands placed on them or because of injury. That's really how I got into rehab medicine. Although the dogs might need to retire, their pain or injury can be managed and they can live happily to old age. Speaking of living to an old age, can we talk about Zeke for a moment?"

He nodded.

"I'd like to try the PRP therapy on him. There are no significant risks. Less than with a routine vaccination," she assured him, remembering his concern about experimental treatments. "Look at it as a way of helping the body heal itself."

She explained the process as it would apply to Zeke.

Rick nodded again and raised his glass to her. "I'm fully supportive. I applaud you for your dedication and caring."

She was pleased that he was comfortable with it. She knew his support would be crucial to convincing Officer Jeff Bradford's family to let her proceed. There was a kindness in his eyes that warmed her. She could feel her face flush as she touched her glass to his and took a sip. "Thank you. It's important to me. It's why I went into veterinary medicine to begin with."

"And how do you like it here?"

"I miss my father. But San Diego is exactly what I was hoping for."

"And what do you do when you're not working?"

"Owen and I volunteer at a hospital. Owen is a trained therapy dog. We work mostly with the elderly and children. Give them some comfort and amusement when they need it."

"That's terrific!" he exclaimed enthusiastically. "I've had Sniff visit a children's hospital with me a couple of times. He loves kids and they respond well to him. Now we mostly do drug counseling for inner-city kids."

She liked the sound of that. It also pleased her that they had a shared interest in doing community work with their dogs. "How did you get into it?"

He swirled the wine in his glass. "Let's just say I know the impact drugs can have on a kid's life. I was exposed to the worst of what drugs can do when I was young. I got through it. I survived and moved beyond it, but I don't want to see it happen to any other kid if I can help it."

She remembered someone at the barbecue saying that Rick was born in Mexico.

"What brought *you* here?" she asked.

Rick shrugged and took a bite. "I wanted to…get some distance from where I was born. Strike out on my own, I suppose. Have you had enough?" he asked, pointing at her plate. When she nodded, he flipped both of their service disks over to red, indicating that they were finished with their main course. He sipped from his glass.

Rick's oblique response piqued her curiosity again, but she could tell that he didn't want to discuss it. He signaled for the waitress, and they ordered coffee. They declined dessert because neither of them had room.

They talked about San Diego and its many attractions over coffee.

"Well, I'm glad you decided to move here," he said as he rose to pull out her chair when they were done. "If there's anything you need, anyplace you'd like to see, just say the word," he added when they were walking to his car.

Madison was in a comfortable, dreamy frame of mind as Rick drove her home. She looked over at him, and smiled at the strong profile, the chiseled features and the way his lips curved upward when he must have sensed that she was watching him.

She experienced that little thrill again when he reached over and took her hand. She liked the feel of his fingers, strong and warm, curled around hers. Because she was focused on that, she immediately felt the tensing of his hand before he drew it away and placed it back on the steering wheel. She gave him another sideways glance, but his features were hard and he was no longer smiling.

He signaled right and took an abrupt turn, his gaze alternating between his mirrors and the road ahead of them. He took another sharp turn, this time without signaling.

"This isn't the way to my house," Madison mumbled, grasping the handlebar above her head.

"I know. Is your seat belt secure?"

She tugged at it to be certain. "Yes. What's wrong?"

"We're being followed."

"What?" She craned her neck but could only see the glare of headlights through the back window. She leaned forward and tried to see behind them in the side-view mirror. "Are you sure?"

"Not a hundred percent. But fairly certain. The vehicle followed us around both turns."

His tires screeched as he took another sudden turn. Madison could definitely see a set of lights following them.

Rick got out his cell phone and searched for a number. "Dispatch, this is Sergeant Rick Vasquez," he said, and recited his badge number. "I have a tail…No, I don't…No, I can't see the plate. Can't identify the make and model…Yes. I'll lead them there. I'm driving my own vehicle." He gave Dispatch the particulars of his car. "All right. Thanks. Out."

Madison's nerves were on edge. If Rick had called it in, he was obviously concerned. She had a lot of questions but decided to stay silent. She'd let him concentrate on driving and leading whoever was following them to the location he'd arranged with Dispatch.

She could tell the vehicle was closing in because of the blinding glare of headlights. When the headlights got brighter still and Rick swerved, she held on tight but gasped.

"It's okay. Just hold on."

"What happened?"

"He was trying to pass us."

"Why?" Her voice quavered.

"I don't know. Hold on," he repeated.

Madison assumed they were nearing the location where the police were waiting for them. Her suspicion was confirmed when Rick got on the phone again to tell them they were almost there. She was still watching the side-view mirror and saw the lights behind them recede and then disappear. When Rick moderated his speed, she sat back in her seat and kept her eyes on him. He pulled over, staring into his rearview mirror. Finally, he smacked the steering wheel. "Damn it!"

Madison felt the panic gurgle up her throat, even though she trusted Rick to take care of her. "What's wrong?" she asked again.

"Our tail swerved off to the right. I was trying to get a look at the vehicle to determine its make and model, or at least see if I could find any distinguishing characteristics. But it was too dark, and I saw it for just a second when it rounded that last corner."

Madison had glimpsed it for a moment, too, through the side-view mirror. As Rick had reported to Dispatch, it was an SUV. But she presumed he'd known that from the height and position of the headlights, even though he couldn't see anything else because its high beams were on.

"It was a large SUV, dark color, right?" she asked him.

Edging his vehicle away from the curb, he kept glancing at the rearview mirror. "Yeah. The only other thing I noticed was the reflection on the wheels, suggesting they were chromed, but that was it. Did you notice anything else?"

"No." Madison saw that Rick was still focused on the rearview. She swung around in the seat; all she could see was a quiet street in the glow of muted streetlights. "What's wrong now?" she asked, her voice higher than normal despite her best efforts to control it.

He reached across the center console and took her hand in his. "Nothing. It's okay now. Whoever was tailing us is gone. I just want to make sure they don't sneak up behind us with their lights off."

He called Dispatch again to let them know what had happened. He agreed to proceed to the location where the police were waiting for them, just to be safe. Madison couldn't argue with the strategy.

Rick pulled over again when they saw a police cruiser parked a short distance ahead. He turned to Madison. "Not exactly how I imagined our date would end," he said with a frustrated laugh.

Her nerves were still raw. Who could blame her? Being in a car chase, even sitting next to a cop, wasn't an everyday occurrence. "Well, I did ask for something different, didn't I?" She attempted to make light of it, for her own sake as much as his.

He laughed again, but now it had a genuine ring. "I aim to please." He took a strand of her hair in his hand and ran it through his fingers. The simple gesture caused Madison's heartbeat to accelerate.

"With what happened to…"

She was certain he was going to refer to the officer who'd been killed. Apparently he thought better of it, most likely to avoid scaring her any more than she already was.

"We don't want to take any chances. I'm going to have to go into the division. I'll have one of the other cops take you home, if that's okay with you."

She nodded but regret mingled with concern. "Sure. I understand."

He let the strand of her hair slip through

his fingers. "I'll make it up to you, okay? If you'll let me."

She nodded again.

"Promise?" He gave her an apologetic smile, then pulled away from the curb and parked behind the police car.

There were three cars—two cruisers, and the third appeared to be a private vehicle. Four cops were clustered on the sidewalk. Another sat in one of the cruisers, talking on his radio. They must have known that the immediate threat was over, but based on their stance and body language, Madison could tell they remained vigilant.

"Wait here for a minute," Rick asked before he got out of his vehicle. He huddled with the cops, the fifth one getting out of the car to join them. Rick came back a few minutes later with a cop she remembered from the captain's barbecue. His name slipped her mind. Rick opened the passenger door and helped her out. "Madison, you remember Tom?"

That was it. Tom… Tom Brody. She nodded.

"Tom's shift is almost over. Your place isn't far from his, so he'll take you home." He dropped his voice so only she could hear. "I know he was a jerk at the barbecue, but he's on duty now and he will be until he drops you off. He'll get you home safe, okay?"

"Should I be worried?"

She caught the momentary pause before he shook his head. Her anxiety spiked again, but she trusted Rick. She nodded to indicate that she was okay with Brody taking her home and turned to the other cop. "Officer Brody." She offered her hand, and found his disconcertingly soft and damp. "Thank you for making the time to take me home."

It appeared that she and Rick weren't going to get a moment alone, because Brody was standing there waiting to lead her to his car. "Good night, Rick, and thank you for dinner," she said to him.

"Good night." He leaned in and touched his lips to hers, briefly, gently. "Call me if you want. It doesn't matter what time it is." He gave Brody a stern look before he headed back to the group of cops.

Moments later, she and Brody were in his car on Harbor Road, driving to her house. Madison sat stiffly in her seat and stared straight ahead. Maybe he'd noticed her discomfort because he made an attempt at small talk. He was trying to put her at ease, she supposed, but she wasn't interested. She kept her responses short and evasive, turning her mind to the evening with Rick. She found that just thinking about him diminished her anxiety.

Madison couldn't deny a growing fascination with the handsome policeman. She was drawn by his kind heart and great sense of humor. His devotion to helping kids and their shared love of animals were definite pluses, as well. Although the evening hadn't ended quite the way they'd hoped, she'd had a wonderful time.

When Brody stopped in her driveway, she thanked him politely for the ride. He offered to walk her to her door, but she declined. She took Owen briefly out into the backyard to do his business. Once they were back inside, she double-checked to make sure all the doors were locked. As an afterthought, she switched on her front and back porch lights, just in case. It wasn't every day a person got tailed. As composed as she'd tried to be on the outside, she had to admit to a level of disquiet she'd never felt before.

CHAPTER EIGHT

RICK STAYED AT the division until nearly midnight. They had no idea who'd been tailing
him, nor could they pick up the vehicle with
any certainty on a traffic camera. He just
hadn't seen enough of it to be able to narrow it down. Dark SUVs with chrome wheels
were popular.

He and the other cops kicked the possi-
bilities around, and the probable answer was
some punks joyriding. But they couldn't dis-
miss the idea that it was just too coincidental, happening so soon after the incident with
Jeff, and the fact that it was highly probable
that whoever it was could be monitoring police communications. The tail had abandoned
the chase abruptly when Rick was nearing
the meet location. Just too coincidental…

Rick wanted to call Madison on his way
home to make sure she was okay, and to
apologize again for the abrupt and less-than-
pleasant end to their evening. But it was late

and he didn't want to wake her. He knew she had to be at work in the morning. He had an early start the next day, too.

After taking Sniff for a short walk, he went upstairs and sprawled out on his bed. With everything happening at work, he was surprised it was Madison and their evening together that was still on his mind when he drifted off to sleep.

It seemed he'd just closed his eyes when his alarm went off. This was the first time in a long while that he wasn't up before his alarm sounded. Sniff was doing a little dance, anxious to be fed and to go outside, and Rick obliged him while he had his own breakfast.

Rick thought about Madison all the way to the division, and found himself humming a tune he'd heard, not unlike his mother had a tendency to do when she was happy.

He wanted to *talk* to Madison. Just hear her voice. And that was crazy…but there it was. He looked at his watch even though he knew it wasn't a respectable hour to call. But he'd call her soon.

Brody was on the early shift and Rick had already checked in with him. He'd confirmed that he'd gotten Madison home okay, but that did nothing to alleviate Rick's need to talk to her. Last night had been a rude and early introduction to what it meant to be dating a cop. Other than a natural apprehensiveness, she seemed to handle it well. That might have been her father's influence. He was a Supreme Court judge and a high-profile lawyer before that, so he'd probably dealt with cases that had attracted intimidation attempts. Madison wouldn't have been unaware of or immune to those. Still, Rick didn't want the exposure to the realities of his job to scare her off.

As he entered the division parking lot, he turned his thoughts to the Los Zetas Cartel. The more he considered it, the more he suspected that his tail the night before had been drug-cartel related. He hoped Los Zetas hadn't gotten wind of what the SDPD was planning and decided on a preemptive strike.

He dismissed the idea of that as too far-fetched.

There were too few people who knew about their plans, and those people were all cops wanting to see the end of the cartel's activities in San Diego as much as he did. They were all aware of how dangerous it could be if any of the information leaked to the cartel bosses. Even within his own unit, relevant information was shared only on a need-to-know basis.

Glancing over at the training yard, he swore under his breath, slammed into Park and jumped out of his vehicle. He sprinted across the yard, grabbing a padded decoy sleeve from a bench.

Brody, obviously agitated and out of control, had rolled Nitro partially on his back and was screaming at the dog while he tried to get him to roll the rest of the way.

The alpha roll—a technique used by certain K-9 handlers to assert their dominance over strong-willed dogs—was a controversial technique, not agreed to by all trainers. Rick didn't believe in it. But when used, it had to be done without emotion, in a totally neutral manner. This was essential to ensure that the dog wouldn't perceive himself to be in danger, and wouldn't hold a grudge against the handler. If this wasn't the case, the alpha roll could do more harm than good—particularly if the dog was a forceful animal, feared for his life or felt that the handler wasn't in complete control. In those situations, the dog could go on the offensive the first opportunity he had. An uncontrolled alpha roll could cause irreparable harm to an otherwise great police dog.

It was clear to Rick that Brody wouldn't be able to fully execute the roll. He knew Nitro already feared the man and had a moderate alpha drive—not a good combination, especially under the circumstances.

Rick stuck his right arm into the decoy sleeve as he ran.

When Rick reached them, Brody looked up in surprise. That instant of lost focus was all the opportunity Nitro needed. He gained his feet and, as Rick had anticipated, driven by distress and self-preservation, he lunged at Brody. Rick shoved Brody out of the way with his left arm and raised his right, protected by the sleeve, for Nitro to latch on to. The dog took the bait and sank his teeth into the thick padding of the sleeve, with only his hind legs touching the ground. Nitro was large and powerful, but Rick held his position. He knew if he went down, the dog would get purchase on all fours and, with the added balance, would be more likely to transfer the bite. The sleeve was Rick's only protection and he didn't want to risk letting the dog get hold of him anywhere else.

From his peripheral vision, Rick saw

Brody regain his footing and stumble toward them.

"What the heck! Why did you interfere—?"

With ice in his voice, Rick cut him off. "Calm down, *Officer*." He purposefully reminded Brody of their respective ranks. "Order your dog to 'out,'" he said.

"He doesn't 'out.' I told you that." Brody's voice sounded whiny. "I have to do physical removal."

Rick knew that with handler and dog in a heightened state of agitation, that could only mean trouble. "All right. Walk away slowly and calmly."

"I can't! That damn dog has a bite on you, and I need to teach him a lesson for not listening to me."

"Do you really want to have this conversation while your dog is latched on to my arm?" Rick was incredulous. "Officer. Just so there's no mistake, this is an order. Walk away slowly and calmly," he repeated. "Right now. You don't do it this instant, I'll write you up for insubordination."

"He's my dog, and I'm not leaving."

"I said *now*." Brody was a bigger fool than Rick had thought if he wanted to get into this argument when Rick should have been exerting all his energy on de-escalating the dog. He was wasting energy arguing with Brody, all the while struggling to maintain his stance and not further agitate Nitro. Based on what he'd seen, the dog wasn't to blame, and he didn't want the situation spiraling to a point where the division might have to consider getting rid of him. Or worse.

Despite trying for calm, Rick's anger flared. He wanted to vent it on Brody, but now was not the time. Not with Nitro still biting the training sleeve. He glared at Brody, not blinking, not shifting his gaze until his opponent did. He'd effectively established dominance. Now if he could only do the same with Nitro.

When Brody finally stalked off, Rick turned his entire concentration on the dog. He knew that with the dog frantic and still clamped to the sleeve, he needed to count on his own skill and Nitro's general lack of aggression to make sure the incident didn't end badly.

Rick kept his arm elevated to prevent the dog from gaining a foothold with his front legs, and in a firm and neutral tone he ordered the dog to "out." When he didn't achieve the desired outcome, he tried again, calling the dog's name loudly to get his attention and repeating the command. This time, Nitro listened. Rick lowered his arm, allowing Nitro to stand with all four legs on the ground—a risk if he wasn't going to obey—but Rick had confidence in Nitro's training and temperament. Rick gave the "out" command again. With only a slight hesitation, the dog released the sleeve.

Rick ordered a sit-stay, knowing "sit" would be an easier command for Nitro to obey in his current state than the more submissive "down."

It worked, but Rick tried not to show his relief. He had to remain dominant. He gently checked Nitro to make sure he wasn't injured, praised him and took Sniff's KONG toy out of his pouch to offer to Nitro as a reward. Finally, he tugged the protective sleeve off his arm and noted the beginning of bruises from the pressure of Nitro's bite. Man, that dog had strong jaws. No wonder they'd trained him in apprehension and handler protection, too.

Giving both Nitro and Sniff some play time first, Rick put both dogs in kennels before entering the building. Once inside, he headed straight to Logan's office.

He didn't knock or ask to be invited in. He strode up to Logan's desk, slapped his palms on the surface and leaned in. "Brody's got to go, Jagger. He *cannot* stay in the K-9 Unit."

Logan gave him a narrow-eyed look, then his gaze skimmed over Rick's arm, where the bruises were already a livid blue, green and purple. "What happened to you?"

"I had to intercede with Brody and Nitro."

Logan sat back, gestured to a chair and folded his arms across his chest. "What happened?" he asked again. "And speak freely." He glanced away from Rick, and his unblinking eyes tracked movement outside his office.

Rick looked over his shoulder and saw Brody walking by, glaring at him. He paused, took a step toward the office door, then seemed to think better of it and stalked off to his workstation. There was no doubt in Rick's mind that Brody knew what they were talking about.

"It wasn't Nitro's fault," Rick said, turning back to Logan. "That jackass tried to do an alpha roll."

Logan raised his eyes to the ceiling.

"Unsuccessfully," Rick added, and went on to explain exactly what Brody had done, including his refusal to follow orders. "Brody's got to go, and not only because he can't keep up with the physical demands of this job." He held up his hand when Logan was about to interject. "You gave me permission to speak freely, so let me do that. You know the officer-selection criteria better than I do, and we don't compromise. I know it's a sensitive subject. I appreciate the union will be all over it because of Brody's connections. But bottom line? He can't work with dogs. He can't be trusted."

Logan held Rick's gaze. "What are you going to do about the insubordination?"

"I don't want to write him up. It's not how we work, and it was a high-stress situation…"

"All the more reason for him to comply with a direct order."

"Yeah. I know," Rick conceded. "I don't want to write him up," he repeated. "But I will if I have to."

"I'll leave that up to you," Logan said cautiously.

Rick sensed there was a message there.

With Brody's uncle being the head of the police union local, he understood that Logan had to deal with a potential transfer— essentially a demotion—delicately. "All right."

He rose to leave. "But I'm taking Nitro in for a checkup if he shows any signs of injury."

"Nitro's Brody's dog. Careful how you handle it," Logan said.

Rick's happy mood of that morning was just a memory by the time he left Logan's office. He wanted to talk to Madison, but he knew his temper would push through, no matter how cheerful and relaxed he tried to sound. On top of that, if she had a problem with what had happened the night before and didn't want to see him again, he didn't want to hear about it right now. He was barely back at his desk when he and Sniff got called out to assist the Vice Squad with a narcotics search. From that point on, it was one call after another, and he wasn't back at the division until ten that evening. By then, it was too late to call Madison, and he wasn't up for what might be a difficult conversation. He'd call her first thing the next day, he resolved, and hope for the best.

IT MIGHT HAVE been Saturday and Madison's day off from the clinic, but it wasn't a day of rest for her. She'd risen at her usual time of six in the morning, dressed in scrubs and sneakers and driven to the San Diego Animal Rehabilitation Center. She smiled as she thought of her dinner with Rick the evening before last. He was fun, intelligent, respectful and very pleasing to the eye. And he loved dogs and did valuable work with teens. The end of their evening had been unconventional and admittedly disconcerting, but having a father who was a judge had conditioned her to the realities of law enforcement and the spillover onto families and friends.

She remembered when she was in her early teens and her father was a prosecutor handling a gang-related corruption case. They'd had police protection for a couple of months when threats had been made against him. That reminded Madison of her father's most recent case, and she hoped all was well with him.

Madison was the first to arrive at the center. She might have been early, but she was eager to get going. She was excited about the progress she was making with the PRP therapy. Today, she was going to try the therapy on a mammal for the first time, a white rat named Mickey who'd sustained nerve damage when he'd caught his front leg in an exercise wheel.

She entered the laboratory where she

worked and set classical music playing softly in the background. The animals seemed to respond well to it, and it didn't distract her from her own concentration. She donned a lab coat, then went to her station. The PRP process involved drawing blood from the patient, enriching it with platelets to create a concentrated growth factor that would, theoretically, stimulate the healing of bone and soft tissue or, as in Mickey's case, the nerves. If all went well with the rat, she intended to try the therapy on Zeke next.

She'd already drawn blood from Mickey and treated it with a two-stage centrifugation. Now she was ready to inject the PRP into him. For this part, she needed assistance to help her guide the injection to the proper location with the use of an ultrasound. She got everything ready and called the tech on duty.

After Mickey had been injected and was resting comfortably, Madison went to the aqua therapy area to work with a few animals scheduled for that afternoon. Her final appointment of the day was Zeke. He'd been discharged from the clinic that week, and the fallen officer's widow was bringing him in for a checkup and to discuss therapy.

She was pleased with Zeke's progress and impressed by the young woman's strength. Madison wondered if she could've been that strong if it was her husband who'd died so tragically. With Rick and the dangers he faced in the line of duty on her mind, she headed back to the lab to check on Mickey before she called it a day.

Satisfied that all was well with the rat, she shrugged out of her lab coat and flexed her shoulders, trying to get the stiffness out after nearly thirteen hours of working hunched over the lab counter or the aqua therapy tank. She might've been stiff, but she was satisfied. Mickey hadn't demonstrated any adverse reaction to the PRP therapy. They'd have to monitor him, and the treatment required a series of injections, but the early results were encouraging.

Madison rolled up her lab coat and stuffed it in a plastic hamper. She yawned hugely as she scrubbed up, and was thankful she didn't have to be at the vet clinic until Monday. She could use a little extra sleep in the morning.

It was dark when she left the building, and she was thankful she had Heather to help out with Owen during these long days at the rehab center. At least she'd be home to take him for his last walk of the day.

After that, she'd curl up in bed with a good book and a cup of chamomile tea, she decided as she parked in her driveway. The only downside to her day was that she hadn't heard from Rick. She'd expected to, and couldn't hide her disappointment each time she checked her phone and found that she hadn't missed any calls. She understood he had a lot going on at work and was keeping long hours. She resisted calling, not wanting to bother him.

As Madison mounted the steps to her front door, the high beams of a vehicle flashed on behind her and the sound of a car door slamming registered in her consciousness. She spun around but was blinded by the lights.

She took a stumbling step back and bumped into the door. She heard Owen barking furiously on the other side and dug in her handbag for her keys. Her eyes watered as she stared at the bright lights, afraid to look away. With her key ring finally in her hand, she tried to locate the front door key by feel.

She rubbed her eyes, trying to clear her vision, while Owen continued barking on the other side of her door. She could tell by the thumping sounds that he was jumping up against it, too.

She presumed his barking might have startled the person, since she didn't see any movement or hear any other sound from that direction. The sudden blare of a radio playing some current top hit competed with Owen's barking. Glancing the other way down the street, Madison blinked rapidly. She saw the blue Mustang convertible that her neighbor's son drove turn the corner into her street at a too-fast speed. She took the opportunity to unlock her door and slip inside without letting Owen escape through the opening. Slamming the door shut behind her, she locked it.

Hearing the screeching of tires, she rushed over to her living room window. She peered outside just in time to see the taillights of a vehicle as it sped away. Next door, Jamie, her neighbor's son, and his girlfriend were getting out of his car, laughing and embracing. Usually a little annoyed by his loud music and aggressive driving, Madison thanked the powers that be for the noise and his timing. Although she believed the threat was gone, if it had been a threat at all, Owen was still growling.

"Owen, settle," she instructed, but the dog

continued to grumble. She felt her legs give out and slid down to sit on the floor next to Owen, her back against the wall and her arm around him. She buried her head in the soft fur of his neck and wondered what would have happened if Owen hadn't been there to distract the person in the car or if Jamie hadn't arrived home at that precise moment.

She should call the police, but what would she tell them? Would they investigate without anything to go on? She lived on a quiet residential street, and it was unlikely that the person had just been hanging around hoping someone would come by. Every indication was that he'd been waiting for her.

Was this about Rick? Was it possible that it was the same person who'd tailed them the other evening? Not likely, since this had been a car, not an SUV. Still, she knew from her father that it could get dangerous when there was a lot at stake for those who lived by illegal means. She had no idea what sort of cases Rick was working on, but if they had to do with drugs and smuggling across the border, organized crime was probably involved.

Or was she overreacting? The car chase had been disconcerting and maybe she was jumpy because of it. Calling the cops would serve no purpose, she decided. They'd take a report, do some drive-bys, but that would be it. And she seriously doubted the car would be back tonight. But if it *had* been waiting for her, what about another time...?

She turned her outside lights on for the night for the second time in a week.

She'd talk to Rick about the incident. See what he had to say. Then she'd figure out what to do about it.

CHAPTER NINE

"HEY, PITBULL." LOGAN SIGNALED to Rick when he entered the squad room.

Rick dumped his briefcase and duffel at his desk, and headed to Logan's office. "What's up?" he asked, noting the somber look on his captain's face.

"Close the door, will you?"

He did as he was asked and settled in one of the visitor chairs, but he felt the hair on the back of his neck bristle. He sensed he wasn't going to like what Logan had to say.

"We caught one of the Los Zetas lieutenants last night, coming across the border with a shipment. We brought him in for questioning. We hoped we might get some intel on the cartel that could be useful."

Rick edged forward in his seat. "And?"

"He was carrying a huge shipment and he knew we had him."

Uncharacteristically, Logan broke eye contact and shifted his gaze to the left, over

Rick's shoulder. "He's young. Early twenties. He'd never been caught before. Despite his fear of the cartel leaders, he feared us more. Not the usual circumstance. Never mind *trying* to get him to talk. We wouldn't have been able to stop him if we'd wanted to."

He looked at Rick again. "The kid begged us to let him stay in California, even if it meant serving time."

Rick compressed his lips and shook his head. His disgust for what the kid was doing warred with sympathy. Twentysomething was old enough to know better, but it was also likely that he didn't have much choice. Rick knew firsthand the lengths cartel enforcers would go to for "recruiting" purposes. What if he himself hadn't escaped Mexico when he had? Would that kid have been him? Never mind the cartel enforcers. At what point would his birth parents have expected him to do it?

"Did he say anything useful?" Rick asked in a strained voice. "Do they have any idea what we're planning?"

"I'll answer those questions in a minute."

Rick suspected this was the part he wasn't going to like. What could be more important than intel for their plan?

"He knew about the ambush on Jeff."

Rick could have sworn he heard his heart pounding in his ears, felt the blood rushing through his veins. "Yeah?" he finally muttered, and linked his fingers. Glancing down, he could see his knuckles turning white and relaxed his grip.

Logan rose and walked around his desk to Rick's side. He leaned against it and crossed his arms. "Rick…as we guessed, it wasn't a random occurrence…"

Rick nodded. He could hardly hear through the roaring in his head.

"Jeff wasn't the target."

Rick sat up straight and unclasped his fingers. He thought about the fact that he was supposed to have been on shift that night. He was afraid he knew what he was going to hear. "Then, who?"

"It's you they want. The cartel bosses have you in their crosshairs. Your aggressive stance on curtailing the flow of narcotics across the border has apparently had a huge impact on their operations and therefore their bottom line." Logan's eyes were steady on his. "Rick, you're the target. They're not done yet."

Silence hung between them.

Rick pushed out of the chair, shoved his hands into the pockets of his cargos and turned his back to Logan, staring out the office's interior window into the squad room. He watched the cops out there working, a couple of them sharing a story that made them both laugh.

Cops knew the risks they faced each day they reported to work. It was the nature of the job. But being targeted by the cartel was bad news. That took the risk to a whole different level. Not only did they seldom back down until their target was dead, often mercenaries wanting to ingratiate themselves with the cartel bosses would take up the cause, too. They could strike anywhere, anytime. And in this case, it had cost a good cop his life.

Rick had managed to put the guilt associated with Jeff's death aside, but now it was back with a vengeance. *He'd* been the target, so he had every reason to feel responsible for Jeff's death. His murder. And if the Los Zetas Cartel bosses had it their way, he'd be next. That tail the other night made a lot more sense now. He doubted it had been a chance occurrence or punks out to cause trouble.

Rick had been able to avoid execution by

cartel enforcers in a number of instances by the age of twelve. Could he beat the odds again?

Perhaps he'd known all along that at some point it might come to this. After the initial shock, he now felt a fatalistic calm. Hadn't he believed after he'd escaped the massacre at his home in Mexico that he was living on borrowed time?

Logan was obviously giving him a chance to digest what he'd told him.

Rick faced his captain. "This doesn't change anything," he said unequivocally. "Our plan goes ahead and I remain co-lead." It was a statement, not a request, but he knew he needed Logan's support. Under the circumstances, Logan could call off the plan altogether, have someone else spearhead it or pull him off. He could require Rick to maintain a low profile until the threat blew over.

But they both knew it wouldn't blow over unless Rick did something drastic, like leave the state. He wasn't significant enough to the cartel for them to chase him down if he did leave their sphere of influence. But that wasn't happening. He wasn't going anywhere. The only option was to take down the cartel.

Logan nodded slowly. "Yeah, we go ahead as planned."

Relief flooded through Rick. He was more determined than ever to put an end to Los Zetas. "Thanks," he said, and moved to the door.

"Watch your back, Rick. Keep your eyes open, and *don't* take unnecessary chances. If you suspect anything, call for backup," Logan told him. "We'll put on a protective detail, do drive-bys and so forth, but you've got to watch out for yourself, too."

He wouldn't take chances, and he'd think about all the rest later. He was still on the case, and they'd make their plan work. Now it was personal.

Walking back into the squad room, perversely all he wanted to do was call Madison. Just hear her voice. He felt bad that he hadn't connected with her the day before. He wanted to thank her for the evening they'd shared and apologize for the way it had ended. She hadn't called him, either, and he hoped it wasn't because of that.

Two dates, two days since he'd spoken to her, and he *missed* her.

He took his personal cell and went into a conference room, nudging the door shut behind him with his foot. He didn't want anyone overhearing him. He dialed the clinic number and Heather answered. "Ah, Heather. Hi. It's Rick Vasquez. How are you?"

"Fine, Enrique. You'd like an appointment for Sniff?"

He could understand the uncertainty in her voice. It was usually the SDPD's admin who made appointments for the K-9 Unit's dogs. "No. Ah, is Madison available?"

"Oh?" There was an odd little inflection to the word, and Rick squirmed in his seat. "She's with a patient right now. Can I take a message… Oh, wait. She's just finishing. Hold on a second, and I'll see if she can take the call."

Rick listened to the hold music for a while and was about to hang up when Madison came on the line. "Rick?"

Damned if he wasn't flustered, and he probably had a silly grin on his face, too. "Hi, Madison. Um, do you have a minute?"

He heard the chuckle that sent a wild current of longing through him.

"Yes, I do. Otherwise, I wouldn't have taken the call."

"Right. About the other night… I had a great time, but I want to apologize for how it ended..." His voice trailed off. Why hadn't it occurred to him before that if it *was* the cartel chasing him, and if she was with him, she could be in danger, too?

He'd been worried that *she* might not want to see *him* again because of what had happened. If that wasn't the case, was it right for him to keep seeing her, potentially putting her at risk? He'd just have to make sure that his circumstances didn't expose either of them to unnecessary risk.

"Rick?"

She seemed hesitant. Yes, this was going to be it. He could feel it coming. He knew the drill. He'd dated women who couldn't handle being with a cop and everything that entailed. But it had never really mattered to him before.

With Madison it did matter. And that in itself was something to think about later. If she didn't dump him now.

"Is everything okay? Are *you* okay?" she whispered. Her voice was infused with emotion. It sounded like deep concern.

"Yeah. Why?"

"Because...because I...care," she said softly. "And because of my father, I know that what went on the other night probably

wasn't random. I think it has to do with whatever you're working on." He heard her suck
in a huge breath. "So…are you okay?"

Not too many people surprised him, but
she'd just thrown him a curve. He'd expected
fear, questions, maybe even recrimination
that he'd subjected her to that kind of risk
or—at best—grudging acceptance. But not
concern…for him. "Yeah. I'm good."

"I'm glad." She paused again. "I was worried."

He was floored. In his experience, women
he'd dated worried about themselves, not
him, and he'd been fine with that. But Madison was thinking of *him* and not herself…
Something shifted inside him and settled
around his heart. "It's okay. Really." He
tried to reassure her. "Occupational hazard,"
he said with a small laugh. "I'm just sorry
it happened when you were with me." He
needed to see her again, but he'd have to be
very careful to not put her in danger. And
if at any point it appeared that she was at
risk… Her safety would always come first.
But for now… "I'd like to make it up to you,
if you'll let me."

"Oh, no…"

Here it comes, he thought. Fine words, but

the incident *had* scared her off. He felt regret slice through him like the sharp edge of a knife. He was sure he could protect her from whatever danger he faced, but he didn't want to lose her.

"Please don't feel you have to make it up to me. I had a nice time," she continued. "If you'd like to do it again, I'd love that, but I don't want you to feel it's an obligation."

"That's..." Was he really at a loss for words? "That's great!" He laughed. "How about if you decide what we do?"

"Okay... How about this? If you're not working next Saturday, let's go for a hike. Take the dogs with us. Give them a chance to meet. That's okay for a police dog to do, isn't it? To play with other dogs?"

Rick was grinning again. He was glad he was in a private conference room because he more than likely looked ridiculous. "Yes, of course. Sounds perfect!"

"Rick?" Her voice had turned serious. She hesitated as if debating whether or not to say something.

"What is it?"

There was another short pause. "Oh, nothing. I was just going to ask you a question, but it can wait. See you Saturday."

THERE WAS A LOT happening at work for Rick, between all his regular tasks and getting everything set up for the Los Zetas takedown.

He'd started carrying his gun at all times, just in case.

Even though he was technically off duty, he swung by the division Saturday morning to catch up on some paperwork.

He was at his desk and the only one in the squad room when Brody wandered in. Rick looked up and did a double take. Brody seemed more unkempt than usual. "Morning," Rick greeted him curtly, not wanting to engage, and slouched over the files again.

He wanted to get his paperwork done and get the heck out of there. He was looking forward to spending time with Madison. He heard Brody approach. The man was anything but light on his feet. Sniff, who'd been curled up under Rick's desk, gave a low, uncharacteristic groan, not quite a growl. Rick moved his foot over to gently rest against Sniff's side for reassurance and glanced up at Brody again. He was standing in front of Rick's desk, arms folded across his chest. His stance was confrontational, his face belligerent.

"You want something?" Rick asked.

"Logan had a talk with me. Said there were some concerns raised about how I was treating Nitro. That and the reprimand you wrote up about the…chat we had makes me think you've got it in for me. If you had an issue, why not come to me direct?"

Rick stifled a groan. He couldn't believe Brody would be stupid enough to confront a higher-ranking officer in this manner. He didn't want to get into an argument with him. Certainly not today. He gave Brody a hard stare and the option to back away. When Brody just kept scowling at him, Rick couldn't hold back the frustrated sigh, and he pushed out of his chair. He wanted to avoid a nasty scene, if he could. If it couldn't be sidestepped, it wouldn't end well for Brody, and Rick would have to write him up again.

When Brody still didn't back away, Rick leaned on his desk. This close up, he could see Brody's eyes were bloodshot, a likely indication of a long night of drinking. "Brody, think about what you're doing here."

When Brody opened his mouth to speak, Rick cut him off. "Think long and hard before you say something that could result in another reprimand on your file. Yeah, I talked to Logan, but did you really expect me not to after what happened? I had a responsibility to do it."

Again, Brody started to speak. This time Rick straightened and held up a hand. "Unless it's an apology, I suggest you don't say anything. You've got one reprimand right now. You know how the system works," he said, referring to Brody's family connection to the police union. Because of that connection, he'd get transferred, but he wouldn't be let go. "It's no big deal in the greater scheme of things. But you don't want another strike against you…"

The words hung between them, and Rick gave Brody some credit for the silence that ensued.

"Get to work and let me get to mine," Rick suggested.

Deep ridges furrowed Brody's brow, and Rick could see the calculation in his eyes. To his credit, he uncrossed his arms and took a step back. "If you have a problem with me in the future, just say so."

Rick raised an eyebrow, held his gaze, but didn't respond.

"Just saying," Brody grumbled before walking away.

Rick sank back into his chair, and reached

down under his desk to run a reassuring hand along Sniff's back.

When Brody was out of hearing range, he snorted and shook his head. That guy badly needed an attitude adjustment. He'd drop it this time and not report the incident to Logan, but he'd keep an eye on Brody. Every instinct told him this wasn't the end of it. He just didn't trust Brody.

But right now, his priority was to finish the paperwork quickly. He wanted to go back home and get ready for a date with a gorgeous woman...and two dogs.

MADISON AND RICK had agreed to meet at the Torrey Pines State Reserve north of San Diego. Madison couldn't wait to see Rick, and she thought it would be fun to introduce their dogs to each other. Going for a hike gave them the ideal opportunity to introduce Owen and Sniff to each other on neutral territory. They both knew enough about animal behavior that neutral territory would minimize the potential for any conflict.

When Madison drove into the parking lot, she saw Rick immediately. He was dressed casually, in faded jeans, a soft blue T-shirt and hiking boots. He was leaning against his

SUV, his hands tucked into his pants pockets and his feet crossed at the ankles. Sniff was stretched out beside him. Madison backed into the spot next to him and hopped out of her car. She'd tied her hair back, but the wind teased some tendrils out of the elastic. She swiped at them, then greeted Rick and bent down to rub Sniff behind his ears. When she straightened and her eyes met Rick's, the clear admiration she saw reflected in them caused a light-headed sensation. She gave him a bright smile. "So how do you want to introduce the dogs to each other?" she asked.

Rick clipped the leash to Sniff's collar. "Why don't you let Owen out? I'll start walking Sniff toward that open area there—" he gestured "—and you and Owen can come join us."

That made sense. It was what she would have suggested, too. Casual and no pressure. She nodded, grabbed Owen's leash from the passenger's side and told him to jump out from the back. When they met, Sniff and Owen showed interest in each other but there were no signs of aggression or discord.

Rick and Madison strolled along, side by side, the dogs keeping pace. Once they reached the clearing, they released the dogs and watched while they did the doggy version of meet and greet. Soon they both dropped down on their front paws, back ends in the air, jumped around a bit and sped off chasing each other.

"Sniff's hind legs don't seem to be bothering him today," Madison observed.

"He has good days and bad ones. As you'd know, it can be both exertion- and weather-dependent."

"I'm glad he's not in pain today," she said and turned to Rick. He was standing close, his eyes steady on her. Her breath caught in her throat, and she felt the heat rise to her face. He traced the curve of her cheek with a finger. She had a strange feeling of needing to gasp for air.

"I wondered what your skin would feel like," he murmured. "You're so beautiful."

She couldn't seem to take her eyes off him, even when the dogs ran over to them and in frenzied little circles around them. There was warmth in his dark eyes. A depth and intelligence, too, that drew her in. The crinkles at the corners became more pronounced when he smiled and gave him character. His olive-toned skin was smooth, except for the slight stubble of five-o'clock shadow on his jaw.

Madison was mesmerized.

When Rick stroked her cheek, she exhaled, really more of a sigh. Her eyelids closed. She was certain he was going to kiss her, and yearned for the feel of his lips on hers.

Abruptly, her legs were bumped from behind, and she collided hard with Rick. She cried out from the shock, and would probably have crumpled to the ground if he hadn't gripped her upper arms and steadied her. The dogs, oblivious that one of them had crashed into her, continued their game of chase.

Madison looked back up at Rick and again found it difficult to breathe.

"I hope you don't mind," he whispered as he lowered his head to softly brush his lips across hers, then deepened the kiss. "I've been wanting to do that more than you can imagine. Consider it a proper good-night kiss I didn't have a chance to give you the other evening."

They stood in silence for a long moment. Finally, he took her hand in his and tugged it lightly. "Shall we?"

They entered the forest by way of one of the trails. Owen walked sedately at Madison's side, while Sniff moved in a zigzag pattern ahead of them, his nose held high and twitching. He was favoring his hind leg slightly, but Madison wasn't surprised after all the running he'd done with Owen. They meandered along the path, her hand clasped in Rick's. She loved the feel of it. For reasons she couldn't explain, his touch gave her a sense of security…of belonging.

Walking along the trail, her thoughts drifting, Madison recalled the incident at her home. "Rick. There's something I'd like to ask you."

He glanced over at her. "Sure."

"The other night when I got home from the rehab center, there was someone outside my house. It's possible he'd been waiting for me."

Rick came to an abrupt halt and turned Madison to face him. "And you're only telling me this *now*?"

"I…I was planning to tell you when we spoke, but it just didn't seem that urgent. The person left, and I decided I was overreacting because of what happened the night we had dinner."

"Did you call 911?"

"No. I thought about it, but I had Owen and the person was long gone by then. I don't know what the police could have done…"

Rick grasped her shoulders and bent his head to look directly into her eyes. "Tell me what happened. Exactly."

She explained it to him and was a little startled by the degree of concern he was exhibiting. But he was a cop, she rationalized, and must see all sorts of bad situations on a regular basis. That didn't mean she should worry about it. Did it? "Should I be concerned?" she asked.

He seemed to consider that for a moment, weighing what to say and what not to, then shook his head. "No, but I want you to be cautious."

She nodded mutely.

"It's probably nothing," he said. "Just like you suggested. But be alert. Whether he was there purposefully or not, he now knows where you live."

Madison felt the hairs on her arms stand on end.

"Just be careful," he said a final time. "I'll ask for some drive-bys for your place, but if you see anything else that concerns you, call 911 right away, then call my cell phone, okay?"

"Yes," she said in a subdued voice.

He gave her a gentle shake. "Promise?"

"Yes," she responded with more conviction.

"Okay." He took her hand. As they continued down the path, she could tell that some of the lightheartedness was gone.

They stopped at the end of the trail to buy ice cream cones for themselves and bottles of water for the dogs before they headed back.

Rick followed her home. He'd insisted. This time, he did walk her up to her front door. "I enjoyed the afternoon."

"I did, too," she said.

"When can I see you again?"

She smiled. "The sooner, the better."

"How about next weekend? I'd like you to meet my folks."

She tried not to gape. Their fourth date and he wanted her to meet his parents? That said a lot about him—and how he felt about her.

He kissed her gently before he took the steps back down to his vehicle.

Once Madison was inside, she stood by her living room window and watched him drive off. She knew if she looked in a mirror, she'd have that silly expression on her face again. He was nothing like the kind of person she'd expected to end up with, but everything and more than she'd dreamed.

And he certainly wasn't the person she'd thought he was on their first meeting. There was so much she loved about him…

Loved?

She felt her heart thunder as the realization struck her. Was she falling in love with Rick Vasquez? And so soon?

The thought made her happy, nervous, scared and giddy all at the same time.

CHAPTER TEN

"I THINK WE made a mistake with Nitro," Rick said to Logan. They were having coffee in the unit's kitchenette.

Brody had been transferred from the unit. Logan had told Rick that he hadn't been alone with Brody on the morning of their last confrontation. One of the vice squad sergeants had been passing by in the hallway and had stopped when he'd heard the altercation. He'd reported it, and that was strike three for Brody, if you counted what had happened at Logan's barbecue. Apparently, Logan had included that incident to make his case to the chief to get Brody reassigned. For the time being, Nitro was Rick's responsibility, and he was glad of it.

"In what way?" Logan asked.

"He's an excellent detection dog. Has all the prerequisites. But I think he'd do better with narcotics than explosives."

"Okay, give me your rationale."

"Nitro's got high drive. He's very intense, good in different environments and fast. Man, is he fast! Although I hate to say this, Brody might've been right on one point. Nitro is probably too independent to excel at directed searches needed for explosives or cadaver detection. Nitro might not have wanted to go where Brody directed him to search. And Brody being…well, Brody, I can see how their partnership would've started to unravel from there."

"Is Nitro beyond redemption? Do we need to retire him?"

"No way! The dog is remarkable. I put him out there a few times on undirected searches. He beat Sniff's record in our yard!"

"Huh. So you think he'd make a good narcotics-detection dog?"

"Absolutely."

"Who should we partner him with?"

"Actually, I want to work with him, once you give me the go-ahead to retire Sniff. Sniff's only eight, I know, but his mobility issues are getting worse. His cruciate ligament is definitely causing him problems. It's not so bad that he needs surgery, and I don't want it to get to that point." Rick paused. He and Sniff made a terrific team, but po-

lice dogs often had short careers. He knew
Logan had already requisitioned a replacement for Zeke. Even if Nitro was assigned
to him, they'd still need a second new dog
for explosives.

"That sounds more urgent that I'd gathered
from our last conversation," Logan observed.
He seemed to consider the proposal. "Take
Sniff for a full physical. If Madison agrees
with you, have her write up a recommendation for me."

"And Nitro?"

"Brody has filed a long list of complaints
against the dog. Are you sure you want to
work with Nitro, and take on retraining him
for narcotics at his age?"

"I'm positive," Rick said without hesitation.

"Okay. I'll get back to you on it tomorrow.
Have Madison look at Sniff," he repeated.

Rick started to rise.

"And when we retire Sniff, are you going
to keep him?"

Rick glanced at Logan in surprise. It was
virtually unheard of for a handler not to keep
his or her canine; the bond between them
was so strong. For Rick, there was no question. Sniff was his family. "Of course he'll

stay with me." Logan might have been his boss, but they were friends, too, so he allowed himself a degree of informality. "I can't believe you'd think anything else."

Logan smiled. "I had to ask. Standard procedure."

MADISON'S WEEK WAS exceptionally full. Jane was on vacation, so some of the other vet's workload and regular patients were shifted to her. She also spent extra time at the rehab center because she was excited about the progress she was making with her research. PRP had worked perfectly for Mickey. The rat was as good as new.

The weekend arrived quickly. Too quickly, Madison thought. She hadn't had a chance to get everything done that she'd hoped to, but she was excited about seeing Rick and meeting his family.

Standing in front of the door to his parents' house on Sunday afternoon, Rick stroked a hand down Madison's back. "There's no need to be nervous."

She exhaled. "I'm not nervous. Not exactly. But I'm meeting your family for the first time."

"Honest. They won't bite."

"I want to make a good impression."

Rick smiled at Madison encouragingly. "I repeat. There's no need to be nervous or to worry. My parents are nice people and easy to get along with."

Madison smoothed a hand over her wildly curling mane of hair. She glanced at Rick. "Should I tie it back?"

Rick burst out laughing. "No!" He dropped a kiss on the tip of her nose. "You look absolutely gorgeous the way you are. Stop worrying!"

Madison drew in a deep breath, straightened her shoulders, tugged down the hem of her shirt. "Okay. I'm ready."

"They'll love you. I'm sure of it." With that, he opened the door and motioned for her to precede him into the house.

They'd barely entered the hallway when a shih tzu came charging toward them.

"This is our official welcome party," Rick declared, and they both bent down to greet the dog. "Madison, meet Toby."

The friendly little dog went a long way to putting Madison at ease. The interior of the house did the rest. The muted colors, the soft textures, the family photographs everywhere. The house looked lived in, but it also seemed to be a place of much love. Rick took her hand and urged her toward the back of the house, where she could hear voices with music in the background, and could smell something spicy and mouthwatering.

When they reached the entryway to the kitchen, with all the noise and talk their presence hadn't been noticed yet. That gave her a moment to take everything in. Rick hadn't said much about it, but she'd assumed he was adopted, based on comments he'd made about his childhood. The contrast in physical appearance between him and his family was distinct, and seemed to corroborate her belief. All but one of the occupants of the room were blond, slim and no more than average height.

Rick tugged on her hand and led her into the room. "Hey, everyone," he announced.

Conversation stopped and all eyes turned to her. Rick drew her a little farther in. He gave the elegant older woman a big hug and a kiss. She was barely over five feet and had a cap of bright blonde hair.

"Everyone, this is Madison. Madison, first, this is my mother, Hillary, and..." He smiled at a lanky older man. "My father, Harold."

Rick's mother enfolded her in a hug, then Madison shook hands with his father.

"Moving on, this lovely young woman is my sister, Sophie, and this," he said, motioning to the only other dark-haired person in the room, "is her husband, Mark." He tugged on the white-blonde curls of the child sitting on Mark's lap. "This is the love of my life, their daughter, Emma."

Emma squealed with delight and held her pudgy little arms up to Rick, making noises that were unintelligible to Madison but seemed to mean "lift me" to Rick. He released Madison's hand and hoisted the girl high in the air. He spun around with her and was rewarded with excited shrieks.

"Sorry, Madison, but Emma's my real girl. Any other woman in my life has to come second," he said with a grin on his face. "And this—" he turned to the last person in the room, a younger version of his father but with a lighter shade of hair "—is my brother, Daniel. So now you've met the whole gang."

Sophie stepped away from the kitchen sink and also gave Madison a hug. "It's a pleasure to meet you, Madison. Welcome!" She sent Rick a mischievous look. "He doesn't bring many women home to meet us, so there's got to be something special about you."

Before Madison could protest or otherwise respond, Sophie moved over to Rick.

"Here, let me take this little diva from you, so you can concentrate on Madison."

"Why don't you and Madison go outside, Rick?" his mother suggested. "We'll be eating out there. The men can go with you. Get Madison a glass of fruit punch from the fridge, and Sophie and I'll join you there in a minute."

Ultimately, Madison didn't go outside, but stayed in to help with the preparations. She diced vegetables, washed the salad and shredded cheese.

Over dinner, she chatted with Sophie about fashion, Daniel about construction, since she learned he was an engineer, and with Sophie's husband, Mark, about babies. With Rick's parents, she covered the gamut, and they all expressed interest in her work and research.

When they'd finished the meal, Madison offered to help Hillary clean up, which gave her the opportunity to get to know Rick's mother a little better while everyone else was still outside enjoying the early-evening sunshine.

After loading the dishwasher, Madison crouched down to pet Toby. "Has Rick always loved dogs?" she asked.

Hillary laughed. "Goodness, no!" She paused. "You know he's adopted?"

Madison nodded.

"Well, when he first came to us, we had a little corgi. Rick was thirteen, already over five and a half feet in height and probably a hundred pounds, and he was..." She pursed her lips, considering. "Let's say...mature for his age. And reserved."

Madison could see in the older woman's eyes that, all these years later, it still pained her, what Rick must have endured during his early life.

"I wouldn't say he was afraid of our little Monty," she continued. "But he was... respectful." She laughed again. "He'd do any chore, take out the garbage, wash the dishes, do the laundry...just about anything, rather than walk Monty."

"Oh, let me do that." Madison rushed over when she saw Hillary stretching up to replace a platter on the top shelf of a cupboard.

Hillary stepped aside gratefully.

"About dogs, that surprises me," Madison said, returning to their conversation. "He's so natural with them."

"He certainly wasn't that way when he first came to us." She looked pensive—a little sad again. "He'd had a hard childhood." She glanced at Madison with clouded eyes. "Did he tell you anything about that?"

Madison shrugged. "A bit."

"Before he came to us, he'd never really had a chance to be a kid. Something as basic as a household pet wasn't part of his experience. Our little Monty was a vocal dog. He had a tendency to bark at the oddest things. A noise he heard outside. An unexpected movement. I think the sudden, sharp noise of Monty's barking would startle Rick until he got used to him. It took Rick a while to stop looking around corners and jumping at noises—and just feeling comfortable that no one was going to hurt him."

Hillary's face relaxed and her mouth settled into a bittersweet smile. "By the time we had to say goodbye to our Monty, it was Rick who took it hardest of any of us. We talked about eventually getting another dog, but none of us felt ready. We were still mourning. Then Rick came home one day clutching a bedraggled little dog with half an ear missing. He'd found the stray near his school and decided he'd adopt him. Rick named him Chico. He was only fifteen, but he insisted that Chico was his responsibility and wouldn't let us help financially. He delivered newspapers, washed cars, did whatever he needed to earn enough money to pay for Chico's food, toys and vet bills."

Madison smiled. "How sweet."

"Oh, that wasn't the end of it. He volunteered at a private animal shelter that, as part of its mandate, helped bring strays from Mexico across the border for adoption. If you'd seen him, you would've thought that each and every one of those animals was his personal responsibility." Smiling, she shook her head. "It was almost a weekly thing for him to try to talk us into adding another animal to our menagerie, which had already grown to three dogs, a rabbit and a skunk by that time."

"He never mentioned that." Madison felt her heart swell again for Rick. "A *skunk*?"

"It had been de…skunked," Hillary said. "For lack of a better word. Someone had kept it as a pet and changed his mind." She paused. "Rick was a good boy, with a big heart, and he's grown into a good man. We're very proud of him."

"And justifiably so," Madison said. She'd seen the pictures of him all over the house. What had happened to his birth parents? she wondered. Whatever it was, she was happy Rick and the Stewarts had found each other. Every indication was that they were a close and loving family.

Madison pondered fleetingly how it would go when Rick met her father. Her father loved her, but he was also protective of her, and he didn't bother to hide it. She hoped he and Rick would hit it off as well as she had with Rick's family.

Once everything was cleaned up and the rest of the family had wandered back inside, they sat around the kitchen island, drinking coffee.

Seeing Rick with his family helped her appreciate him even more. It reinforced the traits she'd sensed and had come to love about him. Watching him with his niece, Emma, was a revelation. If she'd thought he was good with animals, seeing him with the delightful little girl took his kindheartedness to an entirely different level. He doted on her,

198 WHEN LOVE MATTERS MOST

and when he was in the room, Emma had eyes only for him.

Madison adored his entire family. They'd made her feel welcome and comfortable. It was as if she'd known them for years. She particularly liked his sister. Sophie had a great sense of humor, was intelligent and down-to-earth, and they'd connected immediately.

Rick's brother, Daniel, was less outgoing but pleasant.

And his parents? They couldn't have been more welcoming. Not having had a mother or even a mother figure in her life, Madison felt a special fondness for Hillary.

"So what did you think?" Rick asked her during their drive to her house.

"Your family is wonderful! Thank you for taking me to meet them." Her lips curved in a smile. "Emma's going to be a heartbreaker when she grows up. She already has *you* twisted around her little finger," she said with a laugh. She reached out and linked her fingers with his. "It's obvious they love you very much. You're very lucky to have them."

"Yeah, I am."

She squeezed his hand. "And they're lucky

to have you," she added softly, and thought that she, too, was lucky that Rick had come into her life.

TENSION WAS ALL but vibrating in the air, and it was etched on the cops' faces when Rick entered the squad room Monday evening. A tip had come in that Los Zetas would be coming across the border that night. Not in trucks or vans, but by runners—by mules. Mexicans who were so destitute they'd make the run for no more than a few pesos despite the risk of getting arrested, or worse.

Everyone wanted to get back at Los Zetas for what they'd done to Jeff, but no one could shake the apprehension that came from responding to a tip from another confidential informant, since the last time had gone so horribly wrong.

Although Rick had been on duty since early that morning, he wanted in. No way was he going home and leaving it to others. It would also gave him an opportunity to test Nitro in the field.

He was part of the team waiting for the mules at strategic points along the border. It was past midnight when the signal went out that they were nearing. The police team was on alert and in radio silence.

Rick had Nitro lying quietly beside him.

Then he heard it. The thrashing through tall grass. Someone was approaching at a fast pace. With the moon casting its shimmering silver glow across the field, he could make out a silhouette. The runner was hunched over, fear evident in the movement of his body. His hair was on the longish side, and he swiveled his head from side to side, no doubt searching for signs of danger. He had one arm extended in front of him—as if attempting to ward off attack—and a satchel slung across his chest.

He was headed directly toward them. Rick signaled for Nitro to remain quiet, but the dog's legs must have been cramping because he extended his hind rear leg. The minor movement across the dry grass was enough. The crunching sound had the figure slowing and raising his head to listen. Although neither Rick nor Nitro moved, and there was no further sound from their direction, that slight noise had spooked the runner. He took off at a right angle to where they were.

"Damn," Rick exclaimed under his breath. He couldn't call out for him to stop because that might alert some of the other runners. He'd have to chase him, and the runner looked slim, sure-footed and fast.

Rick took off after him. He was quick, but with his body armor and other equipment, he was carrying a good seventy-five pounds of extra weight. The runner was widening the gap between them and there was no way Rick was going to catch him, short of shedding his body armor and equipment. And that wasn't happening. He signaled to Nitro, who was loping along at his side. "Apprehend." He whispered the command and pointed at the figure now at least two hundred yards ahead of them.

Nitro shot off like a bullet, his run as fluid as any Rick had ever seen. There was no energy wasted on vertical motion of his shoulders or flanks. He streaked in a straight and level line toward his target.

Rick couldn't see that far in the muted light, but he knew when Nitro reached the runner. He could hear the grunt, strangely high-pitched, and saw his silhouette floundering while he tried to maintain his balance. Finally, he fell over and out of view in the tall grass. Rick heard the crash when his body connected with the ground.

CHAPTER ELEVEN

RICK CAUGHT UP to Nitro as fast as he could. The dogs were trained in apprehension, with "targets" wearing arm and body protectors to avoid having their skin pierced. In real-life circumstances, there was no such protection, and although the dogs' intention wasn't to harm, the longer they held and detained their targets, the more likely injury could result.

Rick's heart was racing by the time he reached Nitro and the runner, but it skipped a couple of beats when he did get there.

"Out, Nitro. Out!" he ordered the dog.

Nitro obeyed the command and released his target. Rick grabbed the runner by the collar of his jacket, pushed up his sleeve and did a quick check of the arm Nitro had been holding. There were some scrapes and a bit of blood, but nothing serious.

He yanked the runner up to his full height. But the runner immediately started flaying and kicking to try to gain his freedom.

He was a kid—a young one at that—just over five feet tall and skinny, likely no more than ninety pounds.

"Whoa! Take it easy," Rick ordered. *"Tómalo con calma,"* he repeated in Spanish, but his words only caused the kid to fight harder to free himself.

"I wasn't doin' nothin'," the kid spat in halting English.

"Yeah, I bet." When the kid's foot connected solidly with Rick's shin, he swore and took a firmer hold of him. "Stop already! Keep this up and you'll only make matters worse for yourself."

"I didn't do nothin'," the kid mumbled, but his flapping slowed.

"Okay. So what's in the bag?" Rick indicated the satchel.

"Nada. Nothin'."

"We'll see." Rick instructed Nitro to check the boy and his possessions for drugs. Nitro sniffed all around the boy, circling him once, and sat to his right, staring at the satchel strapped around his chest.

"You know what that means, kid? It means the dog thinks there are drugs in your pouch."

"No way. I don't have no drugs!"

"Nitro here thinks you do, and he's right

WHEN LOVE MATTERS MOST

over ninety-nine percent of the time. That's almost a perfect record. He seems pretty sure of himself. You know what else? With his track record being what it is, in legal terms that gives me probable cause to search you. Do you understand?"

"Leave me alone," the kid muttered, and renewed his efforts to break free of Rick's hold.

"Listen to me carefully," Rick said in his most authoritative tone. "This is important, and I'm only going to say it once. Got it?"

Obviously intimidated, the kid nodded.

"I'm going to release my hold on you, but don't think about running. My partner here—" he pointed at Nitro "—is going to watch you. If he thinks you're planning to bolt, he'll take you down again. Do you understand?"

"*Sí.*"

"Good. We understand each other." Rick gave Nitro the signal for "wait" and cautiously released his grip on the kid. He held out his hand for the satchel and was pleased when the kid passed it to him, albeit with a nasty look. Keeping his peripheral vision on the kid, he opened the flap and wasn't surprised to find what must have amounted to at least two kilos of cocaine wrapped in plastic. Rick dipped his small finger in to get a trace amount. He touched his finger to his tongue, then spat on the ground. It was definitely cocaine. He brushed the residue remaining on his finger on the coarse grass.

All bluster had deserted the kid. He wouldn't make eye contact, his shoulders had sagged and, unless Rick was mistaken, he was ready to burst into tears. "How old are you?"

"No es asunto tuyo," he said, but the meekness of his voice belied the bravado of his words.

"You're wrong. Since the amount you're carrying means this is a serious felony, how old you are *does* make a difference in terms of what I do with you. If you weren't a minor, you could be locked up for years."

The kid glanced at him briefly with terror in his eyes. *"Catorce.* Fourteen."

"And your name?"

He squirmed visibly.

"How about just your first name?"

"Matías," he mumbled.

"All right, Matías, where were you going with this?" He held up the satchel.

"To meet a man in front of a coffee shop and give it to him."

"Do you know the man's name?"

"Not his name. Just that I answer when he calls me Manuel."

"Is that your real name? Manuel?"

He shook his head. "No. I am Matías. But Manuel is what they said he would call me."

Rick went on to ask about who "they" were, trying to get as much information from the kid as he could about the cartel. Matías didn't know much. He was just a pawn and utterly petrified at this point. Rick radioed in what he'd learned, hoping they'd be able to catch the kid's contact. "Why do you do it?" Rick asked finally, eyeing the sickly yellow-purple bruise on the boy's cheek.

"My *familia*, they make me." He cast his eyes to the ground. "For the *dinero*. The money. If I don't do it, my father hits me."

Rick was feeling sorrier for the kid by the second. "Do you keep any of the money?"

"No!" He looked dismayed at the suggestion. "*Padre* takes it all."

Rick couldn't help thinking back to his own circumstances in Tijuana when he'd been just a little younger than Matías. If his parents had lived and he'd stayed, he had no doubt he would've been forced to run drugs, too.

"After you handed over the pouch to the man, what were you going to do?"

Matías kicked a pebble at his feet. "You know. Go home to my *familia*."

Rick could read the lie as clearly as if it was written on Matías's face in indelible ink. He sighed. "Let's try that again."

Matías had obviously reached his breaking point. "I was gonna run away. Stay in California." He sniffled.

The similarity to his own early life grabbed Rick by the throat and threatened to choke him. "And what then? What were you planning to do?"

"I dunno. Maybe get a job." He looked up and his eyes shone, not with tears but with determination. "Go to school. Make money."

"You know smuggling drugs is illegal?"

"Sí," he acknowledged, and hung his head.

"And you know it's also illegal to enter the United States without proper authorization?"

"Sí..."

The kid was completely dejected. The bravado had deflated right before Rick's eyes. "Even though you're a minor—young," he clarified at the questioning look, "there are still consequences, ah...*consecuencias*?"

Matías had no words left. He nodded mutely. "I'm sorry, *señor*."

Rick looked around him, ascertaining there were no other cops in sight. He wondered, as he always did at this juncture, if he what he was doing was right. It certainly wasn't the legal thing, but he felt he had no choice. "Matías, I'm going to keep your bag…"

"No, *señor*! I'll be in *big* trouble." The panic was evident on his face, in his voice. "My father will kill me."

Rick wasn't sure if Matías was exaggerating or not, but hoped the kid wouldn't have to find out. "Let me finish. I'm going to keep your bag. I'll need to turn it in. I'll say I found it. Nitro and I are going to walk back there." He indicated the direction they'd come from, where they'd set up their surveillance. "When we get there and I turn around, I don't want to see you. Got that, Matías?"

The kid nodded with fervor. "*Sí, señor*. Thank you very much."

"Do the right thing, kid. Go find an organization called Child Services, okay? They'll help you. Do something worthwhile with your life. Not drugs. There's no life there." With those parting words, he called Nitro and they headed back to their surveillance post.

In these circumstances, Rick didn't uphold the law the way he'd sworn to do, but how could he in good conscience? He knew what would have happened to the kid if he'd turned him in. The consequences would be even more dire if he'd sent him back to go to his father empty-handed. He thought of the livid bruise on the kid's face. Maybe it wasn't a stretch to think his father would've killed him. Rick hoped that rather than going back, Matías would choose to keep going forward and he'd find a life in California.

He wished the kid well.

CHAPTER TWELVE

MADISON STOOD BESIDE the aqua therapy tank at the San Diego Animal Rehabilitation Center. It was a huge glass-walled tank, with metal supports, fitted with a hydro-treadmill.

Zeke stood in the middle of the tank, the warm water halfway up his torso, his favorite squeaky chew toy clamped in his mouth. To help him feel more at ease and guide him if he needed it, one of the center's technicians stood in the water with the dog.

"He seems comfortable enough," the technician, Gordon, said.

Madison nodded. "Yes, he seems pretty relaxed. Ready for the treadmill?"

"Yeah."

Madison pushed the appropriate combination of buttons on the control panel, and the underwater conveyor started slowly. It alarmed Zeke and he faltered, but Gordon kept his hands on him, steady and soothing, and Zeke began walking slowly.

"Let's keep it at this pace until he gets used to it. Maybe for the whole session today, since it's his first time."

"Good idea," Gordon agreed.

After a short period of uncertainty, Zeke seemed to adjust to the slow walk. Madison heard the door open. She glanced over her shoulder and smiled broadly. She'd told Rick that she planned to start Zeke on aqua therapy today and suggested that if he could find the time, he was welcome to watch. "I'm glad you were able to stop by," she said as he strode over.

She was sure he was about to give her a kiss, but she didn't feel comfortable with it in front of Gordon. Rick must have read the look in her eyes, because he straightened and instead leaned his forearms on the top rail of the tank. Madison made the introductions. Rick greeted Zeke, too, and the dog showed his pleasure with a tail wag and, toy still in his mouth, a muffled bark. Madison was pleased to see that he didn't stumble on the treadmill. He maintained the steady gait she'd set for him.

"How's he doing?" Rick asked.

"Well. Really well, for his first time in the tank."

They watched Zeke for a few minutes, then Rick broke the silence. "Okay, you have to excuse my ignorance, but what does walking in the water do for him that a normal walk wouldn't?"

"Let's just go for a few more minutes, Gordon. We don't want to overdo it today," Madison said before she turned to Rick. "Aqua therapy's been proved effective in rehabilitating injured or elderly dogs, and helps strengthen the patient's muscles without causing undue stress. The water buoyancy decreases excessive force on the joints and provides resistance for the range of motion."

Rick looked back at Zeke. "He seems to be enjoying it."

"They usually do. We keep the water warm, and that aids with pain management, increases blood flow and circulation and helps with the elasticity of soft tissue. It means he's more comfortable in the tank. Plus, we can adjust the water height to accommodate any size animal. We can customize the workout to each patient's specific needs. Okay, that's it for today, Gordon," she said to the tech, then punched a few buttons and started draining the water from the tank.

Released from the tank, Zeke shook off

the water and hobbled over to Rick. Rick scratched and rubbed him to the dog's delight, but raised his eyes to meet Madison's. "He's limping badly. Did the exercise hurt him?"

Madison placed a towel on Zeke's back and began drying him gently. "He might feel a bit of discomfort, but no, it didn't hurt him. With aqua therapy, most patients are more likely to use an affected limb when they're standing or walking underwater, and we often observe an improvement on land after just one session of underwater treadmill walking." She tossed the damp towel into a hamper and ran a hand affectionately along Zeke's back. "We'll see if that holds true for this boy. I'm hoping the treadmill exercise will provide a quicker return to normal than would be possible otherwise. It has the added advantage of being an energy outlet for him." She clipped the leash to his collar and handed it to Gordon. "Would you walk him around a bit for me? I'd like to see how it affected his gait."

Gordon did as he was asked, and Madison and Rick watched Zeke while he moved around the room. Madison had been correct. He still favored his hind leg, but he wasn't keeping it completely off the ground. Still, she didn't want him to overexert himself.

"Thanks, Gordon," she said, and kneeled to call Zeke to her for some well-deserved hugs. "Please take him back to his pen and give him some treats. Do another session with him today—same speed and duration—before his owner picks him up, okay?"

Gordon nodded.

As she was about to follow Gordon out of the room, Rick placed a hand on her arm. She gazed up at him.

"Thank you." He closed his eyes for a moment. "Thank you for what you're doing for Zeke. For what you do for all our dogs. For caring."

Madison was breathless, looking into Rick's deep, coal-dark eyes. He dealt with violence—with the ugly underbelly of society—every day. Yet here he was, with emotion evident on his face, thanking her for doing what she loved, for taking care of animals that needed help. She raised a hand and placed it gently on his cheek, feeling the day-old bristle scrape against her palm.

She wanted to explain to him that thanks weren't necessary. That she did what she did because she couldn't do anything but. "I'm happy I could help Zeke" were the soft, simple words that came out.

Madison was finished for the day and so was Rick. They drove to a small coffee shop by the oceanfront.

Madison ordered a regular and Rick a decaffeinated coffee. They took their coffees to a corner table by the window and chatted for a while.

"You don't want the kick of caffeine?" she asked.

"Oh, I love my coffee strong and I get enough of a jolt in the morning to last me. If I drank it caffeinated all day long, I'd be bouncing off the walls. I don't need that kind of stimulant," he said with a smile.

She smiled, too, but his comment made her recall something he'd said a while ago, about his exposure to the world of drugs when he was a child, and that made her think of the discussion she'd had with his mother, Hillary, about Rick being adopted. His early life had to define him in some ways, and she wanted to understand. "Your childhood. It couldn't have been easy," she said tentatively.

He finished his coffee, and to her astonishment, he laughed. "That's an understatement!"

Madison cleared her throat and finished her coffee, too, not knowing quite what to say.

Rick took her hand in his. The smile was gone from his face. "Come walk with me."

His grasp on her hand was light, but she felt the tension radiating from him.

Once they were outside strolling along the boardwalk, he said, "Let me tell you a story."

She nodded when he glanced at her. "You already know I was born in Tijuana and lived there until my early teens."

She nodded again.

"Suffice it to say that it was not an easy childhood. Tijuana is a drug-cartel stronghold. A city with high levels of gang violence, especially during the heyday of the drug cartels when I was a kid. They've curtailed crime considerably, but it was very different when I was growing up. My father…" His voice drifted off.

"Let's sit for a while," he suggested, moving toward a large rock near the edge of the ocean. He leaned back and pulled her against him, both of them facing the water. Wrapping his arms around her, he rested his chin on her shoulder. For a few minutes, they watched the waves pound the shore and listened to the mournful cries of seagulls as they circled overhead.

Madison felt the warmth of his breath against her face when he exhaled.

"My father was a ranking officer in the Tijuana Cartel," Rick continued. "He was frequently involved in the turf wars that existed with the competing Arellano Félix Cartel, and the larger and growing Sinaloa Cartel. My mother was an addict. It would have been impossible for her not to be, with my father's position and constant access to any narcotic you could imagine. Violence and the threat of being killed were realities of our daily existence when I was a kid.

"From an early age, I recognized the destructive and dangerous effects of drugs." He rested his cheek against hers again. "When I was twelve, our home was attacked by the Sinaloa Cartel, the biggest competitor to the one my father was involved with. My parents were both killed…executed."

"Oh, my God," Madison breathed, and turned to Rick. His face was hard and unsmiling. His eyes were darker than she'd ever seen them. He said it so matter-of-factly, but it must have been dreadful. "I'm so sorry."

The wind blew Madison's hair into her

eyes and she swiped at it impatiently. "Where were you at the time? In school?" She couldn't imagine what it would have been like for him to come home and find his parents murdered.

He shook his head. "No. I was home."

She had no words. She stared at him in horror.

His eyes were unfocused. "I was aware, even at that age, that if the Sinaloa enforcers found me, they wouldn't think twice about killing me."

"Then, how...?"

He shrugged. "I hid in my closet. In the corner. Bracing my back against one wall and my feet against the other. I climbed as high as I could so they wouldn't find me if they looked in. They could check the floor of the closet and not see my feet. I was shielded by the hanging clothes. When the enforcers searched my room—checked inside my closet—they didn't see me. Even so, they set our house on fire. I was so terrified of leaving my hiding place—not knowing if they were waiting outside—I nearly succumbed to smoke inhalation."

Madison framed his face with her hands. "That's atrocious. What happened to you? Did you go to the police?"

His laugh was short and harsh. "No. The police wouldn't have helped me."

"Did you have other family?"

"I did, but they were all involved in the drug trade. I wanted out. I left Mexico that night. It wasn't the first time my life had been on the line because of my father's occupation—because of the drugs—but I swore it would be the last. I crossed the border into California. Right where I now patrol. A San Diego cop saw me. I was sure of it, but he must have realized I was just a frightened kid. I had nothing with me. No backpack, nothing that would've suggested I was running drugs. He could have caught me, detained me, turned me back, but he didn't do any of those things. He just let me go. I don't think it was because he was lazy. I think he must've understood that I was running for my life.

"That was when I determined to become a cop and dedicate my life to fighting drug trafficking."

"And that's why you volunteer with the school to counsel kids against drugs?"

He nodded. His eyes were bright and intense.

She placed a tender kiss on his lips. "I'm

so sorry for what you went through when you were a boy." She brushed her lips across his again, and he wound his arms around her and held tight.

CHAPTER THIRTEEN

IN THE MONTHS since Madison had moved to San Diego, most of her time had been focused on her work at the veterinary clinic and at the animal rehabilitation center. During the initial months, her social interactions had been limited to the people she worked with—mostly Heather and Jane. Now she had Rick. Thinking of Rick always brought a smile to her face.

Although it was still in the early stages, Madison had also come to value her friendship with Jessica Palmer, wife of San Diego Police Department K-9 officer Cal Palmer. She'd come to like Jessica's husband, too. She and Jessica shared another undeniably strong bond in addition to their training—having a relationship with a police officer.

Madison had learned that Jessica and Cal were only recently married. They were obviously happy. She'd met their two little girls, Cal's daughter, Haley, from a previous marriage, and their adopted daughter, Kayla. She'd been enchanted by them.

Madison didn't normally romanticize— she was too practical and scientific for that— but she couldn't help being touched by how Jessica and Cal had met just after the powerful earthquake that had struck San Diego almost a year earlier. She was happy for all of them that Jessica and Cal had been able to give Kayla a family after the child had tragically lost her mother in the earthquake, leaving her an orphan.

In the months since their initial meeting, she and Jessica tried to get together at least every couple of weeks. A Saturday when Madison wasn't working, but both Rick and Cal were, was a perfect opportunity. Jess and Cal's girls were at a birthday party, and after a taxing week Madison welcomed a quiet afternoon at Jessica's home with tea and girl talk.

"How's everything between you and Rick?" Jessica asked as she placed the tray laden with tea and shortbread cookies on the coffee table.

Madison accepted the cup from her and smiled. "Good. Really good."

Jessica stirred milk and sugar into her own tea. "I'm so glad! I like seeing the two of you together. I've known Rick for nearly as long as I have Cal, and I've never seen him in a serious relationship. I think relationships matter to him, so he's cautious about them. On an entirely selfish note, since Cal and Rick are close, I'm really glad he picked you, someone I truly like and enjoy being with."

"Thanks. The feeling is mutual."

"Rick is a wonderful man and the two of you are terrific together. He's crazy about you."

Madison's smile wavered, and she held a hand over her stomach. "Oh, Jess, you think so?"

Jessica angled her head and gave Madison a quizzical look. "I wouldn't say it if I didn't believe it. Why? Don't you see it?"

"I guess I do, and I feel… Oh, Jess. This is a new experience for me, and I haven't said it to Rick, not in so many words, but I'm falling in love with him."

Jessica's cup rattled as she placed it hurriedly on the table. She rose from the sofa to enfold Madison in her arms. "I'm so thrilled! For both of you. Rick has had some difficult situations to deal with in his life. He deserves to be happy, and I know you make him happy."

Jessica's reference to what Rick had endured reminded Madison of what she'd learned about his early years in Tijuana. Her heart broke a little as it always did when she thought about it. "Rick does deserve to be happy," Madison said in a subdued voice. "He...he told me how his parents died."

Sorrow glistened in Jessica's eyes. "Rick had great courage as a kid. I have to give him that, and a lot more."

Madison was relieved that Jessica seemed to be aware of the circumstances, and she wouldn't be breaching a confidence. She stood and moved to the living room window, not out of a desire to look outside, but because she couldn't sit still. "It's astonishing that he turned out so well. It would've been so easy for him to get sucked into that life."

"Rick's made of strong stuff. He's one of the most principled people I know. But you're right. You heard he ran away and crossed the San Ysidro border into California on his own when he was just a young teen, right?"

"Yes," Madison whispered, still facing the window, rubbing at a spot on the sill.

"Did he tell you what happened when he first got to San Diego?"

Madison turned around and rested her hands on the sill on either side of her. "No."

"He was so afraid of getting caught by the cartel or by the US authorities and being sent back to Mexico, he lived on the streets for the better part of a year. He equated everything bad in his life with drugs. What I know from Cal is that Rick's drug-dealer father and addict mother were self-absorbed and emotionally unavailable. He had no siblings, and I imagine he had no real family life. Well, at least not one that had any love in it.

"He knew the authorities here took a much stronger stance against illegal drugs, but he must've been terrified. Anyway, after spending time on the streets of San Diego, he realized that he needed to get into school if he was going to fulfill his dream of becoming a cop. He found his way to the county's Child Services department. I've heard something about him having received encouragement, maybe even help, from a police officer, but those details are sketchy. Anyway, he was granted refugee status and placed in a foster home."

Still restless, Madison walked back to the sofa and sat down. She hadn't known about his time living on the streets. Her heart broke even more for the young boy Rick had been. "Was he placed with the Stewarts right away?"

Jessica smiled. "Yes. He got very lucky. I don't think it could have been better for him. The Stewarts, the first family he was fostered with, decided to adopt him. They're wonderful people. Kindhearted, with two kids of their own—adults now, older than Rick."

"Yes, I've met them."

"Well, then you know it was probably Rick's saving grace that they adopted him. For the first time, he had positive role models and he was loved. From what Cal says, he exceled at school, got his citizenship and graduated from the police academy. He did what he pledged to do as a kid escaping Mexico. He became a police officer with the San Diego Police Department."

They both turned when they heard the front door open and the scrabbling of claws on the tile floor. Scout ran into the living room. First he rushed to Jessica, then to Madison.

"How are the two most beautiful ladies in San Diego?" Cal asked, and bent down to give Jessica a kiss.

"Just San Diego?" Jessica feigned a pout.

Cal pulled her to her feet, turned her one way, then the other, pretending to scrutinize her. "Okay. All of California."

She grinned and kissed him back. "That's much better!"

"What are you two up to?" he asked.

"Gossiping about Rick," Jessica responded, and Madison felt the heat on her cheeks.

"Hmm, not how I'd want to spend my day off," he joked. "I'll be right back."

He returned a couple minutes later balancing a beer bottle and two glasses of white wine. Jessica took the glasses, handing one to Madison. Cal sat next to Jessica and draped an arm across his wife's shoulders. "As far as the gossip goes, anything I can add?" he asked with a grin.

Madison's flush felt more pronounced.

"The only reason I'm offering," he went on, "is that I think the world of Rick, and I happen to believe you're good for him, just like Jessica does. If I can help bring the two of you closer together, I'm all for it." He raised his bottle and clinked it to each of their glasses. "So what do you want to know?"

Madison waved a hand. "I...I'm not sure. This seems...wrong."

"Don't worry about it. Rick is one of my best friends. I wouldn't say anything he wouldn't want me to. Besides, as I just said, I'm doing the girlie-gossip thing—ouch!" he exclaimed, and shot Jessica a wounded look while rubbing his shin. "Okay, scratch that last comment. Anyway, I'd like the two of you together, so if I can help…" he repeated.

Madison looked at Jessica with uncertainty.

"Okay," Jessica jumped in. "I was telling her about Rick's background and the Stewarts. Why don't you tell her about his career?"

"That's easy." He took a sip of his beer. "What's for dinner, by the way?" He winced when she gave him a gentle elbow in the side. "So Rick's career. He graduated top of his class at the police academy. He made plainclothes detective with the Narcotics Task Force at SDPD. Working in Narcotics, he frequently collaborated with the cops from the K-9 Unit. The propaganda is—" he held a hand up to protect himself before Jessica could elbow him again "—that Rick's focus and determination enabled him to rise up the ranks of the department in record time. He became the youngest sergeant in the history of the SDPD when he was promoted in the K-9 Unit at the age of twenty-seven. He's now, what, twenty-nine or thereabouts?" He turned to Jessica for confirmation, and she nodded. "So at the ripe old age of twenty-nine, it's rumored that he's in line for the next lieutenancy. That's all there is to tell. Anything else you want to know?"

Madison raised her hand again. "Oh, no. I think that's plenty. This is just wrong. I'm feeling guilty enough as it is."

"Don't be," Jessica interjected. "Here's the main thing. Rick's a good guy. He's got a heart of gold, but—as you can appreciate from what you know—he has some scars, too."

Madison felt her eyes sting as she thought of the child he'd been in Mexico. "Can't blame him."

"He hasn't had a serious relationship since we've known him," Jessica said.

"That's enough information," Madison declared. Since it was almost Owen's feeding and walking time, she said goodbye. On her way home, she thought about everything she'd learned about Rick.

Madison's upbringing had been so different from his, she mused. Yes, she'd lost her

230 WHEN LOVE MATTERS MOST

mother at a very young age. Madison could barely remember her, but her father was a force to be reckoned with. He'd never remarried after her mother had passed away. She was raised in wealth and privilege by her loving, doting, protective father. She'd never lacked for anything, love most of all. She'd always felt entirely secure and safe in her father's love.

She couldn't begin to imagine what Rick's childhood had been like in comparison. As she let herself into the house, she felt an overwhelming urge to make up for some of the pain he'd experienced—and what better time to start than that evening?

CHAPTER FOURTEEN

MADISON WAS SURPRISED not to see Rick's police-issue Ford Explorer in his driveway when she arrived at his house. She checked her watch. No, she wasn't early. Not by much anyway.

Maybe he'd gotten a ride home with someone.

She knocked on Rick's front door, but there was no answer. She shifted the bag containing wine and dessert to her other arm and peered in through the lightly frosted sidelight. She immediately felt embarrassed at the thought of peeking into Rick's house, but it was short-lived. She knocked again.

When there was still no answer, she looked in through the sidelight a second time. She could see Sniff, but above his head...

She drew back quickly at the sight of another pair of bright eyes staring at her. It took her a moment, but she laughed when she realized it was a pair of *dog eyes*. Taking a cau-

tious look, she saw the other dog. He was
larger than Sniff, with a near-black coat and
luminous golden eyes.

Sniff must have recognized her. He was
doing a little happy dance and wagging his
tail energetically. The other dog didn't seem
quite that welcoming, but at least he wasn't
barking.

Clearly, Rick wasn't home yet.

Madison placed the bag on a chair on the
porch, and went back to the side light. She
cupped her hands around her eyes to block
out the glare and peered in again.

The other dog must have retreated somewhere, but Sniff was still watching her, his
nose pressed against the glass. She gazed
beyond him.

What she saw startled her. She'd been to
Rick's home before, but hadn't seen anything
like this.

The interior of the house was in disarray.
There was a towel on the hallway floor. Pairs
of shoes were lying haphazardly about. What
looked like a pot had been dragged into a
doorway. In the living room, she saw sofa
cushions on the coffee table and the floor.

She felt like a voyeur. Admittedly, she was
neat to the point of being obsessive, but this

was ridiculous. And Rick was expecting her! What would the place look like if she'd just stopped by unannounced?

"Hey, there!" Her hand flew to her throat and she jumped at the sound of Rick's voice behind her.

"You're late," she said, trying to cover up her guilt at being caught peeping into his house.

He touched his lips to hers. "No, I'm not. You're early." He held his watch out to her. "See? I have two minutes to spare. Joking aside, I hope you weren't waiting long. I'd planned to be home before now—got detained at work." He unlocked the door, grabbed the bag she'd left on the chair and motioned her in. "Don't tell the cops, but I was speeding most of the way to make it on time."

"Your secret is safe with me," she said.

Sniff and a beautiful Malinois stood just inside the door. She scratched Sniff's head and turned to the Malinois. "Who's this?"

Rick gave the dog a hand signal that had him plopping down. "This is Nitro. He's my new partner in training."

Madison glanced up at him. "Does this mean Sniff's retiring?"

"Yes. His retirement has been approved."

"Yay!" She did a little fist pump. "That's wonderful news." She bent down to rub Sniff's head again. "Hey, pal. Congratulations! You can look forward to a life of leisure now." She turned her attention back to Rick. "You having Nitro? Does that change anything about your plans for Sniff?"

"No, of course not, but now he'll have a buddy to keep him company."

Madison smiled at Nitro. "He's beautiful."

"Yes, he is."

"Malinois?"

"Malinois–Dutch shepherd. Come in. Let me take this into the kitchen first. Get you a drink."

Turning to follow him, Madison was confronted by the disorder she'd noticed from outside. She stepped over a running shoe and what looked to be a dish towel, and followed Rick into the kitchen. It *was* a pot sitting in the doorway. She picked it up and placed it in the sink.

Rick, meanwhile, retrieved the tea towel and tossed it into a laundry hamper inside the open door of a cupboard. He scooped up some kibble from a canister and poured it into two metal dog dishes. Sniff and Nitro both sat patiently until he released them to eat.

"Now, what can I get you?"

"A glass of white wine would be nice, thanks."

Drink in hand, she followed him into the living room.

With an embarrassed laugh, he hurriedly replaced the cushions and chucked a sneaker that had been on a chair into the corner of the room. "How's that?" he asked with a grin. "At least you can sit down now."

Instead of sitting, she joined Rick in his backyard while he barbecued the steaks, potatoes and vegetables for their dinner. She helped by putting together the salad and making garlic bread. She loved the easy good humor they shared. As she set the patio table, she glanced at the two dogs sleeping in the shade of a large tree.

"Isn't Nitro too old to be training as a police dog?" she asked.

She could see Rick's face harden. "Nitro's been with our unit for a few years. He was Brody's dog. You remember him?"

She nodded. Based on what she'd seen of the man, she felt bad for the dog. "So why's Nitro with you?"

Rick stuck a fork into the potatoes to test them. "Brody's no longer with the K-9 Unit."

"Oh." She didn't like the man and wasn't sorry he'd left. "He quit the police department?"

"If only. No. He was transferred to the financial crimes unit, although I doubt he has the smarts to do much good there." His gaze met hers, and she could see the dislike Rick harbored for the other cop. "Anyway, Logan's going to fill Brody's spot in the unit, but we decided to retrain Nitro for narcotics detection. With Sniff retiring, I asked to be partnered with Nitro."

At the mention of their names, both dogs lifted their heads, but Rick signaled them to relax and lie back down.

Madison took a sip of her wine. "Explain to me how it works. I've heard bits and pieces. How do they search houses and cars, for example, for drugs?"

Rick lowered the top of the barbecue and joined her at the patio table. "A dog will do what's called a perimeter search of a structure or a vehicle. With the dogs' track records for accurate detection, if he indicates that drugs are present, that gives us probable cause to search inside. More often than not, it leads to arrest."

"I see."

"We also patrol the border. Often we have tips from CIs—confidential informants— that there's a shipment coming across the border by vehicle or mules."

"Mules?"

"Yeah. Runners working for a cartel, coming from Mexico on foot with drugs to deliver to dealers on this side of the border."

"They walk across?" She thought about the length of the border and how daunting it must be to patrol all that distance, not just the roads.

"The dogs help there, too. There are some common crossings. Once they're on this side of the border, they're illegal aliens, so we can apprehend them even without the suspicion of drugs. Most of our dogs are trained in suspect apprehension, too, and can catch a suspect if he runs."

"What kind of person would risk coming across the border like that, smuggling drugs?" she asked.

"All kinds. Poverty can do strange things to a person, and the cartels can be...persuasive." His face sobered. "Often they're no more than kids."

"It must be hard to arrest them if they're

kids." She was dismayed that children would be used in such a manner.

Rick sighed and got up to check the steaks. He came back to the table with two full plates and placed one in front of her. Just when she concluded that he'd assumed her question was rhetorical, he cleared his throat. "I don't. Not always," he said quietly.

"What, then?"

"I...I sometimes let them go."

Madison stared at him. "Even if they have drugs?"

He nodded.

"But they've broken the law!"

He shrugged, watched her as she tried her steak. "How do you like it?" he asked, changing the subject.

"It's perfect. Thanks." But she was too curious about what he'd said not to pursue it. "So what happens to them if you let them go?"

"Do you really want to know?"

Her mouth full, Madison nodded, but she was no longer certain she did.

"All right. I'll give you an example." He told her about a young boy called Matías, whom he'd caught at the border with a couple kilos of cocaine and a nasty bruise on his face. He'd taken the drugs, gotten as much information from the kid as he could and let him go, hoping he'd continue into San Diego as opposed to going back.

While they ate, Madison kept thinking about Rick's role in law enforcement compared to the one he sometimes chose out of compassion. He understood the law and in every other respect seemed committed to uphold it. She realized he couldn't disregard his own experience. Still, he wasn't doing what he'd sworn to do. She tried not to dwell on it, at least for the time being.

After their meal, Madison offered to retrieve the dessert she'd brought, but Rick had his own plans. He brought out four sweet buns with a streusel topping. "It's a Mexican dessert," he explained. "It's called pan dulce."

Madison tasted one of the buns and licked the tasty, sticky streusel off her fingers. "Delicious! Is this something you ate when you were a child?"

Rick bit into his own bun. "Not in Mexico. It's one of the things my mom—Hillary," he clarified, "did for me when I came to live with them." He smiled. "She did it to make me feel at home."

As they finished their coffee and dessert, Madison's thoughts drifted back to what she'd learned about Rick. She considered her father, and what he'd have to say about a law enforcement officer choosing when and when not to uphold the law, even if that officer had the best of intentions.

"Is everything okay?" Rick asked when he walked her out to her SUV at the end of the evening.

Her moral dilemma must have shown on her face. "Yeah. Sure," she said, but her voice lacked conviction, even to her own ears.

As she drove home, she continued to think about everything they'd discussed that night. Was it so wrong for Rick to be helping boys who'd already suffered in ways no child should have to suffer? Was he seeing himself in those boys and was that why? Still, the law was the law. She'd learned that as far back as she could remember. Apart from her father, how did *she* feel about it? Compassion versus convictions waged a battle. She truly cared about Rick—was more than halfway in love with him—but she might have discovered a basic incompatibility that they needed to understand and resolve…or accept.

And if she did accept it, she'd have to keep

it from her father. Of that she was certain.
Her entire life, she'd never lied to him, had
never kept anything from him. Having to do
it now would create a whole new dilemma
for her.

MADISON WAS UP to her elbows in flour. Since
she had the day off, she'd decided to try her
hand at making Rick the pan dulce pastries
he remembered so fondly. Without Rick's
knowledge, Madison had gotten the recipe
from Mrs. Stewart and wanted to surprise
Rick with it after dinner. She'd just started
to knead the dough when Owen raised his
head, let out the typical malamute woo-hoo
and bolted for the front door.

Madison glanced at her kitchen clock.
It was much too early for Rick to arrive.
When she heard the doorbell, she brushed
her hair back with her forearm and rushed
after Owen.

She swung the door open and squealed.
"Dad! I didn't know you were coming to California." She hugged him, trying to be careful not to get flour on his dark suit jacket.

He didn't seem to have the same reservation and wrapped his arms around her. "Oh,
it's so good to see you, honey," he murmured.

When she stepped back, he brushed at the flour on her forehead.

"Sorry, sorry," she said, gesturing at the generous amounts of flour she'd managed to transfer to his jacket.

"Don't worry about it." He dropped a kiss on her forehead and walked in. "Hey, Owen."

"It's great to see you, Dad, but why didn't you call or send me an email to let me know you were coming?"

Patrick Long followed his daughter and gave her a blank stare. "I asked Holly to send you an email," he said, referring to his assistant. "Didn't you get it?"

Madison shook her head. "No, but it doesn't matter. I'm just happy to see you! What brought you here and how long are you staying?"

"I was asked at the last minute to fill in for a speaker at a conference. I had to work on my presentation, which is why I asked Holly to send you the note. Unfortunately, I have to return first thing tomorrow morning. So let me take you to dinner tonight." He chuckled when they entered the kitchen and he saw the clutter on every available surface. "When did you start..." He took a closer look. "Baking?"

"Today," she acknowledged, a little embarrassed by the uncharacteristic disarray in her kitchen and the mess she was sure *she* was. She rubbed her nose with the back of her hand. Her father laughed and brushed off the flour she must have deposited there. "As for dinner…" She thought about calling and canceling with Rick, but if her father was leaving the next day, she didn't want to miss the opportunity to finally introduce him to Rick. "Um, how about having a home-cooked meal here instead?"

Her father knew her well and was aware of her lack of interest in cooking. He raised a skeptical eyebrow. "That's sweet of you, but I don't mind taking you out. Spare you the trouble."

"It's not that simple." She washed her hands and mixed her father his favorite whiskey sour. "I'm making dinner and, as you can see by the chaos around us, dessert… for someone."

"Am I correct in presuming it's a man?" He seemed even more disbelieving, and that made her laugh. She wasn't surprised by his reaction.

"Uh-huh." They'd had a cook and housekeeper when she was growing up. Madison had always been more interested in her studies and sports, and had had little time for domestic work.

"This man you're cooking for. It's serious, then?"

She was certain she was blushing. "I think so."

Her father leaned against the kitchen counter and took a slow sip of his drink. "Why haven't you mentioned him to me?"

Another tough question. "I don't know, Dad. It's early days still. You could meet him tonight," she suggested with a mixture of excitement and trepidation.

Patrick put down his glass and moved over to Madison. He wrapped both arms around her, resting her head against his shoulder. "I miss having you close to home, honey. I miss knowing about the developments in your life."

He sounded despondent, and that made Madison feel guilty for not having told him about Rick—and sad about the physical distance between her and her father. For most of her life, it had been just the two of them. She tightened her arms around him. "I miss it, too, Dad. As for Rick, I'm sorry I haven't mentioned him to you, but I'd like the two of you to meet. It would mean a lot to me."

"I'd like to meet him, too," Patrick said.

Madison grinned up at her father. "I'd better call and give him a heads-up. It wouldn't be fair if he showed up and I just sprung you on him!"

"I can remember when I was a young man and first dating your mother," he said with the dreamy look he still got whenever he spoke of her. "I'd say that's an accurate statement. Make your call and then tell me about him."

AN HOUR LATER, Madison opened the door for Rick.

He brushed his lips over hers and handed her a huge bouquet of flowers.

"Thank you. Nice," she commented, and gave him an appreciative smile.

"I'm glad you like them."

"I do. They're beautiful. But you…" She motioned with her free hand. "I've never seen you in a suit before. *Very* nice."

Rick straightened the collar of his shirt. "It's not a suit exactly. Just pants and a sports jacket. There's nothing wrong with wanting to make a good impression on your father.

It also isn't every day a person meets a Supreme Court judge."

"He's just Dad to me." Madison raised the bouquet to her nose and inhaled the sweet scent of roses, lilies and freesia—her favorite. Rick had remembered! "Thanks again for these. They're beautiful. Come on in. I'll put these in water and introduce you to Dad." She glanced back while they walked toward the kitchen and flashed him a brilliant smile. "You look great all dressed up. Just so you know."

AFTER DINNER, RICK watched Madison walk her father out and hug him goodbye.

When she reentered the living room, he was sitting in the middle of the sofa, his head against the cushion. He was sure his face looked as glum as he felt. "That couldn't have gone much worse," he said.

Madison flopped down on the sofa next to him and reached for the mug containing her now-cold tea. "I don't know… He didn't threaten to have you removed from the police force."

Rick's chuckle was strained. "I guess. But other than that, we seem to be at the opposite ends of the spectrum about subjects that are basic to each of us—policing, the judicial system and burden of proof, to name a few."

"You could've let some of the subjects go," she suggested gently. "I did try to change the topic once or twice, particularly when you were talking about the predicament of underage drug smugglers."

He sighed heavily and took her hand in his. "No. I couldn't have. It's not who I am. Not when they're things that define me. Some of those kids deserve a break." He rubbed a callused thumb across her knuckles. "Will I be able to keep seeing you, or is he likely to get a restraining order?"

Madison's laugh sounded uncomfortable. The fact that she didn't answer concerned him. He placed his other hand on top of their joined ones. Whether he'd been joking or not, the thought of not seeing her again scared him. He was falling for her, and hard. He'd even tossed the word *love* around in his head. "I care about you. A lot. I wish your father and I could have gotten along better."

Rick appreciated how much Madison's father meant to her. He could see in her eyes—in the lines of her face—that a grudging acceptance between the two of them for her sake wasn't what she'd hoped for. He gave her hand a gentle squeeze. "If I have another chance with him, I promise I'll try to be less opinionated. More conciliatory. I care that much about you."

She responded with a slow nod and a small smile.

Rick had to believe her father would try to make the best of it, too, if that was Madison's wish and in her best interests. He just hoped fervently that her father thought *he* was in her best interests.

Time would tell.

CHAPTER FIFTEEN

RICK SAT ON the patio at Buster's Beach House Bar. Passing his bottle of beer from hand to hand, he watched a schooner sail past. He thought again about Matías and wondered where the kid was and what he was doing. It had been nearly a month since he'd run into the kid. He hoped Matías had followed through, stayed in California and gone to Child Services. He hated the idea of him being back with his family in Mexico and doing the bidding of the cartel. He glanced up when he heard booted footsteps approaching his table.

"Sorry I'm late," Logan said, and pulled out the chair opposite Rick.

"No problem." Knowing his captain had a preference for Coronas, too, Rick signaled to their waiter to bring two more beers. "You were interviewing for a replacement for Brody, weren't you?"

"Yeah." Logan took off his black ball cap

with the SDPD K-9 Unit insignia and placed it on the vacant chair. "There's a lot of interest, as usual."

"See anyone promising?"

"A couple actually. One's a ten-year veteran from Vice. The other's a rookie who's showing great potential. Ethan Gillis and Veronica Monroe. Thanks," he said to the waiter when he brought their beers. "Do you know either of them?"

"I know Gillis to see him, but I don't know anything about him as a cop. Veronica?" He shook his head. "Never heard of her. Usually you don't look at rookies."

"I'm obliged to consider everyone who applies."

Rick smiled at Logan. "Yeah, yeah. Let me rephrase, Captain. Generally, rookies don't demonstrate the requisite levels of experience and maturity needed to take on one of the most dangerous roles in policing, blah, blah, blah. Are you being pressured to meet a quota?" Rick asked with a more serious tone.

"Nah." Logan took a sip from his bottle. "Veronica is smart, balanced and has already distinguish herself in her own unit. She's also good with the dogs. She seems to be a natural."

"Sounds as if you've decided."

"The jury's still out, but those two are at the top of the list and, like I said, both look promising." Logan watched a tall brunette wearing shorts and a tank top sashay by. "How I love the hot California sunshine!" he said with a grin when she was out of earshot. "So what's on your mind?"

Rick took a drink, too, and thought about how Madison's own views, and the discussion with her father over dinner, had caused him to question even more what he'd been doing with the kids coming across the border. "You tend to be a black-and-white sort of guy," he began slowly. "We all understand and respect it. We always know where you stand and where we stand with you."

Those piercing blue eyes of Logan's narrowed. "Someone have a problem with that?"

"No." Rick was quick to assure him. "But do you ever see any gray between the extremes?"

"In what way?"

"On the job." Rick could see that Logan was trying to work out in his mind where the conversation was heading. If the deep creases in his brow and the hunching of his shoulders were any indication, he didn't seem too pleased about the prospects.

"The law is black-and-white. There's not a whole lot of gray there."

Logan sounded like Patrick Long. Rick knew he had to choose his words carefully, especially since Logan was not just a friend but his boss. "We don't issue speeding tickets to people who're a few clicks over the limit, nor do we arrest a kid who's got a joint or two in his back pocket, despite the fact that in both cases they're breaking the law."

"True. We don't have the manpower to process all those minor infractions, nor is there a huge downside. If we catch them, we give them a warning. That's usually de-terrent enough, at least for the short-term." Even white teeth flashed when he smiled. "How many times would your younger self have been hauled in if we enforced to the let-ter of the law?"

"About as often as you would've been," Rick shot back. "But never for drugs," he added. "So there's some gray at times that *is* acceptable," he concluded.

Logan's lips turned down and his gaze was steady on Rick's. "Did you get written up for something? Speeding? A brawl?"

Rick's loud laugh attracted a few curious glances from nearby tables. "No! C'mon, Jagger. You should know better than that."

"So what's this about?"

"What if someone just needs a break? Those examples you cited, they show there's some flexibility in the system, right?"

"The law is the law, but resources and consequences need to be considered. The examples you used are very minor infractions that would just bog down the system. It's accepted that we use our discretion in those cases."

"Exactly!" Rick pointed with his bottle and thought again about Matías and the life he would've had in Mexico, working for the cartel. "And in others? Where upholding the law might cause more harm than good?"

Logan drained the last of his beer. "Our job is to uphold the law. We aren't judge or jury. It's not our job to consider extenuating circumstances or decide punishment for a crime. If we did, we'd have anarchy. Each one of us would apply the law in a different way. Make allowances in an inconsistent manner."

They locked eyes for a long moment.

"If there's something specific you want to

discuss with me, do it," Logan finally said. "If not, I suggest we change the subject, because I can't help you with esoteric questions."

"No, there's nothing specific." Rick looked out at the ocean. He was reminded of his discussion with Madison's father, and the fact that Logan's position seemed to be consistent with Patrick Long's. "You and Madison's father would get along well," he speculated.

When he slid his gaze back to Logan, he could see that his captain had relaxed.

"That's what this is about? The views of the Supreme Court judge are a little more rigid than yours?" There was a mocking light in his eyes now.

Rick wished that it was that simple, but he decided it was best to leave it at that, at least for now. He got the distinct impression that Logan wouldn't be sympathetic to Matías's predicament and what Rick had done about it. He watched Logan's face when his captain glanced at another young woman pass by. That might be unfair. Logan was a good cop, and he had a big heart. He'd be sympathetic but inflexible. In some ways, that would be harder to bear, Rick mused, knowing that upholding the law might not be the best outcome in a situation but upholding it regardless.

If he could do it over again with Matías, he knew he'd do exactly the same thing, so he turned the conversation to another topic that had been eating away at him.

"I think we have a snitch."

Logan's eyes snapped back to Rick's. "Why do you say that?"

Rick shrugged. "It's just too coincidental, if you ask me, that the last number of times we've moved on the cartel, they've been a step ahead of us. Someone must be feeding them information."

"Yeah. I've been thinking the same thing."

"So where do we go from here?" Rick asked.

"We find the leak and shut it down" was Logan's unequivocal answer. "And we do it before we make our big move."

RICK CONTINUED TO struggle with what he was doing. His chat with Logan had done nothing to alleviate his ambivalence. Just the opposite. He'd established that his captain would *not* approve of his actions, which merely added to his discomfort. Out of guilt as much as for pleasure, Rick ramped up his drug-abuse awareness work with school kids. That was something the department wholeheartedly supported. Although he still planned to use Sniff, he wanted to introduce Nitro to the process, too, so he brought the Malinois mix for the session at Del Mar High School.

The murmurs in the school gymnasium subsided the minute Rick and Nitro walked in. Rick was pleased to see the large group. A few students asked if they could pet Nitro and Rick encouraged them to do so. The kids were more receptive if they felt comfortable with the dog, and it was a great orientation for Nitro. After the usual cursory overview by the teacher, Rick introduced Nitro, explained a little about his own job and how he and the dog worked together. He went on to talk about drugs and the harm they caused, the consequences that could result if someone chose to risk it and either use or sell drugs. He could see he'd made an impact on the kids by their wide-eyed looks and their body language. That mattered to him.

It was time to lighten up the session and leave them with a positive message. Rick walked Nitro around the semicircle of chairs so that each student could touch the dog and not be afraid of him. "Are you ready for a demonstration?" Rick asked the kids.

There was a chorus of excited yeses.

"All right. I'm going to ask Nitro to search for drugs in this room. Nitro is very thorough. While he searches, he'll stop and check each one of you. He won't hurt you, I promise, but he will get close and sniff you, including your pockets, shoes and so forth. Are you all comfortable with that?" Rick met the kids' eyes to see their reactions. He'd done this exercise often enough to know that if any of the kids were early users—or worse, schoolyard dealers—their discomfort would show. When that happened in the past, he'd allowed the kid to excuse him- or herself, but followed up with a private meeting in the presence of a school counselor. Getting those kids off that path and back on the straight and narrow was the most rewarding part of his volunteer work. He was pleased to see only enthusiasm from these kids.

"Okay. Here we go." He unclipped Nitro's leash and sent him off with a hand signal. The kids giggled while Nitro checked each of them, at times inadvertently tickling them when he sniffed their hair or clothes. When

Nitro completed his search and came back to sit at Rick's side, the kids were all smiling.

One hand shot up. "How do you know if he finds drugs somewhere?"

"He does what's called a passive indication. Let me show you." Rick motioned for the teacher who'd been standing at the back to bring in the box of canisters he'd left outside the gymnasium. When she returned, he asked her to place the half dozen canisters in various locations throughout the room. While she did so, Rick explained that one of the canisters contained a trace amount of narcotic residue and the others were clean. He further explained that the canister that contained the residue had a big red X on the bottom. This would allow them to determine if Nitro had the right canister or not.

"Ready?" he asked the kids when the teacher had placed the last canister. With a hand signal, he put Nitro to work again. The kids' faces glowed with excitement.

The dog methodically searched the room again at a rapid pace until he got to one of the canisters. He sat down abruptly and stared at it. Rick was pleased to see how well Nitro had done, considering the short time he'd been working with him.

"What's he doing?" one of the kids asked.

"That's what I said is called passive indication. It means he can smell the trace amount of drugs in the canister. Why don't you see if he's right by checking the canister? Has it got the red X on the bottom?"

With a huge grin on his face, the boy ran over and lifted up the canister. He let out a loud whoop and showed the big bold X on the bottom to everyone in the room. "Nitro was right!"

"He usually is. He's correct ninety-nine point six percent of the time. How many of you get scores like that on tests?" Rick asked with an easy smile on his face. The kids all laughed.

Rick thanked them for their attention and participation, and he and Nitro said their good-byes. When he turned to leave, he noticed a blur of movement through the glass pane of the hallway door. He increased his pace and saw a small figure rounding the corner at a run. He was more curious than concerned, but picked up his speed. When he saw the dark-haired boy about to push through the crash bars of the exit door, he called to him to stop. The boy's shoulders slumped and he glanced over at Rick. Rick recognized him immediately. This time he called the boy by name. "Matías! Wait."

His eyes showed fear. Rick knew kids well enough that he could tell this one was about to scram. "Hold on," he said. "I just want to talk to you."

Matías froze and Rick jogged over to him. He unobtrusively signaled Nitro to do a quick check; he wanted to make sure the kid hadn't been running because he had drugs on him.

He was clean.

"You decided to stay in California, did you, Matías?" he asked conversationally.

The kid looked around anxiously and, with a finger over his lips, he whispered. "Shh. I'm just Matt here. Just Matt. And yeah. I stayed."

Rick realized the kid was trying to fit in by Americanizing his name. He himself had used Rick rather than Enrique almost from the time he'd set foot on American soil for the same reason. When a teacher approached them from the opposite direction, Matías appeared panicky. "I didn't want to miss my class," he said vehemently. "I got the highest mark on a math test and I don't want to get in trouble or ruin my grades."

"Good for you," Rick said quietly. Then he

dropped a hand companionably on Matías's shoulder and spoke to the teacher. "Is Matí—uh, Matt in your class?"

"He is. But not right now," she said with a warm smile at the kid. Then she glanced at the SDPD logo on Rick's shirt and frowned. "Is Matt in trouble?"

"Jeez," Matías grumbled under his breath to Rick. "See what you've done?"

Rick applied just enough pressure to his shoulder to both bolster him and keep him from fidgeting. "No, he's not. We…met a few weeks back. I wanted to see how he's doing, that's all."

The teacher relaxed noticeably.

"I understand he should be in a class right now. Could you let his teacher know I want to spend a few minutes with him?"

She nodded, and Rick said, "We'll be outside. Thanks for taking care of this for me."

She gave him an inviting little smile, but when he didn't reciprocate, she headed off.

"So why were you running away from the gym?" Rick asked Matt casually while they walked outside and toward the baseball diamond bleachers. His hand still rested on the kid's back, and he felt him tense. He wondered again if somehow the kid was still involved with drugs. The thought troubled him. "I'm asking as a…friend, not as a cop."

Matt jerked his shoulders. "I heard a cop and his dog were comin' to talk about drugs. I kinda wondered if it was you and your dog. Anyway, I wanted to find out what you were gonna say."

"Why's that?" Rick asked when they'd sat down on a bench.

"'Cause drugs are bad. Kids should *know* that," he said with a resolute nod of his head.

Rick had an odd feeling he couldn't quite describe. Was it pride? Was it hope that Matías—Matt—was going to turn out okay? "I'm glad you know that. How did you manage to stay here and get into school so quickly?"

Matt hopped off the bench to retrieve an overlooked softball. He tossed it from one hand to the other while he walked back to the bench. "I did what you said. I went to Child Services. They put me in a home with a bunch of other kids. It was okay. Better than back home, but then they moved me in with a family. They speak Spanish, and they…they don't hit." A grin appeared on his face. "We have a dog!" He pointed at Nitro. "Can I throw the ball for him?"

"Yeah. Sure."

The ball went flying, and Nitro shot off after it. The kid had a good arm, Rick thought.

"They don't hit and they *listen*," Matt said, his voice serious, his back to Rick.

Rick remembered even after all these years what it felt like to get backhanded by his birth father or mother. More than the physical hurt, it was the emotional pain that lingered. "That's good."

Matt threw the ball once more. He laughed like a hyena when Nitro fielded it in midair. When Matt caught his breath, he turned to Rick. "I want good grades because I want to be a teacher. I want to teach kids so they don't end up like…like some of the kids back home. So they can make money and take care of their family."

RICK'S SELF-DOUBT ABOUT what he'd been doing had been heightened by Madison's views and the subsequent discussion he'd had with Logan. But now, driving home from the school—having seen Matt and witnessed his passion and commitment to becoming a teacher to help other kids—he was glad about what he'd done. He could relate to Matt, since he'd felt the same way about wanting to be a cop at nearly the same age.

Watching Matt's beaming face and the glint of conviction in his eyes, Rick knew he'd done the right thing, no matter what Madison, her father or Logan thought.

CHAPTER SIXTEEN

"MADISON, MADISON!" HEATHER CALLED even before she swung open the door to the treatment room Madison was working in. "Oh, I'm so sorry, Mr. Yarby," she said to the gentleman with the rottweiler. "But I need to speak to Dr. Long."

"I'll just be a minute," Madison told the man apologetically and followed Heather out of the room, closing the door behind her. "What's up?" Heather's distress was clear.

"It's horrible." Heather grabbed Madison's hand and pulled her toward the reception area, where she had the radio playing softly. "Listen…"

Madison did. She heard a commercial for a new-model Nissan. She looked at Heather quizzically. "You want me to buy a new car?"

Heather waved her arms frantically. "No, no! The news was on before that. There was an explosion. A police officer was badly injured."

Madison's heart rate accelerated and a chill snaked up her spine. "That's terrible! Did they say who?"

"No. Just that he's with the SDPD, and he works narcotics," Heather said quietly.

Madison reacted quickly but she felt as if she was moving through molasses. She picked up the phone, called Jane and asked her to handle her patient. The whole time, a terrified voice inside her screamed that it couldn't be Rick.

She drew Heather into an office. "Tell me what you heard." There were tears in Heather's eyes, which only added to Madison's trepidation.

"The reporter said they'd been trying to crack the largest Mexican drug cartel. Los Supo…or Zapos or something…"

"Zetas. Los Zetas," Madison supplied. "Go on." Madison was so cold she thought if she moved, her bones would shatter. Rick had told her Los Zetas was the largest and most dangerous cartel they had to contend with. She understood it wasn't just a job for him. It was personal, and that could be even more dangerous, especially for a man who'd learned at a young age that life could be fleeting.

"Tell me," Madison repeated.

"So they had a tip from a confidential informant, the reporter said, and they were executing a search warrant for a warehouse in Miramar. There are some light-industrial areas there. Apparently, a police dog determined that there were drugs inside the building. So they went in and the dog, um…" Heather's voice trailed off.

"Indicated," Madison murmured, and the full significance started to sink in. If a dog was involved… "Oh, my God."

"Yeah. So the dog indicated that there were drugs inside the office area. The door was rigged to explode when they tried to enter. The reporter said they were lucky because there were sufficient explosives to destroy the entire building, and…"

Heather was hyperventilating.

"Take a couple of slow, deep breaths, then continue," Madison instructed, resting a hand on Heather's back.

Heather did as she was told. "Okay. Apparently, only a portion of the explosives that were there went off. Something faulty about how the way they were rigged—thank goodness. But the explosion badly hurt a cop. The dog and everyone else were far enough away so there were no other injuries."

Madison covered her mouth with her hands and sank down on the low cabinet behind her.

Heather rushed to a cooler, ran some water into a paper cup. "Here…here." She forced it into Madison's hand. "The reporter said it was a trap. Said the cartel had declared war on the SDPD because of their aggressive stance on drug smuggling, and this was payback."

"Would you call the division for me?" Madison asked in a strangled voice. "Ask if Rick is okay?"

"Sure." Heather picked up the phone and dialed. She knew the number because she often had to call for appointments and follow-up.

Madison's eyes felt huge and she stared at Heather, unblinking. "What did they say?" she asked as soon as Heather hung up.

"They wouldn't tell me anything. They need to talk to the police officer's family first."

Madison's terror was mounting. She tugged her iPhone out of her pocket. She wasn't thinking clearly or she would've thought of that first. She called Rick's cell phone number; it went straight to voice mail. *That doesn't mean anything*, she tried to convince herself. He'd be busy—they all would be—with what had just happened. *Please, God, let him be okay.* But if it wasn't him, it would be one of the other cops in the unit or the department. She scrolled through her contacts and found Jessica's number. Pressed Send.

Madison watched Heather leave discreetly as she waited for the call to be answered.

"You heard?" was the first thing Jessica said.

Oh, God, it can't be. It can't be. "Is it… Was it…?" She couldn't get the words out. At least she knew it wasn't Cal, because they'd reported that it was a narcotics cop.

"Calm down, Madison. It's not Rick, if that's what you were thinking."

"What?" Madison's hand was shaking so badly she could barely hold the phone to her ear, but she hoped she hadn't misheard her friend.

"It's not Rick." Jessica enunciated the words. "Rick is fine. The injured officer is with the Narcotics Task Force, not the K-9 Unit."

Now the tears came—tears of relief, of pent-up terror and panic, of sympathy for the injured officer and his family. "Oh, thank God," she whispered. Then she caught herself, realizing that a police officer was still injured. His family would be worried sick. "I'm sorry. I'm so sorry," she repeated. "Do you know the officer?"

"Yeah. I met him, his wife, his son and his daughter a few times at police functions."

"I'm so sorry," she said again. "Can you call me if you hear anything, either from Cal or about the officer?"

"Of course I will."

As soon as Madison hung up the phone, she bent over, trying to catch her breath and keep from vomiting.

RICK CALLED MADISON a couple of hours later. She sounded relieved and upset at the same time, but seemed very glad to hear his voice. She wanted to see him and said as much.

"I'll come over when we're done here, if you're okay having the dogs, and if it's not too late."

"Of course the dogs are welcome, and don't worry about the time. I won't be sleeping."

When Rick finally showed up at her house

well after midnight, Madison threw herself into his arms.

"I was so worried about you! At first I didn't know it wasn't you. Heather heard about the explosion on the radio. About a narcotics cop and the Los Zetas Cartel. I thought it might be you."

She buried her face against his neck, and he stroked her back reassuringly.

"Hey. It's okay. I'm fine."

"But you were *there*?" she almost wailed. "You know the officer who was injured?"

"Yes. Fortunately, Mike will be fine."

Madison took a step back. "But from what I heard, you could all have been killed. I heard there were enough explosives in there that the whole warehouse could've blown up, along with everyone in it."

He grabbed her elbow, guided her in and closed the door behind them. "That's true. More or less. There was a fault in the detonator cord. The fact that all the explosives didn't go off likely saved us from additional… injuries. We're all upset that Mike's hurt, and his family is distraught. He has two kids."

Rick led Madison into the living room, the dogs trailing behind them. He nudged her onto the sofa.

"I know what you're thinking," he continued. "We know there are risks. It's the reality, and I can't change that. We accept it as part of the job." He wondered if *she* could accept it, but didn't voice the question, especially under the circumstances.

He was afraid of the answer.

Madison sprang up, spread her arms, dropped them again. "You *accept* it? The fact that you could *die*? How does Mike's wife accept that she almost lost her husband in that raid today? That her kids could've been left without a father? What about Jeff's family? How should *I* accept it if our relationship gets serious?"

Rick was afraid he'd gotten his answer without having asked the question. He'd had a very long, hard day, and he was losing his patience. "Will you *please* sit down and let me get you a drink?"

She shook her head, disbelief evident on her face, but did as he asked and perched on the edge of the sofa. Her anxiety was transmitting itself to the dogs, and Rick gave them a signal to calm down. He tried to keep himself calm, too, as he went into the kitchen to get her a glass of water.

"The cop… Mike?" she went on when he

returned. "He's a colleague. You *know* him. Doesn't this make you worry that it could happen to you, too? Doesn't it make you think about quitting?"

Rick stopped abruptly and glared at Madison. "You don't think I'm *bothered* by this? You don't think it *matters* to me? Well, it does. Damn right it does! Like you said, he's a colleague. Although we might not be close—mostly because his family means everything to him and he spends every spare minute with them—we've been on the job together since I joined the SDPD."

Rick's anger fizzled out and he sat in the armchair across from Madison, forearms resting on his knees, fingers linked. "As for thinking about quitting... No. *Never*." The last word was an emphatic whisper. "This is who I am. It's *what* I am. Something like this only makes me more determined to do what I do and do it to the best of my ability. My job is to take down guys like the ones who did this to Mike...and to Jeff. To keep them from hurting kids, and injuring or killing good cops or innocent people." He exhaled. He didn't want to think about the fact that all indications were, once again, that he was the one they'd targeted. They didn't care about the collateral damage. All the explosives could've gone off and the entire building blown up. In fact, he expected that would have been a plus for them—a message sent to the entire department. "Is it so hard to understand why I feel this way?" he asked.

Madison's face paled. "I'm sorry. I...I don't know what to say other than sorry. I just don't understand how you can be so... accepting... *Accepting* isn't the right word. Resigned, maybe? About the dangers you face *each day*."

Rick leaned back and considered how to respond. At the best of times, cops' partners had a heavy burden to bear, knowing that any day there might be a knock on their door to let them know their spouse had been killed in the line of duty. And his current circumstances were far riskier, since the cartel was targeting him.

If their relationship was to progress, she had a right to know about the extent of the dangers he faced because of the demons that drove him. She'd already put into words her concern about being able to accept it...and therefore accept him. And that didn't include the possible risk to her. There hadn't been any further occurrences and Logan had arranged for frequent drive-bys, but that didn't negate the possibility. If he was completely honest with her, would his candor drive her away?

He was *falling in love* with Madison.

If she couldn't accept him and his circumstances, which applied to both the danger he faced on the job and what he did on occasion with Mexican kids crossing the border, he'd rather know now than when his heart was even more deeply invested. He needed to make her aware of whatever information he could, but he wasn't at liberty to discuss that the cartel was targeting him.

"I *need* to make a difference. I have to do what I do. It's who I am," he said again.

And then he started to tell her why and hoped she'd still want him when he finished.

MADISON LISTENED INTENTLY while Rick told her more about his childhood, about living in Tijuana. Details he hadn't shared with her before—about his life there, his birth parents, their occupations and preoccupations.

And their execution.

She rose to move around the room and found it easier to listen to some of the most painful parts with her back to him, not having to look at this strong, brave man and see in him the terrified, neglected, *abused* boy he'd been. She didn't want to feel sorry for him, because he'd overcome his early experiences and achieved so much. But her heart shattered yet again for the little boy he was never allowed to be.

Rick segued into the present—what he did and why. The strength and reach of the cartels, the difference the SDPD had made in recent years and his own role in it. And that all translated into the dangers of his job and having to live with knowing what could happen to him any day he was on duty. He was going up against the largest cartels, the most notorious organized crime syndicates. In the short few months she'd known Rick, one officer had died and another currently lay in the hospital. Either time, it could have been Rick.

How could she live with that?

She turned and faced him, her vision blurred by tears. When he stood up to come to her, to take her in his arms and hold her, she had a new, nearly debilitating fear.

She wondered if she could live without him.

CHAPTER SEVENTEEN

RICK HAD A restless night. He wasn't sure where he and Madison stood, and he remained frustrated and angered about how he and other members of his division had walked into another ambush the day before. Logan was in no better mood when Rick saw him. He was convinced he'd failed them all by not going along with Boomer to check for explosives. Rick understood what Logan was feeling. It wasn't unlike what he felt about not being on duty when Jeff had lost his life. Logically, Logan would know they couldn't protect against every possibility. Finding explosives set to detonate in the warehouse had not been an anticipated risk. It had happened only because the cartel had set a trap. But it was Logan's job to expect the unexpected.

And that brought it full circle for Rick—thinking it was his fault since the cartel was targeting him. Why wouldn't they just shoot him? They'd had all sorts of opportunities, but he knew the answer. It wasn't only about taking *him* out. If that was all, there were many other cops who'd step into his shoes. He'd become a martyr and the department would want vengeance, even more so than they already did because of Jeff. So it was also about making a statement to any who might think of following his footsteps.

Logan, Rick and the others in charge had a bigger problem. This tip had come in through a CI the division knew and trusted, but it had been a setup. They were getting intelligence through a snitch or some other means. Could they be certain that the cartel had no knowledge of what they were planning for the takedown and when they intended to do it? Los Zetas seemed to have been a step ahead of them again. There had to be an informant working both sides. Was that person close enough to the SDPD to know of their plans?

Well, they'd been taught another costly lesson. Now they *would* expect the unexpected and prepare for it. Which meant that, for now, they'd have to rethink their plan and revise the timing. They couldn't risk moving forward with their current strategy. And the information related to it would be shared on an even more restricted basis.

"Do you have a minute?" Madison asked from Jessica's office doorway.

Jessica swiveled around on her chair and gave her friend a wide smile. "What a nice surprise! As it happens, I do. Come in. What brings you here in the middle of a workday?"

"It's my day off." Madison looked around the small, cluttered office. "Can we get a coffee somewhere?"

Jessica rose and stretched her back. "Sure. I'm assuming you don't want the toxic stuff we have in our lounge. There's a coffee shop just around the corner."

"That would be great."

Jessica grabbed her jacket from the hook on her door, and they made their way out of the building that housed Care Across Continents' corporate offices and down the street to the coffee shop. With mugs of steaming coffee in their hands, they settled at a table by the window. "What's bothering you?" Jessica asked.

Madison choked out a laugh. "That transparent, am I?"

She shrugged. "I can read people pretty well, but the frown lines on your forehead are hard to miss. Also, you've never stopped by my work unannounced before."

Madison inclined her head in acknowledgment. "How do you do it, Jess? How do you live with the fact that any day you might get a call that the man you love has been injured or killed?"

Jessica's face sobered and she sighed. "It's not easy, and I can understand your feelings. Look. We could leave here, I could cross the street and get hit by a bus."

Madison frowned.

"I'm sorry. I don't mean to trivialize it, but what I said *is* true. We need to make the most of each day. None of us knows how long we might have. With Cal's job, I had to resolve in my own mind that he chose to be a cop, that he does the job he does because he wants to make a difference. He does it very well, but unfortunately there are risks. I love him for who he is. I can't ask him to change for me. I trust him to do the best he can *not* to get hurt." She shook her head. "Yeah, when I hear about cops being killed in the line of duty, the terror that one day it might be Cal resurfaces and part of me wants to beg him to quit." She sipped her coffee. "The scary thing is that if I asked him, if I told him I couldn't live with the fear anymore, I believe he loves me enough that he *would* quit. But that wouldn't be right, and I'd have to live with knowing I forced him to sacrifice something so important, so elemental, to him, for my peace of mind."

She looked out the window. "He might not want me to tell you this, but that's what caused his first marriage to fail. His ex couldn't tolerate being the wife of a cop anymore. Well, there was more to it, but that was what precipitated their breakup."

Madison was at loss for words. She stared at the people walking happily along the sun-dappled sidewalk, seemingly without a care in the world. She realized they could do that as a result of people like Rick and Cal, who dedicated their lives to keeping them safe... and at times made the ultimate sacrifice to do so.

"The divorce was messy and very difficult for Cal." Jessica broke into her musings. "Haley was lost to him for over a year. That's why I say that if I gave him the ultimatum, he'd quit. But it wouldn't be fair or right, and it could drive a wedge between us that I suspect we'd never overcome. But it's different with Rick. What he does is essential to his very existence. He has more personal reasons for doing what he does."

"I think it's different, too, but I wondered if I was overreacting because of my feelings for him. I listen to Cal, and I feel he understands the risks he faces, and he mitigates them the best he can. With Rick…" She shrugged and lifted her mug. "With Rick, I feel he doesn't care about his own safety. No, no. That's wrong," she amended quickly at the challenging look on Jessica's face. "Of course he cares. But I feel that's secondary to his determination to take down Los Zetas. That's what I mean. And don't get me wrong. I know he's smart and wouldn't do anything foolhardy. But to what degree would he put himself in danger if he felt he could make some headway against the cartel? Sometimes I want to shake him because I feel he cares more about that than himself."

Jessica's smile was melancholy. "Yeah, it can appear that way. But he does care what happens to him. He wouldn't want to hurt his family—or you—by doing something reckless. He's dedicated. Determined. And yes, perhaps a bit fatalistic. When you face death repeatedly in your youth the way he did, I think your coping mechanisms kick in and you somehow learn to live with the possibility that any day might be your last. Not to be preoccupied by it every waking moment of your existence, but it's there. Yeah, I appreciate why it would be more difficult for you with Rick because of that."

"You're supposed to be making me feel better, not worse."

Jessica tilted her head. "I think you want to talk about what's bothering you, but you also want me to be honest. If I wasn't truthful, what kind of friend would I be? You have to go into a relationship with a cop with a full understanding of what that entails. I want to see you two together, but if it isn't a good fit for either of you, I'd rather you found that out now."

Madison nodded slowly. "I agree. I'm aware of how and why Rick committed his life to policing."

"I'm glad he shared it with you. He doesn't do that often. To be honest, if I was married to Rick, I'd be even more apprehensive about his safety than I am about Cal's, for the reasons we just discussed." She paused and her eyes were the color of angry storm clouds. "I don't think Rick fears dying. Not like the natural fear most of us have. As a result—and I know this from Cal—Rick won't shy away from taking on the most dangerous assignments at work, and he doesn't hesitate to face off with the cartels when necessary. His fearlessness and his refusal to back down from any situation are what earned him the alias Pitbull."

Madison stared out the window again and grappled with the overwhelming fear she had for the well-being of the man she loved.

RICK HAD BEEN on border patrol all night. He'd expected it to be a quiet one, since they hadn't heard any rumblings about major drug runs. That didn't mean it wouldn't happen, but it was less likely that there'd be anything on an organized scale. He was close to the spot where he'd caught Matías, and he spent the early, uneventful hours of his shift thinking about the kid, with no small measure of pride for what he planned to make of himself. Yeah, Rick told himself, he'd do it all over again, if the need arose.

He thought about those words—doing it all over again, given the opportunity—as he drove home in the first watery glow of sunrise at the end of his shift and wondered if they'd been a premonition.

He'd caught another kid running across the

border. This one was younger, yet had more conviction than most of the others.

He'd dared to defy the cartel.

Rick glanced at the thin boy in grubby clothes huddled against the passenger door of his Explorer. He twitched and occasionally whimpered in his sleep. Rafael was his name, and Rick had really stuck his neck out this time, but he'd felt he had no choice. The kid's life had been in imminent danger because he'd dared to oppose the cartel by ditching the drugs he'd been entrusted with and making a run for the border.

Rick had to acknowledge that the kid had guts. But by doing what he had, he'd incurred the wrath of the cartel, and they'd been after him. Rick didn't think they'd worry about Rafael for long—he was too insignificant, too inconsequential, in the grand scheme of their operations—but the immediate threat was real. Rick had to protect the kid. He couldn't take him into the division and he couldn't leave him with Child Services.

Rick had decided to take the kid home with him. He had a couple of days off and he'd have time to figure out what to do about Rafael. But today and tonight, he'd keep him at his house. The kid *trusted* him. And he didn't think Rafael trusted easily—with good reason. For now, the kid could sleep easy, or as easy as it was possible for him to do.

He really had crossed the line this time, Rick thought as he pulled into his driveway.

CHAPTER EIGHTEEN

RICK MUST HAVE just dozed off on his sofa when he was startled awake by the banging. Disoriented, he tried to place the sound until he heard it again.

It was someone knocking on his door. He glanced at his watch. Almost ten in the morning on Sunday. He wasn't expecting anyone.

"Who is it?" Rick called when he heard the knock again.

"It's me," Madison called through the door.

Rick stared up at the ceiling. The fates were conspiring against him. He couldn't very well *not* open the door for her. If he hadn't called out, he might've been able to pretend he wasn't home. But that horse had left the barn.

"I'll be right there," he called back, and rose, somewhat unsteady on his feet. Lack of sleep could do that to you.

He took a quick peek into the spare bedroom. Rafael lay on the bed, long dark lashes resting on the pronounced hollows under his eyes, his chest moving rhythmically in his sleep. Instead of resting his head on the pillow, he had it clutched to his chest. For comfort? For security? As Rick watched, Rafael let out a little whimper and tightened his hold on the pillow.

Despite how exhausted the kid must've been after his ordeal, he still couldn't seem to escape, even in sleep, the horrors that haunted him. Rick silently closed the door and backed out of the room, just as the knocking on the front door began again.

"Hey," he greeted Madison, and lowered his lips to hers, while both Sniff and Nitro danced around them. "We didn't have a date, did we?"

"No. I was at the rehab center this morning, and thought I'd stop by to see if I could buy you brunch."

Keeping one arm extended and a hand on the edge of the door, effectively blocking her from entering, he forced a smile.

"So can I entice you to have brunch with me?"

He rubbed a hand over his stomach. "Actually, I'm not all that hungry. I think I ate something last night that didn't agree with me. I should just stay home."

"Okay." She looked at his outstretched arm. "Are you going to invite me in?"

What choice did he have? Rick released his hold on the door and shoved his hands into his pockets. "Ah, you know, I was…" He was interrupted by the creak behind them and a child's cough. They both watched as Rafael, wearing one of Rick's old SDPD T-shirts that skimmed his calves, walked into the hallway.

Madison glanced from the boy to the man.

"¿Puedo tener un vaso de agua por favor?" the boy asked, rubbing his eye with a fist.

"Sí. Claro," Rick replied. "Of course you can have some water."

"I'm sorry," Madison murmured. "I'm interrupting. I'd better get home to Owen," she said, and turned to go.

"Wait!" Rick called. He grabbed her arm, but she pulled away and ran down the steps.

Rick rushed after her and placed a hand firmly on the door of her SUV before she had a chance to open it. "Can we talk about this?" he asked.

"That boy?" she said, pointing toward Rick's open front door. "He's not a relative or the son of a friend, is he?"

"No, he isn't."

She looked furtively around and lowered her voice. "Then, he's here illegally, correct? You caught him coming across the border?"

"Yes."

"I know he's just a young boy and I'm sure he's got a sad story, but you have him staying with you…"

"Uh-huh."

"I don't mean to be insensitive, but doesn't that make it worse? You're not just letting him into the States, you're harboring an illegal alien."

Rick dropped his arm. She clearly had a problem with what he'd done. He didn't want to detain her if she was determined to go. "Something like that."

"And if I know and I don't do anything about it? What does that make me? An accessory after the fact?"

Rick remained silent.

"I'm certain you're helping that child in a crucial way, but… I'm sorry," she whispered, and got into her car.

Rick stuffed his hands into his pockets again and watched her drive away. Once her vehicle was out of sight, he went back inside.

Seeing the fear and worry on Rafael's face,

he first reassured the boy that he had nothing to worry about. He explained that Madison wasn't with the authorities and she wouldn't tell anyone about Rafael being in his house. At least he hoped she wouldn't.

He brought Rafael the water he'd asked for and got him settled down. He stayed in the room with him until he fell asleep again. Rick could understand why the kid needed so much sleep after everything he'd been through. He thought of the terror he'd seen in Rafael's eyes when a car had backfired, and later, when one of his neighbors had started up a lawn mower early that morning. Rick understood what it felt like to fear for your life and imagine that every sharp, sudden sound was a gunshot. He'd been there.

He had another day off tomorrow, and he'd take Rafael to Child Services. But today and tonight he'd keep him at home. The kid felt comfortable with him. Maybe it wasn't even comfort. It was probably as simple as not knowing who else to turn to and the fact that, in his view, Rick was the lesser of two evils. Rick was fairly certain that despite Rafael's having thrown away what amounted to thirty thousand dollars' worth of drugs, the cartel wouldn't bother to search for him for long.

Still, it wasn't outside the realm of possibility. That was why he hadn't brought him to Child Services right away; Rick was a cop and he could protect the kid. Tomorrow they'd take the next step.

Rick dropped back down on his sofa.

Why had Madison had to stop by announced today of all days? Yes, she knew what he was doing and had already been struggling with it. But seeing the effect of his actions firsthand in the form of Rafael, her mind had immediately jumped to how that could implicate her, which was obviously an entirely different matter. She'd sure hightailed it out of there.

He was tempted to call her, but he figured it would be best to give her some time to reflect. He'd go see her tomorrow after he'd sorted everything out with Rafael. Maybe he'd take her to that Brazilian churrascaria again, if she was willing. It was hard to be in a bad mood in that environment.

THAT NIGHT WAS a quiet one, thankfully. Rafael slept right through, not always peacefully, but he didn't wake. Rick knew, because he'd slept lightly, on alert, and had checked on Rafael a number of times.

Monday morning Rick took Rafael to the

county's Child Services department. He promised the kid he'd visit him wherever they ended up placing him. Child Services agreed to let Rick know, so he could keep his word. Rafael didn't seem distressed or terrified. He was quietly accepting, although he was shy with the people he met. Rick thought his detachment was natural under the circumstances.

He and Rafael were both relieved that the social worker assigned to his case spoke fluent Spanish, and the agency was hopeful that they could find a foster home where at least one parent spoke the language. Rafael could probably get by with his broken English, but it would give him a sense of comfort. Of fitting in.

Rick was optimistic about Rafael's future and this time he felt no guilt about what he'd done. His worry was focused on Madison and where yesterday's occurrence left them.

After Rick finished at Child Services, he called the clinic. Heather advised him that Madison was in surgery. He asked her to tell Madison he'd see her after work, if that was okay with her. No point dwelling on the negative or delaying the inevitable. He had to believe that he and Madison had a strong enough relationship by now that they could work through it. Hoping for the best, he made a reservation at O Touro and bought her some flowers, too.

Madison returned his call while he was at the gym. She left a message suggesting he come to her place at seven. It buoyed Rick, and his optimism persisted through the afternoon.

He arrived at her house right on time. When she opened the door, he held out the bouquet with a wide smile.

His mood was squashed by the look on Madison's face.

She didn't seem happy, and she took the flowers with the most perfunctory thanks. He followed her into the kitchen, where she stuck them—cellophane, tissue paper wrapping and all—in a vase she filled with water.

He decided to confront her, rather than allow the situation to fester. "You're still upset about Rafael? Let's talk about it if it's bothering you."

"*If* it's bothering me?" she echoed as she spun around. "You've let people come into California illegally. And now you're harboring aliens. What's next?"

"The kid threw away the drugs he was asked to smuggle into the country. He's only ten years old and needed a break."

His comment about Rafael's age seemed to give her pause, but after a moment she continued. "He threw away the drugs? What if he hadn't? Or someone else doesn't? If they're smuggling drugs and maybe even have drugs with them when you take them into your home, you're harboring criminals."

"That's a lot of ifs, but I didn't have much choice with Rafael. The cartel knew he'd ditched the drugs and were after him, probably to make an example of him for his rebellion. I thought it would be safer for him to stay with me than take him to the authorities right away, just in case the cartel was still looking for him. You left in a huff, and I didn't get a chance to explain."

Madison's eyes were wide, her mouth agape. He might have been a bit harsh, but he was feeling the effects of not having had much sleep, and he was getting tired of going around the block with her on this subject again. He'd thought she'd understand and would appreciate that he wanted to help a kid whose life was in peril. He loved her for who she was. Couldn't she do the same with him?

He loved her...

Great. He had to pick the worst time to

realize that. "What?" he asked when he'd missed what she'd said.

"I wasn't in a *huff*! I don't know how to deal with what you're doing."

Rick had just about had enough. If she wasn't worrying about the dangers of his job, it was this. Maybe they weren't meant to be together. "No one asked you to be involved—and you're not!" he retorted. He shook his head in frustration and confusion. Owen had moved to her side and Rick wasn't entirely comfortable with the steady stare the dog leveled at him.

He stepped forward and around the dog. He wanted to touch Madison but was afraid she'd shrug him off. "Rafael hasn't had it easy. He deserves a chance," he said in a quieter, soothing tone. He was being entirely reasonable, he thought. He knew Madison had a good heart. How could she not feel for the kid? "You can't imagine what his life has been like to this point."

"Where is he now?" She didn't seem to be swayed.

He checked his watch. "If he's lucky, he's meeting his foster parents."

"If he didn't have drugs, why was he running?"

"When you dump roughly thirty thousand dollars' worth of drugs, the cartel doesn't take that lightly. According to Rafael, they wanted to make an example of him. He said he was running for his life."

"Oh." Her shoulders sagged and the indignation seemed to melt away. "But why didn't you take him to Child Services as soon as you got back to the city?"

Rick rubbed his temple, where a massive headache was brewing. They'd have to go through all this again, he thought, and see how Madison with the federal court judge father would feel about what he'd done. "Can we get some coffee first?" he asked, stalling.

With mugs of coffee in their hands, he told her about the stakeout that night, the drug busts made by other members of his team and about the terrified, near hysterical boy who'd stumbled upon him and Nitro. The kid, having been raised in a family that earned its livelihood by smuggling drugs, didn't trust police any more than he did the cartel. Rafael had genuinely feared for his life. Rick went on to describe Rafael's reaction when he'd suggested taking him to the division for protection.

"So I brought him home with me." Rick re-

membered the discussion—no, *argument*—
he'd had with Patrick Long about the law and
leniency, and he had a good idea what Patrick's opinion would be. His concern was
whether the man's daughter would feel the
same way.

Madison's expression was inscrutable. She
didn't appear to be angry any longer, but she
wasn't cheering his good deed, either. She
must've been mulling over what he'd told
her, if the creases on her forehead were any
indication.

"Was his life truly in danger?" she finally
asked.

"Based on the information he gave me, I
believe it was." He watched her carefully.
How she judged him would predict whether
they could have a future together.

"What you did was illegal, wasn't it?" Her
eyes were clouded, troubled. "Aiding and
abetting?"

Rick inclined his head. "Yes."

"And the fact that you harbored him for
only a day doesn't negate the seriousness
of that, either. The law doesn't differentiate
based on duration."

"Correct." He felt a constriction in his chest.

She was her father's daughter, it seemed, and Rick's judge and jury.

Madison nodded.

The constriction intensified. He could feel every beat of his heart in his throat. He didn't want this to be the end for them. He loved her.

"This is something you'll never stop doing, is it?"

Rick shook his head.

"I saw Rafael. I can't deny feeling sympathy for the boy, and I can't say I'm not touched by your kindness."

"There's a double negative in there," he observed, wanting to lighten the mood.

"Hmm. The thing is, people can't pick and choose, even for a good reason, when to obey the law and when not to. I know your actions were well intentioned and probably in the best interests of the boy, but you *are* an officer of the law. Shouldn't you be held to the highest standard?"

He exhaled deeply, but remained silent.

"As much as you're a product of your upbringing," she continued, "so am I. I have a deeply ingrained respect for the law." She managed a short laugh. "It's not that I'm putting my father ahead of you, but can you imagine his reaction if he knew what you did?"

She paused. He could see the twitch of the pulse at her temple, and he could tell she was struggling with what he'd done.

"When does lenience become vigilantism?" she challenged.

"Come on..." Rick objected.

She raised a hand. "Isn't it just a matter of degree?"

Rick had no words in his own defense.

"Where do you draw the line, then? If we leave the law open to interpretation—if we selectively decide when it should apply—that would invalidate everything my father stands for. Everything I've always believed. How can I say that's okay?" Her eyes shone with fervor. "I accept that there are times we might not fully agree with the law, but we have to trust the system to work as it should. Rafael should've been turned over to the proper authorities from the start."

"Laws aren't always just or fair. You know that. In those cases, they eventually get changed. As for Rafael, what if he'd died as a consequence? Or simply ran away because he was so scared the cartel would get to him?"

"I understand the moral dilemma. I'm *not* disagreeing with your motivations. I know your intentions were compassionate. Even admirable. I can go as far as to say that I'm empathetic to what you did." She bit her lower lip and stared out the window. "I love and respect my father. I recognize that he can be obstinate at times, but I've never known him to be wrong about the law. He's been my moral compass my entire life, and in many ways, I'm the person I am because of him. And if what you've been doing came to light, it could tarnish my father's reputation. When he was being considered for the bench, we were both subjected to intense personal scrutiny. His professional and our personal lives were examined under a microscope. My father's always lived his life above reproach, and I can't risk his reputation being tainted through me and my relationship with you."

Rick's blood was throbbing in his ears, making it hard to think straight. "What are you saying?" He didn't want to lose her, but he was afraid that was where she was heading.

"Just what I've already said. I have to think about this."

It felt as if his heart had been ripped right

out of his chest. He *loved* Madison! He didn't want to contemplate that tonight might be the last time he'd see her on a personal basis. But there was nothing he could think of to say, nothing that would change her mind. He'd made his case. He walked to her door in silence.

As he stepped over the threshold, she took a deep breath and he braced himself.

"Rafael is a fortunate boy to have happened upon you."

"Thank you," he whispered. He knew, coming from her and under the circumstances, that was a huge concession, and it gave him a glimmer of hope. But understanding wasn't acceptance. Still, he closed his eyes for a moment. She'd just validated what he'd done. Whatever came next, he'd find a way to deal with it, he thought as he walked out the door.

CHAPTER NINETEEN

RICK HADN'T HEARD from Madison for nearly a week, nor had he called her. Her reaction to what he'd confided had only intensified his own personal quandary about what he was doing, but he couldn't...*wouldn't* do anything else, even if it ultimately compromised his job and cost him his relationship with Madison. Intellectually and emotionally, they were at odds. He knew he was breaking the law and there could be serious consequences for him. He wondered what he'd do with his life if he could no longer be a cop. That then brought into question what kind of cop he was if he could repeatedly not just ignore but potentially break the law.

On the emotional side, he was a product of his childhood. He was alive and enjoying the freedom and quality of life that he had only because he'd crossed the San Ysidro border into California and found a home in San Diego.

Madison's silence was driving him crazy. He had to know, one way or the other, where they stood. Finally, he called her and she agreed to have dinner with him. Considering the weighty subject they had to discuss, he offered to make dinner at his place, but she insisted on a restaurant. He felt that didn't bode well. She didn't want to be alone with him. A sobering and ominous thought.

As it turned out, the dinner was what he'd feared. He and Madison were at odds. Being in a public environment precluded making his case any stronger than he already had. Madison said she had feelings for him, but there were issues between them that she couldn't reconcile herself to. Despite her feelings, she told him she needed more time.

When Rick returned home, he let himself into the house, still in a daze. He greeted Sniff and Nitro absentmindedly. He flopped down in his armchair, head back, eyes closed. Both dogs nudged and nuzzled him. Since he continued to ignore them, they finally settled with loud huffs of protest at his feet.

Rick was devastated. The more he thought about losing Madison, the more he realized just how much she meant to him and how much he loved her. He couldn't blame her for her views. He thought about promising her he'd never do it again, but…he couldn't.

He just had to accept that there could be no future for them and move forward with his life the best he could.

MADISON WATCHED ATTENTIVELY while one of the techs walked the Portuguese water dog in circles around the exercise yard. Sure, he still had a limp, but it was subtle, and there was no indication that the limp was caused by pain rather than the imperfect way the bone fracture had set.

"What are we looking for?" she heard the familiar voice ask behind her. She turned her head to smile at Jessica, who stepped up and leaned on the railing next to her. She'd been expecting Jess.

"That's Harlen. The dog I told you about with the femur injury. Closed fracture and soft tissue."

Jessica studied the dog for a couple of circuits. "Based on what you've told me, he's doing extremely well."

Madison could feel her face flush with excitement. "He is. The combination of the PRP therapy and the advanced aqua therapy seems to be doing the trick for Harlen. And Zeke? He's as good as new!"

They watched the dog in silence for a few more minutes, then Madison signaled to the tech that Harlen was done with his therapy for now. They'd give him a rest and later they'd do the aqua therapy.

"Are you still free for lunch?" Jessica asked.

Madison nodded.

As they walked to the restaurant, Madison glanced over at Jess. "Are you okay if I ask you a question about Cal?"

"Sure."

"He's been in law enforcement for a long time, right?"

"Yes."

"Does he talk to you about his work?"

Jessica chuckled. "Of course! It's his life. Good luck trying to stop him. Why do you ask?"

"Does he ever talk to you about how he applies the law or whether he sees any flexibility in the system?"

Jessica gave her a questioning look. "I'm not sure I understand what you mean."

Since Cal worked predominantly search and rescue, it occurred to Madison that he might not face the kinds of quandaries Rick did. "Never mind," she said as they entered the restaurant and were shown to their table. "Forget it."

"No. I wasn't implying I had a problem with your question. I'm just not sure I understand what you're getting at."

"Well…" Madison fidgeted with her fork.

"Does your question have anything to do with the reason you're not looking too cheerful today?" Jessica asked.

Madison rolled her eyes. "That's an understatement."

Jessica asked the waitress to bring them each a glass of Coke. "I understand from Cal that Rick hasn't been in much better spirits recently. Can I assume it has something to do with what's going on between the two of you?"

"Ha! It's more like what's *not* going on between us."

The waitress served their drinks and took their orders. Madison gratefully took a sip. "So what's up?" Jessica prompted when they were alone again. "Last time I saw you, all was well, and you seemed to be deliriously happy and falling in love with Rick." Jessica's eyes clouded over. "Did he do anything to hurt you?"

Madison appreciated her friend's loyalty, despite the fact that Rick was one of her husband's closest friends. That eased the unbearable ache in her heart a fraction. "No. Not in the sense you're thinking. I suppose I'm the one who did the hurting." Madison lifted her glass again. Instead of drinking, she swirled the dark liquid before putting the glass back on the coaster. It felt so good to have the support of her friend, but she couldn't fully disclose the circumstances that had led to their breakup. She owed Rick at least that much. When Jessica remained silent with an expectant look on her face, Madison flipped her hair over her shoulder in a nervous gesture. "We had a difference of opinion that we haven't been able to work through."

"You're both intelligent, reasonable people. Can't you resolve whatever it is?"

Madison picked up a coaster and played with it. "Apparently not. But it's more than that. Even if we could, I have to think of my father, too." Her eyes met Jessica's cool gray ones.

"This sounds serious" was all Jessica said.

Madison almost wished she hadn't raised the matter. She didn't want to alarm her friend, nor did she want to get Rick into trouble. She chose her words carefully. "It's just that Rick and I see things differently, and if my father knew, he wouldn't understand. And…" She considered Patrick's unblemished reputation and the importance of that to his job. "Well, it could create problems for him."

Jessica eyed Madison thoughtfully. "It doesn't take much to figure out that it has something to do with the law, and Rick's upholding of it. Correct?"

"I'd rather not get into it."

"Okay, I'll take that as a yes."

Madison's only response was a long exhalation.

"So let me tell you this. Rick's a good cop. I've never seen a man so committed to the law and, through his drug counseling work, helping at-risk kids make the right decisions to stay clean and off drugs. Knowing what you've told me about your father, I expect there's some gray areas involved in whatever you and Rick argued about."

"We didn't argue." It might have been easier if it had ended badly between them. Maybe she wouldn't still love him so much.

"Okay, disagreed, then. At any rate, your father *interprets* the law. No disrespect, but he does it in a courtroom. *After* the crime or alleged crime, based on facts, to the extent that they're available. Guys like Cal and Rick have to *uphold* the law, and they have to make decisions, sometimes in a split second and often without full knowledge of the facts. Those decisions can mean life or death for them or someone else. What they do isn't always black-and-white, and they do it under considerable stress and often in the most difficult circumstances. Again, no disrespect, but—unlike your father—they don't make their decisions in the comfort of a courtroom."

Madison wanted to jump to her father's defense. And yet, her intellect told her that what Jessica had said was true. "I told you how I met Cal," Jessica continued. "He got injured because he went back into a collapsed building to rescue Scout. He did that in contravention of a direct order. That's insubordination. In the military, he could've been court-martialed for it. He got written up by Logan, which was bad enough for Cal, especially since he was still in his probationary period. Cal knew what he was doing, that it could have cost him his job—even his *life*—

but he wasn't prepared to leave Scout in that building."

Madison was aware of some of this. She knew Cal had been seriously hurt in the incident. He'd been off work and on crutches for a period of time. She hadn't known it was because he'd gone back against orders to rescue Scout. How could she not respect him for what he'd done to save his dog?

"The point I'm making is that Cal did what he thought was right." Jessica took a sip of her soda. "He disobeyed an order. Does that make him a bad person? A lesser cop? I told him then and I'll tell you now. I would've done the same thing. I wouldn't have been able to walk away from that building, knowing my dog might still be alive in there and essentially condemn him to death by doing so. Could *you* have?" she asked pointedly.

Madison glanced away. Of course she couldn't have. She would've gone in, too, if it was Owen. "That's not the same," she said finally. "Disobeying an order and breaking the law are two different things." She hadn't meant to divulge that much, but it had slipped out.

"Are they?" Jessica asked. "Or are they just different points on a spectrum? I don't know what your disagreement was about, and I don't need you to tell me. What I do know is that Rick is a good man. A decent, caring man who believes in the law. I don't have to know what happened to state without the shadow of a doubt that Rick did the right thing—what he believed was right in his heart, if not in his head." She looked at Madison questioningly. "I can understand that who your father is might complicate matters for you, but try to keep an open mind."

After her conversation with Jessica, Madison tried to see it from Rick's perspective, but that had never really been the problem. She'd understood *why* he was doing what he did. Jessica had said she should decide whether she could accept him for who he was, despite his faults. Madison couldn't call it a "fault." Intellectually, she understood Jessica's rationale, but she was certain that her father wouldn't. How could she resolve such basic differences between the two men she loved?

Madison thought about her discussion with Jessica on and off most of the afternoon, at the end of the day as she drove home and, later, when she and Owen went for a long walk.

It was late enough that there weren't a lot

of people out on the beach. She let Owen off his leash, sat on a bench and watched him chase the waves.

Jessica had made a number of good points over lunch. Madison couldn't argue with them. Jess had grasped the situation without knowing the particulars, including the complication concerning Madison's father.

Madison realized that Rick had been grappling with his own doubts and she hadn't made it any easier for him. But she felt conflicted, too.

Her father had taught her never to ignore someone breaking the law or an injustice being done He'd taught her to report any such occurrences. But in this case, those two things were at odds. Rick might have been allowing or aiding the law to be broken, but he was doing it to help right injustices, like little Rafael's need to flee for his life.

She'd almost resigned herself to overlooking what he'd been doing, but his actions were escalating. Taking Rafael into his home was proof of it. Where would he stop?

Now *she* was withholding knowledge of illegal activity—and by the man she loved—from the authorities. Her father had always told her when she was a child that nothing bad would happen if she told the truth, but she simply couldn't see that applying in this case. Nothing would be gained, but for Rick a great deal could be lost when he was only trying to help kids in need.

In her driveway, Madison let Owen hop out of the back of the SUV. Luckily she wasn't holding on to his leash or she would've been pulled right off her feet. Owen bolted for the front door, jumped up against it a couple of times, then rushed down the steps and around to the backyard.

"Owen!" Madison called, and ran after him. "What's gotten into you? Settle!"

Owen seemed oblivious to her command. He was at the patio door, barking aggressively. Madison's mouth dropped when she caught up to him. The sliding door to her kitchen was open a couple of inches. Leaving the door unlocked, let alone open, was something she'd never do.

She grabbed Owen by his collar and led him away, at the same time fumbling in her handbag for her cell. She walked Owen around to the front and put him back in the SUV. Pressing Send for Rick's number, she looked anxiously up and down the street while she waited for him to answer.

"Madison!" He sounded so happy to hear from her she felt awkward.

"I'm sorry to disturb you, but I just got home from a walk with Owen. I think someone's broken into my house."

"Have you gone inside?" Rick's voice was all business now.

"No. I'm outside. Owen sensed there was something wrong when I let him out. We found the back patio door open. I'm always careful about locking up. I didn't leave it like that."

"Okay. Do you see anything else out of place?"

Madison scanned her house carefully. "I'm out front now, but no. Everything looks fine from here."

"Okay. Don't go in. I'm coming over right now. In fact, do me a favor. Get back in your vehicle and park on the road a good ten houses away. Park so you can see your house, but not so close that your presence would be obvious. And lock your vehicle."

"Okay," she said, and climbed back in her SUV.

"I'll be there as soon as I can. Call me back if you want, but I'll see you in about twenty minutes."

He was true to his word. Madison saw his Explorer turn the corner onto her street and drive slowly by her house less than twenty minutes later. She noticed a second police vehicle following Rick's. While Rick pulled up beside her and rolled down his window, the other vehicle stopped directly in front of her house.

"You okay?" Rick asked.

She nodded. "Thanks for coming."

"No problem. I'm glad you called. Have you seen anything since we spoke?"

"No." When she saw Cal Palmer and his search and rescue dog, Scout, get out of the other vehicle, she waved to him. "I see you brought reinforcements." She tried to make her comment sound light, but the fact that Rick considered this serious enough to bring backup added to her anxiety.

"Cal was just returning to the division as I was leaving. I thought he might be able to help," he explained.

She nodded again.

"Was your alarm system armed when you'd left?"

"Yes, I'm sure of it."

"And you've had no calls from the monitoring company?"

"No."

"Okay. Give me your keys and wait here. Cal and I'll check it out."

She'd been calmer while she waited for Rick, but now she was feeling anxious. Her house had obviously been broken into, and there were two cops and a dog inside while she waited helplessly.

She saw them come out the front door and Rick signaled to her. After she'd parked in her driveway, she got out, leaving Owen inside the car. She exchanged greetings with Cal, but his attention was focused on Scout. Rick's face was grim.

"There was someone inside, wasn't there?"

"Yeah. I'll take you in and you can see what, if anything, was taken."

"Okay."

He touched her arm. "There's some damage."

She swallowed hard. "Thanks for the warning." She didn't want to ask how bad it was. She'd see for herself soon enough. But she needed another moment to gather herself before she went in. "What's he doing?" she asked Rick, pointing at Scout running in a zigzag pattern, his nose high and scenting the air.

Rick stood next to her, watching, too. "Cal's trying to see if Scout can pick up a trail."

"Really? Even though the person might be long gone?"

"You'd be surprised how long scents linger, and can be followed by a search and rescue dog. There! Scout's got something."

They watched as he ran along the sidewalk in a direct line, his nose to the ground. "By now the scent is concentrated and he's following it."

Rick put his hand on the small of Madison's back and led her toward the house. At his simple touch, all she wanted to do was turn into his arms and let him hold her.

Inside, Rick walked with her from room to room. She tried to be stoic about it all. The damage was generally broken knickknacks and the like. Most of it could be easily replaced, but she gasped when she saw the shattered remains of a vase that had been her mother's. Her bedroom also gave her pause. While nothing was broken, her dresser drawers were open, and her belongings scattered about. She backed out quickly and ran down the stairs. She felt violated, knowing someone had invaded her personal space and pawed through her belongings.

When they'd finished and brought Owen inside, Rick went out to check in with Cal. She waited in her front hall, not quite knowing what to do. Owen joined her and leaned against her leg reassuringly. Rick returned a few minutes later. He stood in front of her for a moment, then without a word took her in his arms. Her emotions—her love for Rick, how much she'd missed him and the impact of the break-in—swamped her and her tears spilled silently over.

When she finally felt a little steadier, she raised her head and looked into Rick's troubled eyes. "I...I don't think anything's missing. Not anything obvious anyway. Why would someone do this?" She heard the pleading in her own voice and struggled to make sense of the pointless destruction. Before Rick had a chance to answer, there was a knock at the door. She felt unbearably cold and alone when he released her to open the door for Cal and Scout.

"Anything?" Rick asked.

Cal lifted a shoulder, let it drop again. "Scout had the scent. He followed it to where the perp's vehicle must've been parked a couple of blocks down and around a corner. He still had the scent, but there was no point trying to follow the vehicle from there. Unless the guy's a neighbor—which I seriously doubt—we won't find him."

CHAPTER TWENTY

RICK, LOGAN AND CAL sat in the conference room at the division, mugs of coffee in front of them.

"There's only one thing that comes to mind about the break-in at Madison's," Rick stated.

"I know what you're thinking, that it's Los Zetas. But it doesn't make sense. The cartel is after *you*." Logan took a drink from his mug. His voice had a hard edge. "Their goal is not intimidation, Rick, and you know it. Sorry to be so blunt, but they want you dead."

Rick wondered fleetingly why the reality of that didn't affect him more forcefully. He supposed it was because he'd lived with the threat of being killed since he was a kid in Tijuana.

"So what purpose would it serve for them to ransack Madison's place?" Logan continued.

"Yeah, I can't explain that," Rick responded.

"Unless they thought you were there," Cal said.

Rick shook his head. "No reason they

should. There were no vehicles in the drive or the carport. It would've been simple enough to learn my schedule. Heck, if they knew I was supposed to be leading the bust when Jeff died, they'd know if I was on or off duty. Why haven't they made a move directly on me? Why not break into *my* house?"

"You live with two police dogs for one thing," Cal said. "As I said, it doesn't make sense, but what else could it be? That's two incidents that Madison's been exposed to since we learned about the cartel's intentions."

"Her father's a Supreme Court judge," Logan pointed out.

Rick nodded. "Yeah, he is."

"Any possibility this has anything to do with him? A trial he's currently presiding over? Or a recent one that might've had significant consequences for the defendant?"

Rick raised his eyebrows. "I hadn't considered that. I don't know…"

"It's worth looking into," Cal agreed. "If that's the case, I'd suspect the father's been experiencing some problems, too. If nothing else, we should eliminate it as a possibility."

They agreed it would be best for Logan to make the call to keep it impersonal, but Rick asked him to hold off until he'd had a chance to talk to Madison. He didn't want her to hear about it from her father.

Before Rick left to go see Madison, they also decided that it would be prudent to put a protective detail on Madison and on Rick's family.

MADISON'S SHOULDERS SLUMPED when Rick explained what they'd been thinking. Owen was sitting tightly by her side, leaning in against her leg, and she dropped her hand on top of his head. "Yes, there've been times when my father was targeted because of a particularly sensitive trial. He hasn't mentioned anything like that recently, but he did talk about a case in which he considered a jury's verdict to be flawed and he was deciding what to do about it." She stared at Rick, her eyes wide and shimmering with tears. "He said the accused had ties to organized crime. Is *that* what this is about? Is he in danger?"

Rick took her free hand in his, laced his fingers through hers. He was inordinately pleased that she let him do it. "There's no reason to suspect he is. We're just trying to figure out what motivated the break-in. It could be as simple as some kids out for excitement," he said, trying to soothe her. "There's nothing for you to worry about. Honest," he added, sensing that she wasn't reassured.

She pulled her hand back and started to rise. "I have to call him."

Rick tugged her back down. "Let Logan speak to him. Logan said he'd ask your father to call you after they've spoken."

He draped an arm around her shoulders and she rested her head against him. He wasn't sure what this meant as far as their relationship was concerned but, man, did it feel good to have her beside him again.

"LOGAN WANTS TO see you," Cal said to Rick the moment he walked into the squad room the following Monday.

"Yeah?" Rick glanced toward Logan's office and through the glass partition to judge the mood his captain was in. He was reading. Nothing telltale. "Any idea what it's about?"

"Nope," Cal said with a grin. "Better ask the captain."

Rick dropped his gear beside his desk and strode into Logan's office.

"Close the door, will you?" Logan muttered.

Not good news, Rick decided, but he did as he was asked and sat down opposite Logan.

"What's the situation between you and Madison Long?"

Rick frowned, irritated that he didn't know the answer to that himself. "How is that your business?" Rick thought about Logan's reputation with women and got to his feet. "Look, if this is about you being interested in her…"

Logan's cool blue eyes flashed hot, but he motioned to the chair. "Don't jump to foolish conclusions. Sit down and I'll explain why it's my business."

Rick realized how unreasonable he'd been and chalked it up to his own emotional turmoil. He was unaccustomed to the green haze of jealousy. He lowered himself back into the chair.

Logan continued only when Rick was sitting and had forced his body to relax. "We had another incident last night…"

Rick was on his feet again, this time drawing the logical conclusion. "Involving Madison? Is she okay?"

"She's fine. She doesn't know about it yet."

Rick clenched his fists. "What happened?"

"We've been patrolling the area more frequently, as you know, since the break-in at her place last week. A patrol car noticed a suspicious vehicle outside her home last night. When the cop went to approach it on foot, the car took off. By the time the rookie got back in his cruiser, the car was long gone. We have make, model and color, but he didn't get the full plate…" Logan shook his head in disgust. "Rookie mistake, but he thinks he remembers some of it. Since it's a common model, we don't have much to go on."

Rick straightened and shoved his hands in his pockets. "So what are you thinking now?"

"We've eliminated the theory that it has anything to do with Madison's father, as I told you the other day. She's aware of it, too. Her father hasn't taken any action on the case we suspected could have been the cause. Nor has he encountered any problems."

"Are we back to thinking it has to do with Los Zetas?"

Logan shrugged. "That's why I asked about your relationship with Madison. If it's casual, the incidents probably aren't connected to the cartel. But if you're spending a lot of time with her, that makes it more likely. We haven't tracked down the car that was outside her home, but the timing is just too coincidental. With the failure of the cartel's ambush at the warehouse and the most recent bust we've made, I'll bet the cartel bosses are getting impatient…and worse."

Rick dragged his fingers through his hair. "But you think they'd go after Madison?"

"They've been tailing you. We know that much. They might've thought you'd be with her. Her house is more remote—on a quieter street—than yours."

"Aw, damn!"

"You knew this was a possibility," Logan said.

"Sure. It's a risk we all take." He sighed. "And unfortunately, the risk extends to our families and the people close to us." He felt the horror build. "What about my family? Mom and Dad? My brother and sister and her family? Nothing's happened there that I'm aware of, but…"

"We'll add extra surveillance for your family, and for Madison. You should give all of them a heads-up, though, if you haven't already."

Rick thought about his parents, his brother and sister and his sister's little girl. It wouldn't be the first time he'd asked them to be on alert because of a possible threat associated with

his job. The anger swelled in him, intense and
all consuming. The Stewarts had given him a
home, a family, love. They hadn't signed up
for this, and how could he live with it if anything happened to one of them on account
of his job? Although the SDPD would try to
protect them, there was nothing he could do
to put them entirely out of harm's way.

But Madison? That was different. The
threat to her existed only because of her relationship with him, and that relationship
was voluntary. So far, there hadn't been any
indication that the cartel was targeting his
family, but it seemed that they might be targeting Madison.

With his hands in his pockets, he paced
the length of Logan's office, his gaze on
the carpet. "I just don't get it." He stopped
and looked at Logan. "As you've said before, this isn't about intimidation. They don't
want something *from* me. They want me out
of the way. In that case, why involve Madison? Or my family? Why haven't they simply taken me out?"

"I can't argue with you in principle. But
the point you make—about the cartel wanting payback… Maybe they want you to suffer before they go for you. Then the logical

choice becomes the people closest to you. If they hurt them, they hurt you. And as we've discussed before, it might also be about making an example of you to ensure others leave them alone, too. That's why I suggest added surveillance."

"Fine. Do it for my family."

"And Madison?"

"Well, yeah, her, too. But I'll deal with Madison myself."

"Rick," Logan called after him when he was just about to walk out the door. "Don't do anything stupid."

He glanced back. "Let's just move on the cartel soon, okay?"

MADISON HEARD THE roar of the Harley-Davidson when it was probably still a block away. She looked at her watch, then set the pot of water on the stove to boil, wiped her hands on a dishcloth and headed to the front door.

She'd finally come to the conclusion that it was foolish to judge Rick for something he was doing that was so bighearted and decent, even if it ignored the letter of the law. And as Jessica had pointed out, no one was being hurt by his actions. She thought of Rafael. Not only was Rick not hurting anyone, he was helping in a big way. She wanted to make amends. Inviting him over for dinner and explaining what she'd decided and why—telling him she *loved* him—was a good way to start.

Watching him dismount from his motorcycle, Madison felt the thrill of anticipation at just being with him again. She'd been so stupid to think they shouldn't be together.

She swung the door open just as he reached the last step to her porch. She immediately noticed the grim look on his face, but didn't let that deter her from the happiness she felt at simply seeing him again after an interminable few weeks apart. She placed her hands on his shoulders, rose up on her toes and pressed her lips to his. "You're early," she whispered. "Eager to see me?"

"We finished sooner than I expected at the school today," he said.

Madison's smile faded as she held the door for him. That wasn't the response she'd expected, and the good mood he was usually in after one of the school sessions seemed to be absent.

Rick greeted Owen, but Madison could see that even Owen sensed there was something bothering him. She led him into the kitchen, stirred the carbonara sauce and checked the water in the pot. She took a Coke out of the fridge, poured it into a glass over some ice and handed it to him. Then a terrifying thought occurred to her. Was something wrong with one of the dogs? That would certainly explain his mood. But then she would've known because she'd been at the clinic all day. Unless... "Are the dogs okay?"

He took a sip, then lowered the glass. "Yes. Why do you ask?"

"I just wondered... You seem... I was wondering because you didn't bring them."

"Yeah, they're fine."

The water started to boil. She adjusted the heat and stirred the sauce. "Dinner can be ready in ten minutes, if you're hungry, or we can sit out back for a while first." She was anxious to tell him how she was feeling, but there was definitely something off with him. It worried her. "We can just talk for a while, if you like."

He drank again before putting the glass on the table. He bent forward and scratched Owen's ears, which brought a contented moan. When he straightened again, his eyes were almost black, and every muscle in his face seemed tense. He stuck his hands into his pants pockets. "Look, I think this is a bad idea."

Madison's hand with the wooden spoon in it stilled. "What is? Spaghetti?"

He turned away to give his attention to Owen again. It troubled her that he didn't maintain eye contact with her. If she'd learned anything about him, it was that he was always direct, and that he wasn't a coward. "What is?" she repeated.

"Us. I don't think we're a good idea."

She hadn't realized she'd released her hold on the spoon until it splashed in the pot. Ignoring the splatter of sauce everywhere, she gaped at him. "Sorry?"

He cleared his throat. "I just don't think this is working," he said. "Us seeing each other. I think you were right about us being too different."

She felt a sudden panic. She'd finally reconciled herself to the fact that she loved him, that she could tolerate what he did, and what was he saying? Incredulous, she shook her head. Was *he* breaking up with *her*? Owen must have sensed her alarm because he strolled over to her side. "I...I don't understand."

"Like I said, it just isn't working." His voice sounded gruff. She couldn't detect any emotion behind his words.

"But why?" The words came out as a wail. She leaned back against the counter and braced her hands on the ledge. She waited while he moved about restlessly. He seemed to be gathering his thoughts.

"We're just too far apart on…philosophical matters that mean a lot to me." She knew he was referring to her stand on the law and his lenience. "I know those differences would ultimately drive us apart, and I can't change the way I feel or what I do. There it is in a nutshell."

Her mouth was opening and closing, but no words were forming. She felt the sting of tears and squeezed her eyes shut until she was certain she had them under control. "But…but *I'm* okay with it… That's what I wanted to tell you tonight. That I understand, and that…" She couldn't say "I love you," just then. Not because she didn't *feel* it. But because it didn't seem right if he was breaking up with her.

"I'm sorry. I really am." He sounded more compassionate. He sounded like the man she'd fallen in love with.

"Oh, my God," she whispered. She *loved* him. She'd been building up to it, but there it was. Totally. Unquestionably. She loved Rick with all her heart. Would it make a difference if she told him? She couldn't do it now. He'd think she was trying to trap him into staying with her.

"I'd better go," he said, but at least now she saw regret in his eyes. Still, she was too proud—and too hurt—to ask him to stay.

"I'm sorry about the trouble you went to with dinner. You don't need to see me out," he said, and with a final long look at her, he walked out of her house.

Rick sat at a back table at Buster's Beach House Bar. He just wanted a coffee, a light dinner and to get home to bed. He hadn't done much other than work, eat and sleep in the days since he'd broken up with Madison.

He knew he'd hurt Madison badly, but he'd had to do it. He loved her too much to risk seeing her get hurt by the cartel because of him. Ironically, to keep her from harm, he'd hurt her himself. But the pain he'd caused was the lesser of the two. And he'd had to lie to her. If he'd told her it was to keep her safe from the cartel, he knew she wouldn't have let him break up with her. So he'd had to do it in a way she couldn't question or refuse. She'd get over him in time, he was sure of it, but would he get over her?

Rick glanced around the room. He hadn't seen Cal Palmer when he'd entered the bar, but obviously Cal had been there and must have seen him, because he was walking in his direction.

"Mind if I sit?" Cal asked. Without waiting for an answer, he pulled out a chair and dropped into it.

"That's a rhetorical question, since you've already made yourself comfortable." Rick knew Cal wouldn't take offense. They'd known each other too long, both professionally and personally.

"Not to worry. I don't plan to interfere with your brooding. I won't stay for more than a few minutes. I'm here with Jess."

Rick looked in the direction Cal indicated, saw Cal's wife and lifted a hand in greeting. "If I were you, I'd certainly pick her over me."

"No contest," Cal said cheerfully. He waved off the waitress when she headed their way. "It was actually Jess who suggested I come and see you."

The surprise must have shown on his face because Cal continued to grin at him.

"She saw you come in—and this is *not* a professional medical opinion—but she thought you looked, um, haggard."

"Maybe because that's how I feel."

"Does it have anything to do with you and Madison breaking up?"

This time his gaze flew to Cal's. "Not that it's any of your business, but what gave you that idea?"

"Jess had lunch with Madison."

"And Madison *told* her?" Rick didn't know why that annoyed him so much; after all, they were friends, so it seemed natural enough.

"You could've told me, too." The reprimand was mild but it was unmistakable. "And no, she didn't tell Jess, at least not of her own volition. Jess asked how your relationship was going, and she basically broke down."

Rick stared into his coffee cup. He hadn't wanted to hurt Madison. He wanted to protect her and keep her safe. He still thought this was the only way, until they'd dealt with Los Zetas.

Cal remained silent for a long moment. "According to Jess, Madison didn't seem terribly happy about it. So being the brilliant investigator I am, I surmised that you did the breaking up. Looking at you now, I'm not so sure."

"It was me," Rick admitted.

Cal cast a glance over his shoulder, signaling to Jessica that he'd be a while longer. She smiled and nodded. "What prompted that? It doesn't seem to be making you happy."

"It's my problem. Don't keep Jessica waiting."

"She's on her cell phone, writing an email to someone at work. Looks as if she's still at it, so I've got plenty of time." Now he did motion to the waitress to bring him a coffee. "You know you can level with me, and it won't get back to Madison. Or even Jess."

Rick could trust Cal, and maybe he needed to let it out. "We know that I'm being targeted by Los Zetas."

Cal nodded.

"You're obviously aware of the recent incidents with Madison. In addition to the break-in, there was another incident last week. I spoke to Logan, and although it still doesn't entirely make sense, he and I kicked it around some more. We keep circling back to one thing—that the cartel wants to get to me through Madison."

Cal seemed to think that over. "But why ransack her place?" he asked.

"The ransacking... Maybe it was to make sure we knew they'd been there."

"So you figured she was in danger because of you and decided to end it?" Cal concluded.

"That about sums it up."

"And you didn't level with her? Give her a choice, did you?"

"No."

"Idiot." Cal's expression was grim.

Rick raised his eyebrows in response.

"Do you really think she'd want you to try to protect her like this? Make an arbitrary decision about your future together without consulting her, well intentioned—although, in my opinion, misguided—as your actions might be?"

"No."

Cal's voice dropped. "The division can protect her. You know that. Just like your family."

Rick exhaled. "It's bad enough with my family, but I can't distance myself from them. As far as protecting them goes, all I can do is plan for the worst and hope for the best."

"And Madison?"

"That's different. If she has no involvement with me, she's safe."

"What if she was your wife?"

"Well, she's not."

"But if she was, you'd protect her, same as you're doing with your family. You wouldn't push her aside, hoping to keep her safe."

"No," he conceded.

"You care about her. She cares about you. Don't do this. At least be honest with her. Give her the freedom of choice."

Rick was silent for a long time. Finally, he said, "I can't. I've seen the effects of drugs and the drug trade firsthand. The violence." His voice dropped to a whisper. "The senseless loss of life, what it does to families…"

"If you're talking about what happened to your birth parents…"

Rick raised a hand. "I can guess what you're going to say. Their murder was different. Yeah, they were involved with the drug trade. Madison isn't. All the more reason for me *not* to take violence and possibly worse to her doorstep."

Cal shook his head slowly. "I'll never be able to understand what it was like for you when you were a kid. For that reason alone, I can't argue this point with you." He finished his coffee and rose, but rather than walking away he placed his palms on the table and leaned forward. "All the time I've known you, I've never seen you with another woman the way you were with Madison. I can't imagine my life without Jess, and to think I almost screwed that up…" His lips compressed into a straight line. "Do *me* a favor? If you believe Madison could be right for you, think about it at least." Cal gave Rick's shoulder a pat and headed back to his wife.

Rick's appetite was gone. The cold sandwich sitting on the plate in front of him had lost its appeal.

Yes, he loved Madison. She was the person he wanted to spend the rest of his life with. But that didn't change anything in the here and now. *Especially* because of the way he felt about her, he couldn't allow her to be touched by the darkness he was dealing with. Maybe after they dismantled the cartel, he'd go to her, explain everything and ask for her understanding and forgiveness.

He stood up, dug into his pocket for some bills and left a generous amount on the table.

Who was he kidding? Cal was right. She wouldn't approve of what he was doing to keep her from harm. And after the fact? She wouldn't forgive him.

He'd have to live with that.

If he told her the truth now? She'd almost said she loved him. He was sure of it. If he told her what was going on, she'd insist on staying with him. She wouldn't let him distance himself from her, and they'd be back at square one.

Despite what Cal had said, his situation was different from Rick's. Cal dealt with search and rescue, not narcotics.

Madison's safety and well-being came first, and he wouldn't do anything that might compromise that and put her in jeopardy. Not now and not in the future.

CHAPTER TWENTY-ONE

"YOU'VE BEEN EVEN more generous with your time lately, Madison, and we appreciate it," Allison Hartford, the head of pediatrics at Ocean Crest Hospital, said to Madison. They were walking down a corridor toward a common play area for the kids. Madison thought of all the spare time she had on her hands since she and Rick had stopped seeing each other a few weeks ago. She was glad she could at least do something productive that gave her pleasure, despite the constant pain of her broken heart.

"I might have a special challenge for you today," Allison continued. "I believe you and your malamute will be a perfect fit for the two boys I have in mind. They're siblings, victims of drug abuse and associated violence. What these kids experienced is horrific. They have physical issues, not surprisingly, but their emotional wounds are far deeper and more debilitating. Even though they try to act tough, my assessment is that they're two terrified, lonely kids, hurting a lot but not wanting to show it."

It didn't take Madison long to agree with Allison's assessment of Miguel and Diego. They were two skinny, angry brothers with dark complexions, long stringy hair and coal-colored eyes that had seen too much. At nine and eleven years of age, they should've been playing and laughing rather than snarling and talking back. But Allison had also been right about Owen's effect. The large dog caught their interest, and she glimpsed the children they still were despite the tough outer shell. With Owen, Madison was able to reach the boys. The stories they told her broke her already fragile heart. But in that heart, tender shoots of love started to sprout for the two boys who'd endured so much hardship in such short lives.

Madison and Owen began to see the boys weekly, and she learned more about them. She was infuriated by the abuse they'd been subjected to. But every session she spent with Miguel and Diego provided her with greater insight into the man she loved, the man who'd left her. It enabled her to see Rick's actions from a different perspective. From Rick's viewpoint as a child who'd lived it.

Miguel and Diego's parents were both involved in the drug trade in Tijuana. Through the boys' stories, Madison started to piece together more clearly the horrors Rick must have experienced when he was a child. He'd lasted longer with his parents than these kids had. She wasn't certain, but she suspected that would have made it harder for him. He'd likely been exposed to more atrocities and greater abuses. Her heart continued to embrace the two young boys, and the importance of what Rick had chosen to do—and why—began to make even more sense to her.

These boys were alive today because they'd been able to escape their circumstances. Their parents—the very people who should have been protecting them—had been exploiting them. If they'd been turned back at the border or handed over to the Mexican authorities, where would these boys be now?

Maybe she'd decided earlier to *tolerate* what Rick did because she didn't want to lose him, but now she'd come to appreciate the difference between tolerance and acceptance. Now she finally and truly understood and accepted—but it was too little, too late.

Watching Miguel and Diego cuddled up with Owen, both boys resting their heads on the large dog's side, Madison smiled. Diego, the younger boy, was snuggled up against his brother, and Miguel was doing his best to read one of the English children's books she'd brought them.

She wished Rick could have seen these boys with her dog. But that wasn't to be. Although she'd come to better understand and appreciate him and his actions through Miguel and Diego, she knew there was no possibility of reconciling with Rick. Rick just didn't want her.

Thinking of her father at least brought a small smile to her face. He'd promised to visit her for the Thanksgiving holidays. She missed him and was glad she'd be seeing him later that week. Talking every couple of days and the frequent emails they exchanged just weren't the same. She hoped that seeing him would dull the pain of missing Rick, if just temporarily.

When Madison left the hospital, she had a message waiting on her cell phone. It was from Jessica. She called her friend back on her way home.

"Cal and I would like you to join us and

the girls for Thanksgiving dinner, if you don't have any plans," Jessica said.

"Oh, Jess, that's sweet of you, but my father's coming to visit. He's aware that Rick and I aren't seeing each other anymore, and he doesn't want me to be alone. I'm making him dinner."

"You're going to cook?" Jessica joked. "We've been friends long enough that I know it's one of your least favorite things to do. Although when you do it, you do it well!" she amended. "Why don't you bring your father? Haley will be with us this Thanksgiving, and the girls would love to see you again."

Madison thought how much fun it would be to join them. She knew her father would get along with Jessica and Cal. However... "Jess, I have to be honest. I appreciate the invitation. I really do. But I don't feel that Cal's comfortable with me. Not since Rick and I stopped seeing each other."

"Don't be silly! You can't let that bother you. We're friends, and he respects that. He wouldn't want to put any strain on our friendship. He's sorry it didn't work out between the two of you. So am I. But that doesn't mean we can't be friends and spend time together. He knows I'm inviting you to join us, and he'd like to see you, too. Why don't you think about it?"

"Okay" was Madison's hesitant answer.

After considerable debate with herself, Madison ended up accepting Jessica's offer.

She put any worries about loyalties and resentment out of her mind. She was looking forward to seeing her father too much to dwell on negatives.

THE DAY HAD finally come for the multijurisdictional, multiagency takedown of the Los Zetas Cartel. All the members of the task force wanted to have something else to be grateful for this Thanksgiving.

It had not been without risks and had required complex coordination between a number of SDPD units and other law enforcement authorities, including some cross-border cooperation between the United States and Mexico. Rick had been at the center of it all. Leading up to it, they had restricted communications even more than they had previously. All information sharing was on a strict need-to-know basis.

And their plan had gone off without a hitch. They'd raided Los Zetas in all their strongholds simultaneously in the middle of the night. They had the high-ranking bosses of the cartel on both sides of the border behind bars. Rick wasn't kidding himself. It didn't mean that the cartel wouldn't regroup and rebuild, but it would take considerable time and effort. They had all the men who'd held the most power and had significantly impaired the source of their funding, as well.

Rick walked into his house. He couldn't remember being so exhausted but self-satisfied at the same time. He was happy to get home and to be greeted by his dogs, even if his place was a shambles because of how long he'd had to leave them alone. He let them out in the backyard first, and prepared their meals. While they ate, he started to put his living room in order. He went back into the kitchen to get a Corona out of the refrigerator.

He knew the cartel would regroup. Eventually. But for now, the immediate threat had been thwarted. They'd also determined who had put the price on Rick's head. The boss who'd ordered him dead was one of the ones behind bars and would be staying there for a long, long time. With him out of the picture, without the ability to pay and with the cartel in disarray, no one would be championing the cause, and he was safe. The threat to him, personally, had been neutralized, at least for the immediate future.

And no one else had been hurt. Not members of his unit, not his family. Not the woman he loved—not Madison.

He'd driven her away. He'd hurt her. Was there any going back, as much as he wanted it?

He took a long drink of his beer, rested his head back against the cushions and closed his eyes. The knock on his door caused his eyes to fly open. A bit disoriented, he realized he must have dozed off. Another more forceful knock reminded him what had awakened him. "Just a minute," he called out before the person decided to kick his door in.

Swinging the door open, he was surprised to see Cal Palmer. "What are you doing here?"

"The charmer, as always," Cal commented without rancor. "Isn't the proper response when you find a friend at your front door something along the lines of 'Would you like to come in?' or 'Can I offer you a beer?'"

"Yeah, well. I'm not feeling my most hospitable," he muttered, but he opened the door. "C'mon in. Grab yourself a beer."

Cal laughed. "Much better. If you're antisocial."

"I'm not usually, but it's been a long, hard day."

Cal followed Rick into the living room. "Yeah. I heard." He patted his friend on the shoulder. "Good job."

"So that's why you're here?"

"Yeah. I thought you could use some company to celebrate."

"All right. Let me get you that beer."

"No. You sit down. I can get my own beer."

Cal joined Rick on the sofa a few minutes later, carrying two frosted bottles, and handed one to Rick. "Want to talk about it?"

No, Rick wasn't up to reliving it all just now. "Nah, but thanks."

"Okay."

They sat in silence for a few minutes.

"So…what about Madison?"

Rick turned to glare at Cal. "What about Madison?"

"You going to see if you two can pick up where you left off?"

"Are you kidding me? I doubt she'd give me the time of day, let alone anything else."

"You won't know unless you try."

"The last time I spoke to her… No, there's no chance."

"But if you explained to her what this was all about?"

"You're the one who told me she'd be pissed off if she thought I was trying to protect her and not giving her a say in it, remember? Do you really think she'd be more understanding now, after the fact?"

"Like I said, you won't know unless you try. Isn't she worth trying for?"

RICK THOUGHT ABOUT Cal's comments after Cal had left and late into the night. He almost convinced himself that Madison would understand. That she'd forgive him. He wanted her so desperately he was willing to try.

But what would happen the next time he was in a similar situation? And he would be. It was the nature of his job. The cartel would regroup eventually, and they'd have even more reason to go after him then. What if he and Madison were married, maybe had a couple of kids?

That thought made all the others pale in comparison.

Had he really just imagined Madison and him married?

It left him with such an incredible longing he found it hard to breathe.

MADISON HANDED JESSICA the huge bunch of flowers she'd brought and leaned in to give her friend a kiss on the cheek. "Happy Thanksgiving! Jessica, Cal, this is my father, Patrick Long. Dad, my friends Jess and Cal." She beamed at the opportunity to introduce her father to her friends.

"Your Honor, it's a pleasure to welcome you to our home," Cal said.

"Oh, no. Please. No formalities here. 'Patrick' will do just fine. I appreciate the invitation, and the kindness and friendship I understand you've extended to my daughter." He had Madison's arm through his elbow and patted her hand.

"And this is Scout," Jessica said, before sliding her arm into the crook of Patrick's other elbow and guiding him inside the house, with Scout at their heels. "Well, Patrick, we're very glad to meet you. We're both rather fond of your daughter. Girls," she called when they stepped into the living room.

The two little girls turned in unison from a dollhouse they'd been playing with in a corner of the room. They were nearly the same age and dressed in a similar fashion but total opposites in coloring. They were both wearing frilly pink dresses; Kayla, the dark-haired girl, had a bright yellow sash tied around her waist, while Haley, the blonde one, wore a rich brown sash, similar in hue to Kayla's hair. Madison knew that the "switching of colors," as they called it, had been something they'd done since the day Jessica and Cal were married.

"Girls, this is Mr. Long. Madison's father. Patrick, meet Haley and Kayla."

"It's a pleasure to meet two such beautiful young ladies," Patrick said in his clear, deep baritone, and gave them a formal bow, making the girls giggle.

Madison felt relaxed and happy as the afternoon progressed. She almost managed *not* to think of Rick in the company of her friends and father. As she'd anticipated, her father got along well with Jess and Cal, and the discomfort she'd expected to feel in their company because of Rick was nonexistent.

It was obvious that Madison's father was charmed by the bright, sweet, vivacious girls, and he looked meaningfully at her more than once over the dinner table. Madison was fully aware that he longed for grandkids. He'd have to be disappointed, because Madison didn't think it was going to be happening anytime soon. She couldn't see herself getting into another relationship.

After dinner, Jessica excused herself to put Haley and Kayla to bed, and Cal made Patrick a whiskey sour.

"Excellent drink," Patrick said after sampling the rich amber liquid. Her father gave Jessica a warm smile when she reentered the room. "Thank you for the outstanding dinner and your generous hospitality. I'm delighted to see a young couple so obviously and deeply in love and, frankly, so well suited."

Cal reached for Jessica's hand. "Thank you, Patrick. You're a perceptive man, and I'm a very fortunate one," he said, winking at his wife.

"How did you two meet, if you don't mind my asking?"

Madison sat back, enjoying the last of her wine, listening to her friend explain how she and Cal had met in the aftermath of the earthquake. With good humor, Jess admitted that she'd been less than impressed by the injured cop with the bad attitude. She went on to say that they'd also met Kayla that day. Cal had rescued her from a collapsed building, the same one in which he was later injured when he went back to rescue Scout. Jessica had subsequently triaged and treated Kayla.

She also described the circumstances behind Kayla's adoption. "It was so tragic for Kayla to have lost her mother in the earthquake. She didn't have relatives. Cal was trying to adopt Kayla on his own but was facing some roadblocks, being a single male. The San Diego Social Services Agency was concerned that Kayla had only had a mother's influence and that it would've been too much of an adjustment for her to go to a single, male-parent household, with everything else she had to contend with."

Jessica smiled at Cal. "I think it was all meant to be. Cal and I, um, resolved our differences, and the timing enabled us to adopt Kayla. We've been so fortunate in so many ways."

Madison felt a twinge of regret for her own circumstances, watching the glow of love on Jessica's face as she looked at her husband. Jess's eyes rounded suddenly and she turned to Madison. "I can't believe I haven't told you what we've learned!" she exclaimed. "I realize you know all that background, but we just discovered some new facts." She scooted to the edge of her seat and faced Madison. "You remember how I've been trying to get some information on Kayla's history, her medical records and so forth, because of that surgical scar she has?"

Madison nodded.

"Well, Kayla's mother had risked everything, left everything behind in Mexico—her family, her home, her job—and entered the United States illegally. But you knew that part."

Madison thought of what Rick had been doing and shot a quick, worried glance at her father. She couldn't discern any negative reaction on his face. He was watching Jessica with interest, but she knew her father had an excellent poker face. He had to for the bench, because he couldn't let his own views and reactions influence the deliberations of a jury. She slid her gaze back to Jessica.

"I can't imagine the courage that took, to leave everything behind like that." She shook her head. "I've always considered myself a brave, self-reliant person, but I don't know if I could have done that."

"I don't know if I could, either," Madison acknowledged.

"But Kayla's mother did. And here's the news. Kayla had been diagnosed with a rare vascular disorder that progressively narrows the blood vessels and arteries supplying the brain. The condition constricts blood flow, which makes the formation of blood clots likely, leading to a high probability of stroke."

"Oh, no," Madison interjected. She might have been a veterinarian, not a physician, but she understood the risks and ramifications of Kayla's condition. "How old was she at the time?"

"Just over a year. Anyway, the treatment is surgery, and only a handful of pediatric hospitals can perform it successfully. Although they'd diagnosed it in Mexico, Kayla's mother knew that the surgery wasn't possible there. Kayla simply couldn't have received the care she needed in her country."

"The mother brought Kayla to California illegally to get medical care for her?" Patrick asked. Madison was still unable to detect any emotion on his face or his tone of voice.

Cal nodded. "Can you believe that? The extent to which her mother went to get our beautiful Kayla her life-saving surgery."

"Extraordinary," Patrick remarked. Madison thought her father sounded impressed.

She kept her gaze on his profile as he continued. "How did she manage it? She wouldn't have had insurance coverage, would she?"

"We wondered about that, too," Cal responded. "The most we were able to learn from a nurse who works at the hospital where Kayla was treated was that her mother had said she'd been a paralegal in Mexico. She was a single mother, university educated, had a good job. She'd owned a small house that she sold. She took the proceeds from the sale, all her savings and some money her family could spare, and came to California. Her education and experience might have helped her manipulate the system so they could stay here. She had false papers and no legal status."

"But surely a young woman in her circumstances, as accomplished as she was, wouldn't have had enough to cover the cost."

"True." Jessica nodded. "She'd worked a number of jobs here to support herself and her daughter, mostly cleaning houses, but that and the money she'd come with still wasn't enough. The hospital had a charitable program, and the nurse said they covered the rest of the expense."

"Remarkable," Patrick said again. "Quite an extraordinary young woman, I gather."

"I think so, too." Jessica sent her husband a sad smile. "We suspect that if Kayla's mother hadn't come here to get the needed care for her daughter, Kayla would have succumbed to her illness."

"An extraordinary young woman," Patrick said again. "A woman very much committed to her child." Madison was touched by the revelation, but despite her father's words she was anxious about his reaction. A knock at the door drew her out of her reflections.

"I'll get it," Cal said, and strode out of the room. "Hey, good to see you!" Madison heard him say from the hallway. "Happy Thanksgiving!"

"I know I said I wouldn't be able to make it, but we wrapped our family dinner at my parents early, and I thought I'd stop by and take you up on the offer of a nightcap."

Madison froze at the sound of the familiar deep voice, followed by some murmuring. She couldn't quite make out what was being said before she picked up the conversation again. "No problem for me," Rick said. "If she's okay with it."

Jessica glanced at Madison. Her expression was both apologetic and inquiring.

I'm okay. Madison mouthed the words and caught her father's concerned look, too. "Really," she assured him just before Rick walked into the room, Cal's arm slung over his shoulders.

Madison wondered if that was to keep Rick from changing his mind once he saw her. "Guess who decided to stop by for a drink?" Cal said, the note of tension in his voice belying his relaxed demeanor.

"Madison," Rick said by way of greeting.

His eyes lingered on her and she felt her mouth go dry. "Hello, Rick."

He turned his attention to her father, offered a hand. "Judge Long, nice to see you again."

Madison wondered if everyone could hear her heart thundering. She tried to listen to the conversation flowing around the room over the deafening roar in her ears.

"Exactly!" Rick exclaimed.

She'd missed the exchange between her father and Rick, but they seemed to be in agreement rather than contention. Oddly, now that she and Rick were no longer seeing each other, he and her father appeared to get along fine.

Madison sipped her wine, hoping fervently that the feelings raging inside her weren't evident on her face or in her mannerisms. Judging by the heat she felt on her cheeks, she suspected they probably were. She wanted to cry. She'd been fooling herself, thinking she'd get over Rick. Seeing him now, so animated and engaged in discussion with her father and Cal, she knew she'd been kidding herself.

She'd never stopped loving Rick, despite the way he'd cast her aside. He still meant as much to her as he ever had. Watching him surreptitiously, and watching Cal and Jessica holding hands and laughing in unison at something Rick had said, she realized how empty her life was without him. Catching her eye, Jessica formed the word *Sorry*.

Madison responded with an equally silent, *It's okay*, but knew it wasn't and might never be again.

To distract herself from her heartbreak, she focused on the conversation. She was incredulous to hear that Rick and her father had similar views on the topic of immigration. Scout unexpectedly pressed his cold nose against her leg and she gasped in surprise. Everyone's gaze shifted to her, but she only saw Rick and an unfathomable question in his eyes. She forced a smile and stroked the dog's head. "He startled me," she mumbled with a nervous laugh.

Although Cal, Jessica and her father tried to engage her in the conversation, she remained quiet for the most part. When her father finally rose to thank their hosts and say good-night, she almost cried with relief. She'd desperately wanted to go, but knew it would have been rude for her to initiate it.

"That was a pleasant evening," Patrick said when they'd settled down with mugs of coffee in Madison's living room. "They're delightful people, and they're obviously good friends to you."

Madison sipped her coffee and waited for the other shoe to drop. She was certain he'd raise the matter of Kayla's mother. To her considerable surprise, he segued to another topic altogether. She was baffled and too curious not to pursue it.

"Dad, can I ask you something?"

"Of course. Has there ever been a time I didn't encourage you to do so?"

Madison rose from her chair and placed a

kiss on her father's cheek. "No, there never has. Tonight, at Jess and Cal's place, you seemed...impressed by what Kayla's mother had done."

He chuckled. "And why wouldn't I be? It was a selfless thing she did. I expect it took a great deal of courage and conviction, not to mention love for her little one."

Madison felt her lips part. "But...what she did was illegal!"

Patrick cocked his head slightly. "And what were her options? Jessica used to practice medicine and I expect she was very good at it. She said Kayla might not have survived if she hadn't received the needed surgery in a timely manner." He looked at Madison, seeming to search her face. "What would you have done in her place?"

Madison was about to say, "The very same thing," but she realized that would've been admitting to her father the *judge* that she would've been willing to break the law. But her father had also conditioned her to believe that nothing bad could come from telling the truth. She held her father's gaze and chose her words carefully. "I would have done whatever it took to save my child's life." She knew that was the only answer she could ever give to that question, but she watched nervously for her father's reaction.

"There you go," Patrick said, patting her knee. "I'd better get some sleep. How about if I take you out for an early breakfast tomorrow before I leave for the airport?"

Now Madison's jaw did drop open. "Dad?"

"You don't want to have breakfast?"

She made a surprised sound. "Yes to breakfast. But Kayla's mother and what I said—you're *okay* with the law being broken?"

Patrick's face darkened. "Of *course* I'm not okay with the law being broken."

"But..."

He placed his mug on the coffee table and held up a hand. "Hold on a second, honey, will you?" He looked perturbed. "Haven't I taught you to reason? Haven't I taught you to consider risks and consequences when making decisions?"

Mute, she nodded.

"We live privileged lives. There are many people who don't have the same privileges we do. How could we begrudge a young mother's desire to get the best health care for her ailing child? Care that we take for granted?"

Madison exhaled heavily, and rubbed her temples. "Dad, I'm confused."

He lowered his voice. "As a judge, I can't condone the breaking of the law, no matter how minor the infraction. But as a person, I can sympathize—even be outraged—by the plight of those less fortunate than us. A child of ten living on the street and stealing a loaf of bread because he's starving has broken the law. Do you expect me to send him to jail, or even to a juvenile detention facility?"

With her head still in her hands, she raised her eyes back to his, but said nothing.

"Have I led you to believe that I'm heartless?" he asked.

"No, of course not!" she exclaimed.

"I realize illegal immigration is a big problem for California, as it is for Texas. You know I've always supported a number of charities. What you might not be aware of is that for years I've been making sizable donations to an El Paso–based charitable organization aiding refugees from the city of Ciudad Juárez, in Chihuahua, just south of our border. The city is highly dangerous and there are always refugees making their way across the border. These people need help. Yes, we have to trust the system—but the system doesn't always work, so there are organizations that help."

Disbelieving, Madison stared at her father.

"I don't know what happened between you and Rick, but would you have denied him—the child he was—the opportunity to stay in California? Did it cost the system? Maybe some. But look what he's made of himself, and how much he gives back to society. At great personal peril, I might add."

Had it been her own lack of compassion, her own rigidity, that had driven her and Rick apart after all? Madison stayed up long after her father had gone to bed, deliberating on everything she'd learned that evening. Finally, she checked her watch.

It was too late to call Rick now, as much as she wanted to.

The sudden muffled thumps outside her front door startled her. She was on her feet almost as fast as Owen was.

CHAPTER TWENTY-TWO

THE STEADY OFFSHORE wind had Madison's hair whipping around her face. She brushed it back impatiently and gazed out over the ocean. The turbulence of the white-capped waves seemed to mimic her emotions. In the muted light of the full moon, she watched Owen, Sniff and Nitro chasing one another in the sand. She cast a professional eye on Sniff, noting that his cruciate ligament didn't seem to be bothering him too much.

She and Rick stood side by side. The crash of the waves and the occasional bark of a dog were the only sounds around them. "Thank you for coming out with me," Rick finally said. "I know it's late…early actually," he said with a nervous laugh, "but I had to see you after this evening."

"I'm glad you stopped by."

"Sorry that Sniff's tail hitting your door startled you. He knew where we were and was happy about seeing you and Owen."

"With everything that's gone on, yes, the thumping did scare me." Despite her brave thoughts not that much earlier, she didn't know what else to say in the face of her rioting emotions.

The silence stretched out again, then Rick turned to her. "I've missed you."

The simple words tore at Madison's heart. Oh, how she'd missed him.

The three dogs charged into the surf and came rushing out just as quickly, almost as if they were trying to catch the waves.

"Can we talk about it?"

Unsure of what he meant, Madison looked back at him. "About what?"

He hunched his shoulders against the wind and stuffed his hands into his pockets. "About what's going on between us?"

"Sure," she said, the nerves skittering through her.

"Will you walk with me?"

They strolled along the Pacific Beach boardwalk as the dogs engaged in a frenzied game of chase.

"I was wrong," Rick eventually said.

Madison stopped and placed a hand on his arm, getting him to turn toward her. "No. No.

I was wrong!" She didn't want him to give up what he'd been doing. He'd helped so many young boys. She'd finally come to understand and truly value what he'd been doing for those kids, and appreciate even more the man he was. She needed to convince him of that. But looking deep into his eyes, she saw confusion. "Please don't stop," she entreated him.

"Stop?"

"Yes. Please don't stop doing what you've been doing."

"Stop…what?"

Madison shook her head. "What you did."

"I was wrong about what I did."

"No!" She grabbed both his arms. "You aren't wrong!"

A deep V appeared between his brows. "Madison, I don't think we're talking about the same thing."

"Yes. Yes, we are," she said. "What you've been doing with those boys. Helping them start a new life in California. It's so wonderful, and I've been so hardheaded about it, and so wrong. I'd come to conclude that I would…*tolerate* it. That's what I wanted to tell you the night you came over…when you broke up with me. But *tolerate* isn't the right word. I understand and *accept* what you've been doing."

She told him about Diego and Miguel, and the impact they'd had on her. "I'm still seeing them and I'd like you to meet them," she said. "I'm *proud* of you! Even my father would approve!"

"You mentioned it to your father?"

"No. No, but we discussed what Kayla's mother did at Thanksgiving dinner before you got there. About her being in California illegally and with false papers, and he admires her for it. So I know he'd think what you're doing is commendable."

She couldn't read the look on his face. "Can you give me another chance?" she asked. "I'm so sorry for having judged you, and judged you wrong. Is there a chance for us?" She reached for his hands. "I love you…" she whispered.

Rick continued to hold her gaze with what might have been wonder in his eyes. "Oh, Madison. You have no idea how much those words mean to me. How I've longed to hear them from you."

She reached up to hold his face in her

hands, but he grabbed her arms and prevented her from doing that.

"Madison, if you can only say those words to me again after you hear me out." He inhaled deeply, then blew out a huge breath. "We *have* been talking about two different things here. Like I said, you have no idea how much it means for you to say what you did about my actions. But that's not what I was referring to."

"Then, what?" she asked, panic rising inside her. "That's why you left me. Because I couldn't accept or understand what you were doing. I know how wrong I was…"

"I didn't leave you because of our differences in that regard. That was an excuse. I couldn't tell you the truth." He led her to a bench, whistled to the dogs and drew her down beside him.

She felt an incredible chill despite the warm night air. Just when she'd thought that what had driven them apart had been resolved, she dreaded what he was going to say. "Then, why?"

"I did it because I was afraid for your safety."

Rick explained to her what had occurred

with the cartel, the risk he'd faced and why he'd done what he had. "And I was wrong," he concluded. "Even Cal told me I shouldn't have made the decision for us unilaterally, but I wouldn't listen. He told me I was an idiot, and he was right."

Madison didn't know what to say. She felt petrified, knowing the cartel had been after Rick, and it was disconcerting to think she'd been targeted, too. "I can understand, even appreciate, that you were trying to protect me."

He forced a laugh again. "I was wrong."

"You've lost me again."

"The incidents that occurred with you? We decided it had to be the cartel trying to make a point although it made no sense to us. But it wasn't."

Madison was ready to scream. This was too much to take in. "If it wasn't the cartel, then who? Am I still in danger? Are you?"

He gave her a lopsided smile and reached out to tuck a strand of her hair behind her ear. "No. You're not in danger. It wasn't the cartel. It was Brody."

"Sorry. *What?*" She couldn't have been hearing right. "The cop?"

"Uh-huh. There was another incident you didn't know about. After the break-in at your house, we put on extra patrols. One of them caught a car in front of your place, but it took off. The officer got the vehicle make, model, color and a partial plate. We located the vehicle. It belongs to Brody."

Madison was shaking her head in disbelief.

"When we interrogated him, he fell apart. It turns out he'd been feeding information to the cartel. That was how they knew about the bust on that warehouse and were able to set the trap for us. He's the one who got the CI—one of his new ones—to call us about the tip that ended in Jeff's murder. He did it for money, sure. Apparently along with his drinking problem, he has a gambling problem. But also because he'd had it in for me for a while. After his transfer, which he blamed me for, his hatred for me intensified. He saw you at Logan's barbecue, was attracted to you and thought he could satisfy his own craving and get back at me at the same time."

Madison stared at Rick mutely. "My things… He went through my belongings and broke my things. Why?"

Rick shrugged. "All we can figure is that he was drunk and his emotional state was deteriorating. Madison, he confessed to it all. With his confession, and everything Brody's done, he's going to be locked away for a long time. You don't have to worry. And me? I was wrong. I thought I was doing what was best for you, but I didn't even know where the threat was coming from, and it could have cost us our future. I was so very wrong." He cupped her face. His eyes shone with something she couldn't quite comprehend, but it tugged at her heart.

"Madison, I love you. If you can forgive me and say those three words to me again now, knowing what I did… Well, it would mean the world to me."

Madison's cheeks were wet with tears and she tried to find her voice. She was so overwhelmed with emotion—with happiness—she was afraid she couldn't get a single word out. She could see in Rick's eyes that he was expecting the worst. "Oh, Rick. I love you!" she finally cried, and threw herself into his arms.

Her exclamation had alerted the dogs and they came bounding back. They shook themselves, spraying water and wet sand on them.

"Do you think three dogs together are too much?" Rick asked, laughing.

"No, I think three dogs are just right!" Then she sobered and looked in his eyes again. "What are you saying?"

"I'm saying…well, we've had so much to distract us and things we've both been worried about. These misunderstandings and threats. But do you know what I've discovered?"

She shook her head.

"I've discovered that I can't spend my life without you. In fact, I can't spend another day without you!"

"Oh, Rick…"

He placed a finger on her lips. "Shh. Let me finish. I'm not saying that the issues we've had to deal with aren't significant. What I do with those kids. Wanting to keep you safe and protected. These are vital matters. But you know what?"

She shook her head again.

"I've discovered that *you* are the top priority in my life. That my love for you, and yours for me, is what's crucial." He brushed his lips across hers.

"So here's what I've learned," he went on.

"That nothing matters as much as our love. It's love that matters most."

"It *is* love that matters most," Madison repeated in awe, delighting in the certainty that Rick was truly hers and she was his.

* * * * *

LARGER-PRINT BOOKS!

GET 2 FREE LARGER-PRINT NOVELS PLUS 2 FREE MYSTERY GIFTS

Love Inspired®

Larger-print novels are now available...

LARGER-PRINT BOOKS!

GET 2 FREE LARGER-PRINT NOVELS PLUS 2 FREE MYSTERY GIFTS

Love Inspired®

SUSPENSE
RIVETING INSPIRATIONAL ROMANCE

Larger-print novels are now available...

YES! Please send me **The Montana Mavericks Collection** in Larger Print. This collection begins with 3 FREE books and 2 FREE gifts (gifts valued at approx. $20.00 retail) in the first shipment, along with the other first 4 books from the collection! If I do not cancel, I will receive 8 monthly shipments until I have the entire 51-book Montana Mavericks collection. I will receive 2 or 3 FREE books in each shipment and I will pay just $4.99 US/ $5.89 CDN for each of the other four books in each shipment, plus $2.99 for shipping and handling per shipment.*If I decide to keep the entire collection, I'll have paid for only 32 books, because 19 books are FREE! I understand that accepting the 3 free books and gifts places me under no obligation to buy anything. I can always return a shipment and cancel at any time. My free books and gifts are mine to keep no matter what I decide.

263 HCN 2404   463 HCN 2404

Name _____ (PLEASE PRINT) _____

Address _____ Apt. # _____

City _____ State/Prov. _____ Zip/Postal Code _____

Signature (if under 18, a parent or guardian must sign)

Mail to the **Reader Service:**
IN U.S.A.: P.O. Box 1867, Buffalo, NY 14240-1867
IN CANADA: P.O. Box 609, Fort Erie, Ontario L2A 5X3

LARGER-PRINT BOOKS!
GET 2 FREE LARGER-PRINT NOVELS PLUS
2 FREE GIFTS!

⊕ HARLEQUIN®

super romance®

More Story...More Romance